Switchcraft

Mary Castillo

AVON

An Imprint of HarperCollins*Publishers*

HarperCollins books may be purchased for educational, business, or sales promotional use. For information please write: Special Markets Department, HarperCollins Publishers, 10 East 53rd Street, New York, NY 10022.

FIRST EDITION

Interior text designed by Diahann Sturge

Library of Congress Cataloging-in-Publication Data
Castillo, Mary, 1974–
  Switchcraft / Mary Castillo.—1st ed.
    p. cm.
  ISBN: 978-0-06-087608-1
  ISBN-10: 0-06-087608-5
  1. Female friendship—Fiction. I. Title

PS3603.A876S95 2007
813'.6—dc22   2007012686

07 08 09 10 11   OV/RRD   10 9 8 7 6 5 4 3 2 1

*For William and Nicole
and the little birds who have yet to fly home.*

Acknowledgments

Grief can take care of itself, but to get the full value of joy you must have somebody to divide it with.

—MARK TWAIN

I was never alone when I wrote this book. My Little Dude was a passenger while I wrote the first draft, and then willingly hung out in the exer-saucer while I frantically worked on subsequent drafts. My fabulous agent, Jenny Bent, went nuts when I told her about the idea I thought she'd hate. When I turned in the first draft of this story—late!—to my editor, Carrie Feron, and her assistant, Tessa Woodward, I was convinced they'd ask for their money back. But their notes and encouragement inspired me to take this story to what I had dreamed it would become.

Thank you to Nic Villareal and Jose Acevedo at Taléo Mexican Grill in Irvine. If it wasn't for you welcoming me into your restaurant and sharing your passion for food, the character of Kevin wouldn't have been as interesting.

Thank you so much to my home team—Ryan, Mom and Dad, Ilona, Dana, and Jen. When I was tearing my hair out, convinced this story was cursed, you encouraged me to keep going.

One

Aggie Portrero never should've slept with the guy next to her.

Not that he was just "some guy"; he was Kevin. Her next door neighbor and only *real* male friend, and as such, they had exchanged honest accounts of each other's exploits. In other words, if anyone knew better than to get in the sack with him, that person should have been her.

For three years Kevin listened to her vent about everything from PMS, business, and the latest jerkoff she'd dated; while she helped him plot his exit strategies from numerous relationships. They enjoyed the kind of intimacy old married couples had, but without the cumbersome matrimonial ties. But now Aggie really screwed up by calling him up semidrunk last night and then sleeping with him.

Aggie unstuck her shriveled tongue from the roof of her

mouth, wincing at the nasty taste. Last night's multiple rounds of green tea martinis at Laurel had been the perfect tonic after another depressing day at her ailing boutique. Sitting in the white and black bar, under a glass chandelier, she'd been feeling chic and sophisticated with her dinner date.

But then, without warning, she thought, I've gotta call Mama tonight. All the air sucked out of the room as she remembered that she couldn't call her mama tonight, or any other night for the rest of her life. While her dinner date seemed to go on mute, a full-frontal assault of loss pelted her with the cold certainty that she couldn't take her mama to their weekly Sunday brunch, or fight about the latest loser Mama opened her door to.

Never again would she be embarrassed when people made faces at Mama's signature, skunk-striped hair, or because she still lived in that double wide in the Keystone Trailer Park next to the Bay Theatre. And she would never get another chance to tell her mama "Love you," because the person she loved most in this world was mowed down by an eighty-one-year-old pink-haired woman who had been startled by a backfire in the parking lot of Wal-Mart.

Last night had been one of those nights Aggie knew she wouldn't survive alone, which was how Kevin ended up in her bed.

The sheets whispered over Kevin as he turned, brushing his hot skin against hers. She snuck a look at him, his hair glowing like antique gold against his dark surfer's tan. Long lashes rested on the delicate skin under his eyes, hiding eyes that had seen it all and weren't impressed. She raised her fingers, wanting to touch his plush lower lip. But she let it hover so as not to wake him and give him the wrong idea.

After her mama died, she didn't need a shrink to explain

why she'd decided it was time to grow up and settle down. It was a need that started out slowly, almost innocently, when Nely, Aggie's best friend, took her hand, put it on her belly, and said, "The baby's moving."

It was one of those piss-in-your-pants moments, and after that, Aggie began noticing that the world seemed full of pregnant women. And then one day she filled out a subscription card to *Working Mother*. She knew she was in trouble when she caught herself walking through the doors of Babystyle, because that's when her case of baby fever went from the sniffles to chronic.

All she wanted was someone to love and to love her back. Someone to belong to and who belonged to her.

Aggie pulled the covers up to her nose in case she started crying and Kevin woke up and tried to make her feel better. But she couldn't drag her gaze away from him as she was hit with the senseless need to roll over and snuggle against his side.

Before she did anything else stupid, she snuck out of bed with the vague discomfort that something important had slipped her mind.

"I always knew you'd have great taste in underwear," Kevin grumbled in his sleepy voice, catching her tiptoeing around the foot of the bed. Until then, she'd forgotten about the see-through black mesh bra and panty set. Her robe was nowhere to be seen.

Although she knew she looked good—she'd better, having given up mashed potatoes and other carbs after her thirtieth birthday—this was not what anyone would call a power position. Unless of course, she was trying to seduce him, which of course she was not.

"You have to go," she said as if she weren't standing there

in her see-through underpants, and Kevin didn't look like a Herb Ritts portrait with the hazy morning light caressing his cap of close cropped curly hair and his taut shoulders.

Her mouth watered as she took in his chocolate colored nipples, the pattern of hair that started at his belly and then trailed down to his groin, covered by the sheet that barely clung to his skin. When his face squinched into a yawn, she bore down on the lust that spiraled through her belly.

She bent down, deliberately picked his pants off the floor, then pitched them over the bed. He caught them and flung them over her pillow.

"Oh come on. You were a lady last night and I . . ." He pointed to his chest. "I was a gentleman. Nothing happened."

"Really? I could've sworn I was wearing my vintage Diane von Furstenberg wrap when I met you at Laurel."

"You were. But I thought you'd be more comfortable in that." His eyes sparkled in the way of a wolf that just spotted an easy meal.

Aggie thought about all those unfortunate women who tried to tame him. They hadn't stood a chance, although she—

No, she told those thoughts.

"Okay, well, see you later," she said before pivoting on the ball of her foot.

"This how you want to do it?" He dry-scrubbed his hands over his face. "And don't go making this my fault. You called me."

"You're the one who came running," she shot back.

She was surprised his stare didn't bore a hole through her head.

"You have no—" he started, then caught himself. He

grabbed his pants, holding the sheets over himself as he swung his legs off the bed. "What? Are you going to watch?" His gaze slammed into hers as he surged to his feet, and she no longer had to wonder what he looked like naked.

She opened her mouth and then shut it. Her whole body flushed hot. But it took a lot of willpower to stare at the floor.

"Don't you have somewhere to go?" he prompted, yanking up his zipper but not buttoning.

And then she remembered that today was Saturday, and unless she hustled, she'd be late picking up Nely for their girls' weekend at the exclusive Ventana de Oro. Aggie had read Guru Sauro's book, *Seekers of the Dead*, after her mama died. She immediately signed herself and Nely up for his revolutionary transcendental meditation ceremony. On the website, people who had done it claimed they saw the future, missing people, and dead relatives. It was unlikely that she would get that lucky, but maybe . . .

She mentally rolled her eyes at herself. She probably had a better chance of asking God what the hell he was thinking, taking her mama when she still needed her.

"Aggie!" Kevin called her back, concern softening his frowning brow. "Are you all right?"

She pulled it together, determined not to appear weak. "Lock the door after you leave, please."

When she made it to the bathroom, she shut the door, turned on the shower, then sat on the toilet seat lid, overwhelmed by the collision of mortification, jealousy, lust, and oddly, loss. She was mortified that she'd called Kevin drunk and lonely; the lust was self-explanatory. She couldn't lose him, and yet, if she wanted a husband and a baby, she would have to eventually.

If she were more sophisticated, this morning wouldn't ruin their friendship. But she wasn't and—

The door clicked open, and his brandy and gravel voice beckoned from the crack. "Can I talk to you before I go?"

"Nely hates it when I'm late," she said, then told herself that she wasn't crying. It must be really dusty in there, and if she hadn't had to let go of the cleaning service, she wouldn't be—

"Are you crying?" he demanded through the door.

"No."

"Can we talk?"

Her heart slammed against her chest and she realized she was tugging too hard on the rhinestone star pendant she'd worn since seventh grade.

"I think we have something worth saving, don't you?" After a few moments, he snapped impatiently, "Stop crying. Nothing happened."

"Was I really that drunk?"

"To call me?" he asked with wry humor. "You didn't do anything to embarrass either of us."

She got up from the toilet and wrapped a towel around herself before yanking the door open and facing him. "You could've explained everything when I was standing there in my underpants."

Kevin crossed his arms over that chiseled chest. The flare of heat in his eyes should've melted her on the spot.

"I'm sorry, but I really have to go," she said, confused, and awkward with the way things had changed between them. He acted like they hadn't, but they had, and she didn't want to be the one to admit it. "My friend has really been looking forward to this trip."

It seemed he was about to say or do something to tempt her beyond the safe boundaries of friendship. But then a self-deprecating laugh huffed out of him and he shook his head, pushing himself off the wall.

"We'll talk when you get back," he said, turning away. "I hope this doesn't turn out to be one of your games, Aggie."

She opened her mouth to say something, but as he walked away, he cut her off: "Just get dressed."

"Aggie, are you on the freeway coming to get me?" Nely asked her friend's voice mail as she rushed out of the steaming bathroom wrapped in a towel. "I'm having second thoughts. I've never been away from Audrey this long and I don't have anything to wear—"

"Simon's hand snuck up from behind her and landed on her breast. A spark exploded the dust off her libido as he whispered, "You're going."

"Cut it out," she chastised him, but he gently squeezed, pushing her toward the wall. "I'm on the phone—"

He plucked it out of her hand, hit the End button, and threw the phone on the bed.

"She's always late," he said with that feral growl that always made her an easy mark. "And Audrey's asleep."

He swung her to face him before her back bumped against the wall. His kiss, wet and deep, and leaving nothing to the imagination, frightened away all of her worries about the weekend. She gave a start when his tongue thrust into her mouth and his hand ripped her towel open.

He broke the kiss to whisper the kind of things that no one would imagine a father of an eighteen-month-old daughter would whisper to his wife. Dirty, disgusting things that

made her hitch her leg up on his hip as he wrestled himself
out of his pants, not bothering to take off his clothes.

"You want this," he said, teasing her with the tip. "How
bad, baby, how bad?"

But then a crash sounded from Audrey's room and her
reply froze in her mouth. *She'll be fine*, Nely prayed. But
Simon jerked away when Audrey's cry sounded over the
baby monitor.

"Sorry," he hissed, and then, with a peck on her lips, ran
out of the room.

"Anyway . . ." Nely sighed, bending down to retrieve her
towel.

It was better this way. She never found the time to get all
the things she'd wanted to do done, like fold and put away
all of Audrey's laundry, shop for clothes to wear to Ventana
de Oro, much less have hot, grinding sex with her husband,
who had been working insane hours on a case.

"Where are the clean bottles?" Simon shouted from the
kitchen.

"They're in the dishwasher," she shouted back. She
squeezed the toothpaste too hard and ended up with a blob
oozing between her breasts.

"What?"

"Dishwasher!"

"Why weren't they put away?"

Just like that, any desire to have sex with him vanished.
Was she wrong in remembering that her husband had once
been a competent adult? The man held the power to enforce
the law of the land. He carried a gun. Shouldn't he be able
to fend for himself?

"Nel!" Simon called over the sound of him wreaking
havoc in her kitchen cabinets.

"What?"

"Get down here!"

She looked out the window at the flawless blue sky, the first blue sky in a whole week, and thought about Aggie. She probably packed her bag last night with Bebel Gilberto or Diana Krall bossa novaing softly from the stereo while taking sips from an expensive bottle of pinot grigio. And she could do so without any guilt. Little bitch.

"Will you just come down here?" Simon shouted. "She just threw up."

Throwing her toothbrush into the sink, Nely paused, hoping that when she was arraigned for Simon's murder, she got a female judge with a husband and toddler. Only a woman would understand.

In record time she yanked on her uniform of jeans, tank top, and flip-flops to go downstairs and clean up a vomity, hungry toddler.

"Thanks for not having these ready," he growled at her while Audrey screamed from the high chair.

"F-you," she hissed on her way to rescue her daughter.

"I wish," he hissed back, and she couldn't help but smile. But only for a second. He had no right to shout at her for not having the bottles ready. Did he see her getting a massage any time this week?

She cleaned Audrey up and then calmed her with a bottle of juice and some crackers.

"Sorry for yelling at you," he said. "I hate it when she cries like that."

Her anger snapped off like a light. She never quite got over the fact that her tough, mean-looking husband could sit in the same room with rapists, murderers, and people who would sell their kids for heroin money. But one peep from their daughter and he was completely worthless.

"I'll throw her sheets into the dryer," she said in concession to his apology. "But I have to pack."

"Go."

Nely hurried into the laundry room then froze in place, like a deer that sensed the hunter. Sniffing Estée Lauder Youth Dew in the air, she knew it could only be La Cacuy.

"Oh, I'm so glad I caught you before you left," her mother-in-law, Simona Mendoza trilled, popping up from behind the dryer door. "I hope you don't mind but the door was open and I saw all of this dirty laundry that hadn't been done."

Nely forced a smile on her face. Aggie better have her ass in that car.

"Thank you, Simona."

Slamming the dryer door shut, Simona handed a folder to her.

"What is this?" Nely asked through her clenched teeth.

"I signed you and Audrey up for Miss Cheryl's Toddler Time," Simona said.

"But I said I wasn't sure if we were going to do it again," Nely replied, trying not to emphasize the word "again" but failing.

"Well, I really wanted you to join the group at the church," Simona said, as if she hadn't spoken. "You know, you still have to get her baptized. Or else she'll still have her *cuernos*—her horns from original sin."

Nely told herself that her mother-in-law only had their best interests at heart. Remembering to respect Simon's mother, she said, "Thank you so much for doing the laundry but Aggie will be here any second and I have to finish packing."

She edged toward the kitchen door, hoping Simona would take the hint and go away. But the woman who named her son after herself had no intention of leaving until she drew as much blood as she possibly could.

"Are you really wearing that?"

In the glow of Simona's Ann Taylor casual, Nely felt heavy-footed and slatternly. She'd never seen Simona's hair when it wasn't teased dramatically off her face and sprayed firmly in place. She wished she'd put on lipstick and tied her frizzed-out hair into a ponytail.

"You know," La Cacuy continued, "my son really deserves to have his rest since he's the only one who works. By the way, have you found something to do?"

This woman knew where it hurt.

They could only stretch Simon's paycheck for so long. More often than usual, she caught herself fantasizing about Audrey's first day of preschool. Maybe it was time for her to think about going back into the real world. But when she left her old job, she'd been burned out from the vague sense that she should be doing something else. She just didn't know what it was.

"I've been keeping you," Simona said, her blood thirst assuaged. For now. "Oh, and don't worry while you're away. I'm sure Audrey will get used to you being gone."

Nely's guilty conscience snapped at the bait, but she held it back from taking a full bite.

Simona sighed. "Still, I hope you'll let me put Audrey on the baptism list. You never know what could happen."

Simona walked by Nely and into kitchen, shutting her out of her own house.

Leaving the folder on the washing machine, Nely slipped out the side door, ran around to the front door and then up the stairs, where she heard Simona singing a child's song to Audrey in Spanish.

At her chest of drawers, she blindly threw fistfuls of clothes into the open bag. When it was stuffed to the max, she hurried to her dresser to sift through her jewelry box for her wedding band and engagement ring. She was about to push them down her finger when she hesitated. They hadn't fit since she was five months pregnant with Audrey.

But perhaps they could after this week's diet of Slim Fast and her interrupted attempts at the postnatal Yoga Boogie tape Simona had given her the day she and Audrey came home from the hospital. Unfortunately, her last minute regimen still left her body resembling the Michelin tire man.

With a deep breath, she slid the rings on. But they refused to budge past her knuckle.

Predeparture homesickness flooded her again. What if something happened to Simon or Audrey and she was too far away to get back in time? Or what if something happened to her?

Was she a bad wife and mother for leaving them, for not baptizing her baby and possibly making her a candidate for that special place in Purgatory for children?

Nely caught her reflection in the mirror. Stop torturing yourself with guilt, she told herself. That's what her mother always said. Then again, her mother hadn't been around much when she was growing up.

She would only be away for a weekend, and maybe the distance would be good for her. She returned the rings to the box.

Two

She should've lined the driveway with peach Bellini's to lure Nely out.

"This isn't going to be easy," Simon warned her, effortlessly holding Audrey in one arm while carrying his wife's bulging bag in the other. "My mother got to her again."

"Oh," Aggie said, checking out the sharp sinew of muscle under his tanned skin, the hint of steel in his black hair. Why did Simon have to be an only child? When she imagined the perfect man, he was the one. Except she didn't have any attraction to guys like Simon. Too serious.

"Hi, sweetie," she cooed to Audrey, reaching out to touch a chubby arm. Audrey snatched it back, her dark eyes narrowing at her as if to say, *Stop checking out my daddy.*

"So where's the little mama?" Aggie asked, wondering what she did to make Audrey hate her so much.

"Take this in the car," he said, handing her the duffel. "I'll bring her out."

Tossing her hair out of her eyes, Aggie walked to the trunk of her mother's black and white 1969 Dodge Charger. With the way that kid screamed every time she called, it seemed Nely would've been waiting with hands pressed to the window to get out. With a heave, she swung the duffel into the trunk next to the monogrammed doctor's bag she'd bought as a present to herself. Her Sidekick vibrated that she had a voice mail and she told herself to ignore it.

Then Simon brought Nely out and they looked so adult, standing in front of their two-story, stucco tract house. Aggie swelled with jealousy, thinking about how at thirty-two she still rented, barely made her car payments, and didn't even own a cat much less a baby. She felt so childish while they seemed so . . . so grown up.

You could have that, a voice whispered from the farthest, darkest corner of her brain. *Just stop sleeping with the wrong men.*

"All right, you two, break it up," Aggie hollered. "Nely, get your ass in the car and let's go get us a cabana boy."

She slammed the trunk down and noticed Simon's thuggish glare. "For me," she teased.

His stoic Indian face, with the long nose that was ever so slightly wide at the nostrils and the flat cheekbones, was built to intimidate criminals and keep small children in line. But she knew him long enough to see the teasing glint in his eye.

"Please keep my wife out of trouble," he warned as Nely blinked her red-rimmed eyes. "But make sure she has a good time and doesn't call every five minutes."

"I'm your woman," Aggie replied. "Come on," she urged

her overly maternal friend. "Back away from the baby and get in the car."

"I don't know." Nely hesitated after she gave Aggie a tepid hug.

"Get going, babe," Simon gently encouraged. "You'll run into traffic."

"Don't forget she'll be hungry in an hour," Nely told him as Aggie escorted her to the car.

He nodded. His glance at Aggie told her to jump in and start the engine.

"And she likes to sleep with Peter Rabbit, not that weird spider thing your mother got her."

"Weird spider thing is out," he said.

Aggie watched Simon place his hand on top of Nely's head and push her down into the car. He ducked his head into the window. "I promise not to maim, paralyze, or kill our daughter. Go and have a great time."

To Aggie, he said, "Hit the gas while you still have a chance."

Aggie released the parking brake, separating mother from child, hearth, and home. The tires crunched the grit as they slowly rolled away from the sidewalk.

"And her sheets are in the dryer!" Nely shouted out the window.

"Okay."

"If you need more breast milk—"

Aggie, who had allowed the car to creep away, slammed her foot to the gas pedal. The engine roared exuberantly as they sped down the street.

"You'll only be gone for thirty-six hours," Aggie reminded her. "Give yourself a break. She'll be fine."

"I know but—okay, you're right. I work twenty-four/seven and this is my chance to sit down, have a drink, maybe read a book without someone screaming at me from the kitchen or a suicidal child trying to throw herself off the couch."

Aggie smiled at her friend. Some women got pretty worked over by motherhood, but not Nely. Aggie envied her flawless pale skin, brandy-colored eyes, and black hair. Even as she sniffled and wiped her tears off her face, Nely still had an untouchable grace and elegance that Aggie knew she would never achieve.

"You don't think I'm a bad mother, do you?"

"What? Why would you even think that?"

Nely answered with a listless shrug, and Aggie saw no reason to trouble her already troubled friend with this morning's "incident," or any of her other looming disasters. This was their chance to hang out, which they hadn't been able to do since Audrey arrived.

Aggie concentrated on driving them out of the labyrinthine streets of the Eastlake neighborhood that spiraled out toward the nucleus, a suburban mom's mecca of Old Navy, Target, Baja Fresh, and Starbucks. Eastlake had a very Munchkinland quality to it without the scruffy, cooler-than-thou edges of Golden Hills where she herself lived.

Then again, people out here seemed nice. They actually acknowledged each other as they pushed strollers to and from the family SUV. Aggie indulged herself with a brief fantasy of holding the door open to Jamba Juice while Kevin pushed a stroller.

"Oh my God!" Nely screamed when Aggie swerved into the other lane, cutting off an SUV full of kids in soccer uniforms.

With her heart running like a terrified rabbit, Aggie

yanked the heavy car back into her lane. When the tire dust settled and the SUV took off with a middle finger salute, Aggie reached over and switched the radio on. Creedence Clearwater Revival sang "Bad Moon Rising."

"Is your car in the shop?" Nely asked after their brush with death.

"No," Aggie half lied. The Charger was a beast on wheels that was slightly musty with a totally white-trash paint job, but it made her feel closer to her mother.

Even though they'd been friends since move-in day at USC, Aggie didn't want to trouble Nely with the fact that she'd had to sell her snappy little Nissan Z to pay the lease on the store.

Nely cranked the window up when they reached the 805 freeway. A sombrero danced from the rearview mirror, and the gigantic motor quickly heated up the interior.

Aggie's eyes darted behind her tinted glasses like startled fish in an aquarium. Based on fourteen years of friendship and many nights of holding each other's hair out of their faces after too many drinks, Nely sensed that her friend was trying to keep a secret.

"So what did you do last night?" she asked casually.

"Nothing," Aggie cried out, then moderated her tone. "I mean, nothing."

Nely knew there was a man in this mystery, and her spidey sense told her that he wasn't just some ordinary man. He meant something to Aggie.

"Do I know him?" she asked, twirling her hair around her finger.

Aggie hesitated. "Not really."

A swirling light went off over Nely's head. *Dear God, no.* "It's not Kevin, is it?"

"Is my private life that entertaining to you?" Aggie snapped. "Or is your life that boring?"

Nely started to back off, then remembered they were friends, and friends didn't let friends sleep with men like him. "Can I ask one question?"

Aggie's silence told her that no, she couldn't, but Nely asked it anyway. "Kevin *Kevin?* The one who sleeps with every—"

"Yes, *that* Kevin."

Nely didn't know what else to say other than, "Does he live up to his reputation?"

"I don't know. We slept together in the technical sense. There was no sex, just sleeping."

Nely had met Kevin twice. First, when Aggie took her and Simon to his restaurant, Sazón, for their second anniversary, and then again at the memorial party for Helen, Aggie's mama.

Nely's impression of him was an arrogant, tough guy who should've run a biker bar rather than a sexy, sophisticated restaurant in the Gaslamp Quarter. But he'd run Helen's party with quiet authority, bringing out trays of food and directing the wait staff. Nely remembered thinking that he had the swagger of a man who had won every fight and had any woman he wanted.

But he had never been far from Aggie's side. Nely caught him glancing at her, concern softening the playboy glint in his eyes. But just when Nely started to like him, she'd walked into the ladies' room and caught him wrestling with a girl who looked like she had celebrated her eighteenth birthday the night before.

"So what does that mean?" Nely asked now, returning to

the subject at hand. "Are you falling—" She caught herself. "No, Aggie. No you can't let yourself—"

"I'm not that stupid!"

"But—"

"I had too much to drink and Kevin brought me home. He was acting in the role of a friend."

Nely kept her silence on what kind of friend he was.

"Don't give me the eyebrow," Aggie whined.

"What eyebrow?"

"That thing you do with your left eyebrow."

Nely narrowed her eyes instead.

"The situation is under control," Aggie rushed on. "In fact, it's not even a situation."

How many times had Nely heard that?

"Is it?" she asked. "Under control, I mean. Or was he taking advantage of the fact that you're still mourning your mother, and your need to have a baby, which stems from that loss?"

Aggie lips tightened. Nely saw that she had struck two nerves. "I never said I wanted a baby," she muttered.

"You've got a *Parents* magazine in the backseat."

Aggie sunk lower in the seat, having been caught.

"I'm not judging you. I think that's wonderful. If you want those things, then I want them for you."

"You don't think I'm pathetic, do you?"

"No," Nely said, though she didn't see her flighty friend as a mom. "Just a glutton for punishment."

Aggie swung her head in alarm. "But I thought you loved being a mom!"

Nely loved nothing more on this earth than her daughter. But there were moments, like this morning, when she wondered if she was really cut out to civilize another human being.

"You do, don't you?" Aggie asked.

"Of course I do," Nely sighed, getting a chill when she suddenly remembered Simon pushing her up against the wall.

She cleared her throat. "If you're thinking about settling down, maybe you need to start hanging around the kind of men who want the same thing."

"You mean stay away from Kevin?"

"I didn't say that." Nely scratched her arm, ran her fingertip over her left eyebrow, then looked out the window. If she told Aggie the sky was blue, Aggie would insist it was red. So she had to be careful. "But yeah, that would be a good idea."

Aggie sighed in that wistful way she always did when Nely hoped she wouldn't do what she'd probably end up doing anyway.

Three

Kevin ended up at the Influx Café up the hill from the bungalow duplex he shared with Aggie. When he walked in, Johnny Cash sang about looking for someone who's never weak but always strong over the sound system.

Kevin glanced up at the mirror behind the counter and saw a coward's face reflected back at him. He'd answered Aggie's SOS call with every intention of seducing her and then keeping her in bed for the rest of the weekend and quite possibly longer than that.

But then he couldn't when he saw what condition she was in last night. So he got her undressed, trying not to look, and when that proved to be too hard, he just told himself not to touch. And he didn't, which he now regretted because when he saw her in her underwear this morning, it physically hurt not to be able to touch her. Normally this sort of thing wouldn't have stopped him. But Aggie had this flashing neon Do Not Touch Me sign around her neck and he'd choked.

"That'll be six-fifty, sir," said the barista with a safety pin stuck through his eyebrow.

"Do you mind changing the music?" Kevin asked.

"It's the Cash."

This pretentious moron probably never heard of Johnny Cash before the Joaquin Phoenix movie, he thought.

"I know it's Johnny Cash," Kevin said, "and it's depressing."

The barista sputtered his lips and thrust out a hip full of attitude. "I don't know how to change the CD player."

He then turned his attention to the customer waiting behind Kevin. "What can I get you?"

Kevin nearly turned into the guy with the bags under his eyes and a baby strapped to his chest. The little kid was cute.

Jesus.

He strode out the door. A bus roared up Golden Hill toward the mini-downtown area where Victorian mansions had been converted into law offices and families still shopped at a 1940s-era market. It was a typical San Diego morning, rich, gold light pouring out of a sky that mocked him with its pristine blueness.

He knew what to do. He had to find some woman who would erase the shame that he'd been rejected by Aggie, who thought of him—him—as only a friend. For a guy, being "just a friend" was worse than death.

"Kevin? What are you doing here?"

He looked up and saw his buddy from his days as a dishwasher at the Hotel Del, Pierce.

"I've been wanting to call you, what's up?" Pierce said.

Kevin cleared the knot out of his throat. "Not much, what's up with you?"

Pierce glanced over his shoulder and then shuffled his feet nervously. "You mind sittin' down with me for a second?"

"I really have to—"

"Dude, this is serious. I really need to talk to you."

Kevin needed a moment to clear his head of Aggie, of the thought that he'd come this close to begging her to give him a chance. "Yeah, man. Why don't you get yourself a coffee and I'll hang here."

"Dude, I owe you one."

Pierce ran off, almost tackling the dad and baby. Kevin pulled his eyes off the baby and onto his espresso. He wasn't sure when this—looking at babies and Aggie in the same train of thought—had happened to him. At some point in the recent past women started to all look alike. Sure he noticed them—he wasn't dead, just stupid—but he never chased, never gave them a second glance. Rather, he found himself comparing them to Aggie.

"I can't thank you enough," Pierce said, shooting into his seat and spilling coffee on the table. "Here's the deal. I'm asking Marcel to marry me."

With a shaking hand, Kevin reached for his espresso, wishing it was tequila.

"And I want to do it at your place," Pierce finished.

"My place?"

"Yeah. The restaurant. She thinks that your wedding soup tastes just like her grandmother's."

"Fine. I'll reserve you a table."

"But I need you to serve that soup. It's crucial."

"It's not on the menu."

"Dude, please. Her sister has this guy she's dating, and Marcel can't stop talking about all the shit this guy does. I have to make this special. I want her to look back on this night and remember it for the rest of her life."

Pierce had always been intense, but he was so tense now, Kevin could feel the vibrations across the table. And what he saw chilled his blood. He had to do something fast before he ended up like this pathetic fool sitting across from him.

"Why are you trying so hard?" popped out of his mouth.

"Because I love her, man."

"But does she love you the same?"

Pierce jerked back in his seat. "Of course she does. Are you telling me I shouldn't do this?"

The espresso kicked into high gear, rattling Kevin's teeth. He had to get out of here. He had to get out of his own skin.

"It's cool, man," he said, pushing his seat away.

"So can I do it at your place or not?"

"Yeah. Call me with the date."

Shit, he had to talk to someone about this. Talk? Blech. He never talked. Talk was for pretty boys who had feelings and wore jewelry and stuff like that.

But like it or not, his choice was down to talking or crying. On his way out the door, Kevin reached for his cell phone and flipped it open.

A man knew that he'd cut all ties to his bachelorhood when (a) he swapped the porno version of *Snow White and the Seven Dwarfs* for the Disney one, (b) his beer run ended with him wrestling his screaming eighteen-month-old daughter off the coin operated merry-go-round, and (c) he had danced, sang, bribed, and then finally wrapped his daughter with her favorite blanket so tightly that she looked like a bubble-gum-colored burrito, all with the goal of getting her to sleep so he could have a beer.

Not even five minutes had passed since Simon tiptoed out of Audrey's room, avoiding all the creaky places in the stairs, when the phone rang. His whole being flashed red as he dived across the floor for the phone, hissing curses at the idiot who could've ruined his whole evening with one ill-timed call.

"Simon, it's me. I'm just calling to say good night."

It was his mother calling *again*, even though she'd stayed most of the day, cleaning and cooking. He appreciated everything she did, but damn it, he'd wanted a father-daughter day all to himself. His father had stuck around long enough to put his name on his birth certificate. Simon promised to be different. But between his wife and mother hogging Audrey, he wasn't getting the time he really wanted.

He closed his eyes and counted to three before he said, "Good night, Mom."

She didn't take the hint. "So what are you doing?"

"My laundry," he lied, hoping she'd let him go.

"Didn't Nely do your laundry before she left? Why didn't you tell me? I would've done it for you!"

His mother was the only person he knew who could be insulted if he didn't ask her to do something for him. "Mom, you know that Nely has never done my laundry in the eight years we've been together."

"Oh, I see. I just thought that since she's not working she'd do a little more around the house."

"Mom . . ." he warned.

"I'm not—"

"Mom."

"Did I tell you about this new program I found on TV?" Simona asked, changing the subject.

With the cordless wedged between his ear and shoulder, Simon opened the refrigerator for a beer, prepared to listen in a nonlistening yet dutiful son sort of way.

"It's one of those reality shows about spouses who cheat. This one woman signed up for one of those Internet dating services. Anyway, she pretended to be a different woman and met a man. So one weekend she told her husband and three children she was going away with a friend, but what she really did was meet that man at a hotel."

He never should've picked up the phone. "When are you ever going to like my wife?" he asked. "Or at least appreciate that she brought your one and only grandchild into the world?"

"Simon—"

"In fifteen minutes I'm going to sit down and watch the repeat of the USC game, and I'd like to do it in peace."

"Simon, I love Nely. You know I do."

He didn't even blink an eye at her blatant lie.

"Well, I'm trying," she admitted.

"If that's your way of trying, stop."

She sighed. "If I make your favorite breakfast Sunday, could I watch Audrey before Nely comes home?"

A real breakfast and a morning without his mother presented two very difficult choices. But if she kept Audrey entertained, he might be able to pull off the special dinner he'd been planning for Nely and he wouldn't hurt his mother's feelings.

On the other hand, he'd never have sex again if Nely returned to see the house in its current, spotless condition, because somehow she'd know Simona had done it and not him.

He drummed his fingers on the counter, wishing he didn't have to play diplomat to his wife and mother.

"How about lunch?" he asked. "I want to take Audrey out for a jog in the morning."

Simona made a huffy sigh.

He then appealed to her sense of fantasy. "Just pretend she left me and I needed you to move in and help me with my recently orphaned child."

She brightened. "Sounds perfect, *mijo*."

Relieved to get her off the phone, Simon tasted his beer and then listened carefully to the house. It was a lonely, slow quiet without Nely, or at least the Nely he'd married.

But she hadn't changed so much that she'd pull a stunt like his mother had so subtly described. He practically had to attack her just to see her naked. If she couldn't be naked in front of him, then she definitely wouldn't be in front of another guy.

Shaking his head, Simon fell into his recliner and turned on the TV, but he just flipped through the 400 channels they had through the satellite, seeing nothing except the sofa where he and Nely used to make love, and the crack in the vase they had broken when they first tried having sex against the wall.

A grin cracked across his serious face. He missed that. It wasn't so much the sex—not that his wife would ever believe him if he told her—it was the feel of her skin. Afterward, he'd always draw his knuckles down and up the slope of her waist and hip as they'd lie together.

In those moments they would either doze off or make the

most important decisions of their lives. Or they'd be silent, just listening to each other breathing.

Back then he felt that his wife had loved him. But now it seemed like Nely loved Audrey even more. He told himself not to be jealous of that love. Would he prefer that she hate their kid? But he couldn't help but want a little of that love for himself.

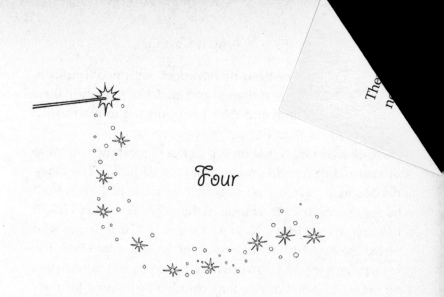

Four

"Do you think we should stop drinking if we're going to the guru's transcendental mediation tonight?" Nely asked, lolling her head over to Aggie.

"Absolutely not," Aggie answered, reaching for her drink.

"Do you really think you can talk to the dead like it says you can?" Nely asked. "I don't know what I'd say."

Aggie hoped so, having thrown herself deeper into debt to spend the weekend up here. Maybe Mama would have some wisdom about how she could get untangled from all the loose ends in her life, or at the very least what she should do about the e-mail from Kevin waiting in her Sidekick in box.

They lounged in a private, poolside cabana attended to by an all-American cabana boy named Luke who had natural honey-colored highlights in his hair and a generous smile.

y had been massaged by hot rocks, wrapped in unpro-
unceable herbs, exfoliated and moisturized until their
skin shone like satin and their bones melted to warm jelly.
This was better than pot.

Ventana de Oro stood on top of the highest mountaintop
skirted with avocado groves, just west of Julian. The original Moorish palace with sugar-white walls had been built
by some eccentric steel baron in the 1920s. A year ago it had
been renovated into a New Age resort by Guru Sauro, who
wrote the *New York Times* best-seller, *Seekers of the Dead*. The
resort was a mecca for overworked A-types and movie stars
on orders to detox or else they couldn't be insured for their
next production.

Aggie thought that if there was a place where she could
stop running around in circles and get some answers, this
would be it. She'd gone to sleep every night this past year
hoping it would be the night when Mama would visit her in
her dreams. It seemed like everyone who lost a parent had
at least one dream of them . . . everyone except her.

But then Kevin's stupid e-mail ruined everything.

"Earth to Aggie?" Nely called her back.

"What?"

Nely stared at her for an impossibly slow moment while
Aggie tried to force her uncooperative lips into a smile.
Good God, why was she tying herself up into knots over
Kevin? They hadn't slept together, so no damage was done,
and yet while she knew sleeping with him would've been a
disaster, she regretted that they hadn't.

And then she remembered that Nely had said something.
"What did you say?" she asked.

"Nothing." Nely flicked three pages of her magazine.

An exasperated sigh escaped, and then Aggie explained, "I got a message from Kevin."

Nely's head popped up. "What did he say?"

"I don't know. I didn't open it."

Nely opened her mouth and then shut it. "I can just imagine what he would have to say," she groused. "Nothing you could believe anyway."

Hearing the crisp disapproval in Nely's voice, Aggie almost spoke up in his defense. He was her friend, after all, and in a lot of ways he was the male version of her: driven, honest, and always needing the best and beautiful of everything, including lovers.

Aggie stared at the negative edge pool that seemed to spill off the cliff—into the narrow valley below. She reminded herself that she had better remember who she was dealing with before she tripped and fell with nothing to catch her. But she couldn't stop the riptide of memories that pulled her back to the day she met him.

"If there's a God in heaven, he's buying those for his girl-friend and not for himself," her then-assistant manager Dana had said when Aggie walked back into her new boutique after her lunch with a rep from Nanette Lepore.

"Who are you talking about?"

Dana had licked her lips as she pointed across the store. "Him."

Him, or rather, *he*, made Aggie's heart stop.

Six feet of broad-shouldered, taut-tushed, and barbarously sexy male stood over the table of lingerie, picking up a pair of Dita Glamour French Heel stockings. He peered through the package without any embarrassment.

Dana made a grab for her arm. "I spotted him first, he's mine."

Aggie flicked her eyes down to Dana's tummy. "Dude, go put your feet up or I'm calling your husband and your mother."

"But—"

Aggie barely registered Dana's protest, much less felt her feet touching the floor, as she made her way toward the man. But she swished her hips to the throbbing bass of Madonna's "Erotic," which just happened to start playing over the sound system.

Usually she didn't care for men who wore jeans during the work week. But the two men she'd been dating at the time weren't doing it for her, and the time neared to cut them loose. David kept sneaking the conversation into the religion territory, which made her suspect he was one of those super Christians. And Aaron's predilection for bright pink drinks made her wonder if he'd yet come to grips with his sexual orientation.

But this man inspired her to broaden her horizons, especially the way he wore those jeans locked tight against a narrow waist, notches and stains all along the worn denim, and tattered hems over scuffed motorcycle boots. A silver pendant with a wolf hung from a strip of leather around his neck, and she recognized the light blue T-shirt from Abercrombie and Fitch.

When she neared, piercing eyes under satyr brows flicked her way and then back to the panties dangling helplessly in his grip. "Do you work here?" he asked.

"I do." She locked eyes with him, not minding that he nearly dropped her merchandise on the floor.

"Are you kidding me? Fifty bucks for this? And what about that little jacket thing? How much is it?"

Eyes blinking as if someone had just dumped a cooler of ice over her head, Aggie stammered, "Those are from Dita von Teese's exclusive line."

"Did she wear them?"

"No, but—" Who the hell did he think he was, making her explain her merchandise? Only one store carried that line in San Diego, and that happened to be hers. No one insulted her stock or her boutique or her friend Dita.

"Maybe I can help you find something in your budget," she suggested.

His eyes never once released their hold on hers, and she didn't give into the urge to look away. It had been the first time a man sized her up without dragging his eyes all over her body. Finally, he hitched the corner of his mouth into a lopsided grin.

"She'll like these," he said, picking up a pair of the stockings. "And that jacket over there."

"It's a Milly beaded bolero," Aggie corrected. "And her size would be?"

"She's about twice the size you are—no, make that three."

Aggie smiled tightly, eager to take his money. She walked to the rack, pulled out a size eight, and held it up for his inspection.

He frowned at it for the longest time, making her wonder if she was his human clothing rack.

"Cool. Wrap it."

"Are you sure this is the right size?"

He thought about it and then his eyes fastened on her chest. "She's bigger than you. I don't know . . . a large?"

She couldn't wait for him to see the price. But when she gave him the total, he paid for it without another word and walked out the door.

Aggie wasn't sure how many days went by before that grumpy yet sexy stranger walked back into her boutique. When he did, her skin prickled as if hot, sultry wind gusted through the open door. Every female in the store sensed the presence of hot male and paused to take notice.

This time he wore his white chef's jacket, pin-striped pants, and thick, rubber-soled shoes. He dumped the bag on the counter, avoiding her gaze as he dug his wallet out of his back pocket.

"Did it not work out?" she asked, all saccharine sweet.

He didn't spare her as much as a glare. "No." He smacked his American Express card on the counter.

Although she prided herself on her professionalism, something about him irked her, so she continued to put away the spools of ribbon before her with excruciating slowness.

"Hey, do you mind? I've got other things to do."

It was the strain in his voice that got her, as if he were . . . She looked up to see if she'd heard wrong.

He stared down at the floor with one hand braced on the counter and the other hitched over his hip. But he seemed haggard and raw, as if he were trying not to cry. Did the girlfriend break his heart, leave him at the altar . . . walk off with another woman?

She took the bag on the counter, which was misshapen and torn. It crinkled in her hand. Then his hand clamped down on hers.

"Don't." Her hand began to sweat under his heavier, rougher one.

"Don't what?" she asked.

"Never mind," he said gruffly. "Just take it back."

He shot out of the store and straight into a couple out for an evening in the Gaslamp Quarter. An eruption of "Hey" and "Watch it" sounded right outside her door, but he stormed off across the street.

Holding her hand to her chest, she glanced down at the credit card with the name Kevin Sanchez. She then took the merchandise, credited his card, and sealed it in an envelope with a note to Dana to call her when he returned. On second thought, she opened the envelope and tore up the note. It wasn't her business to know why he'd acted so weird.

But then Saturday morning, as she turned the corner, he was waiting.

"Thanks for the refund," he said in greeting. "Can I have my card?"

"I was just going inside to do some paperwork," she said, because she didn't know what else to say.

He jerked his head for her to open the door, and they went into the dark store. Her scalp tingled as his steps sounded behind her. She lectured herself on the dangers of men like him. She'd just dumped a born-again freak and an accountant whose intentions were to score discounted women's clothing.

"Here's your card," she said, handing him the envelope.

He swallowed hard as he took it from her. "I hope you don't—" he started, then pressed his lips together. "That was for my mother, she . . . it just didn't work out."

She couldn't help it, but the words just shot out of her mouth. "You bought Dita von Teese stockings for your mother?"

He glanced up, and she expected to have her head ripped

off. But he was grinning. "You had to know her," he said. "She, uh . . ."

He struggled for a moment, and Aggie prayed he wouldn't break down in front of her, embarrassing them both.

"She died. Cancer. I thought she'd like—" He jerked his thumb over his shoulder to the beaded bolero still on display as he backed out of the store. "She liked pretty things."

She reached him before he got to the door. "I have coffee," she invited. "If you'd like some."

"What kind?"

She held up her cup of Pannikan Coffee, but he didn't look at it. His eyes connected to hers.

"You have enough to share?" he asked.

Silent, she nodded yes, and for once it wasn't a man's quality of ass or shoes that compelled her to make a move. Actually, it hadn't been a move, so to speak. It was more of . . . well, love at first sight. Except not the kind that morphed into the white dress and a Tiffany-cut diamond. What they started that day was a zero-bullshit kind of love, and it made her feel rather chic to have a real male friend who wasn't a lover or gay.

And when she lost Mama, Kevin had been her rock. He didn't speak platitudes of wisdom, or awkwardly say the things people said to you when your very soul had been ripped apart by loss. There was something comforting in knowing that she had a friend who knew when to talk and when to shut up.

Then again, maybe her love for him was the kind that—

"You're going to read it, aren't you?" Nely asked, snapping Aggie out of the past.

"Later," Aggie said after a second. She tucked her rhinestone-encrusted Sidekick into her bag and then pushed her fake Dolce & Gabbana sunglasses up a bit higher. "But can I ask you a question?"

"Yeah."

"How did you . . . When you met Simon, did you know he was the one?"

Nely seemed surprised, then wary. "Actually I remember thinking his date had really big teeth."

"Dude, you know what I mean. When did you know?"

"I don't know, it . . . kinda snuck up on me. I mean there was chemistry there, but he came after Jason and I broke up so I wasn't looking for 'the one.' I just thought we were having a good time and then— Don't you ever get tired of hearing this story?"

Aggie shook her head. It gave her hope.

Nely smiled, her eyes lost in the past. "I knew when he picked me up for a date and the Batman theme blasted out of the radio. He played it to pump himself up for the date. It was so cute and dorky and he was so embarrassed." She shook her head. "That's when I knew."

Aggie almost sighed. Every time a guy so much as displayed one tiny flaw, she dumped him. Perhaps she'd been too picky. Maybe she had even let "the one" go before giving him a chance.

"It feels like that day happened forever ago," Nely said, staring out at the pool. "And then sometimes it feels like yesterday."

"So that's why you're obsessed with my sex life," Aggie teased.

"Because I don't have one?" Nely cracked a grin. "But I might have sex again when Audrey graduates from high school."

Shocked, Aggie's mouth fell open, and stayed that way long enough for a fly to do a U-turn. She then shook herself loose. She had seen the kiss Simon gave Nely, with her very eyes and could not accept that her friend was not having regular sex with a man like that.

"May I refill your drinks, ladies?" Luke asked.

Red crept up Nely's chest and neck to the top of her hairline. She shot Aggie a look that said, *You could've warned me,* before diving behind her magazine.

"Two more tequila sweets," Aggie said, thinking how grown up she was that she didn't want to sleep with Luke, the cabana boy. But she wasn't so old that *he* didn't.

"You've had quite a few of those," Luke said.

Nely thrust the magazine down. "Aggie, how much are we paying for this cabana again?"

Luke did an abrupt pivot and vanished.

"As I was about to say," Nely turned to Aggie, "we have sex. Just not all the time."

Or, in a really long, long time. Actually, she couldn't remember the last time she let Simon see her naked. Not that he hadn't asked to.

"I'm going for a swim," Aggie announced, gracefully getting to her feet, but then gently swaying. "Come on in with me."

Nely swung her legs off the lounge, ready to join her, and then saw the teeny tiny rhinestone belt that rested on Aggie's fat-free hips. Silver hoops held the front and back of her bikini bottom, while a giant hoop holding onto the strapless top rested between her breasts.

Aggie's bone-straight, caramel-colored hair was pulled into one of those stylishly messy twists. Without makeup, her skin was dewy and her lips pouty pink. Nely knew that if she went into the pool, she'd have to lose her wrap, and there was no way she'd stand next to sleek little Aggie in public.

Pressing her back into her chaise lounge, Nely said, "I'll stay here and wait for the cabana boy."

"Be nice or we'll have to leave a really big tip."

"Don't drown. I'm too buzzed to save you."

Left alone and semidrunk, Nely's physical longing for her family threatened to gouge a hole in the pit of her stomach. She starved for Audrey's sleeping weight against her chest and the sudden awareness of Simon's presence before he walked through the door after his shift.

She eyed the phone sitting under the flat-screen TV mounted on an elaborately carved trunk. She'd called yesterday when they arrived, last night before bed, and then this morning. She wanted to call again now, but Simon had told her not to.

"Enjoy your time away," he'd said. "That's what you've been wanting all this time."

She wasn't so sure what he meant by that. Did he think she'd been dying to get away from them and was being sarcastic about it? Or did he truly want her to have a good time?

Lately, she felt so out of synch. She constantly questioned if she was a bad mom or a good mom; traitor to the feminist movement or acting within her rights as a woman. She didn't always relate to most of the other mommies whom she met once a week at Miss Cheryl's Toddler Time, nor to Aggie half the time.

It felt like Aggie left her behind, out there doing things and meeting interesting new people while she took care of her baby.

Nely fussed with her wrap to make sure it covered her thighs. She knew better than to envy Aggie. She knew Aggie's life wasn't perfect.

If she didn't know Aggie, she'd hate her at first sight. But ever since Aggie lost her mama, Helen, the loneliness throbbed off her. For a woman who had it all—a great body, personality, contacts in the fashion world, and money—Aggie wanted so badly to have a husband and family.

Nely mentally flicked through the faces of the single guys Simon worked with. They either had girlfriends or were like Kevin, the kind she wouldn't wish even on La Cacuy.

You know Aggie's going to sleep with him, the voice of experience said, getting back to the question at hand. Ever since Nely turned thirty, that voice no longer whispered, and it no longer stayed in her head. She could tell that her outspokenness against Kevin was driving Aggie away.

Sighing, she promised to stay quiet. Like a train wreck, there was nothing she could do to put a stop to it. She'd just have to stand there and wait for the pieces to land until she could step in and put Aggie back together again.

Five

Many weeks after this night had passed, when she'd wake up in the hospital, Aggie would realize that alcohol really could fuck things up. In other words, that she shouldn't have attempted transcendental meditation with seven tequila sweets on an empty stomach.

But at the moment, she wouldn't use the word "drunk" to describe her state of mind; that was a bit strong. She'd use "tipsy," or perhaps, as her mama used say, she was feelin' *sass-eh*.

Or she was trying to. Her heart felt like it had seized up and ceased to beat, waiting for that moment when she'd make contact with her mama. She'd feel stupid if she admitted that to Nely. She really didn't believe it would happen, and yet she hoped with her whole being that at the very least she could return to her tattered life with something.

When the golf cart turned onto a torch-lit path, she would've tumbled out into the shadowed garden if it hadn't been for Nely's fast grab.

"You might want to toss out what's left in that bottle," Nely said in that mom voice of hers.

"It's just water." Aggie held up the free water bottle she got from that morning's Pilates class. "And I'm not drunk. Just fuzzy around the edg-esh."

But when the golf cart jerked to a stop at the top of the hill, she couldn't move.

"Aggie, we're here," Nely said. "Unless, of course, you want to go back and order room service."

"Wha . . . ?"

"Oh my God. Are you okay? You're sweating."

Aggie wiped her upper lip with the back of her trembling hand. "It's the fire," she said, shrugging it off, but still not able to get off the cart. "And I'm fu-fu-fine."

A shiver ripped through her knotted muscles.

"You haven't eaten much today," Nely said. "Driver, would you—"

"No!" Aggie cried, and the people around them turned to watch what was going on. "I want to do it."

She had to do it.

Carefully feeling for the ground with her foot, she stepped off the cart and somehow walked on wobbly legs toward the roaring bonfire in the center of several large stones. A smiling woman who wore her ebony hair in a Frieda Kahlo braid tacked up at the top of her head greeted them.

"Welcome, star sister. Please walk the circle until your rock calls to you."

"Wait a second," Nely said. "We have to sit on those?"

The star sister smiled and nodded. "They are the fingers of the Mother Earth. They will keep you grounded."

Aggie grabbed Nely's hand, tucking it under her elbow. "Just go with it," she said with shameless bravado. But in fact she felt like the Cowardly Lion worrying his tail with his hands while chanting, "I do believe in spooks, I do, I do, I do believe in spooks."

"Easy for you to say," Nely hissed back. "You didn't have an episiotomy a year and a half ago!"

"Is that all you can talk about?"

"What the hell is your problem?"

"All you talk about is the baby and being pregnant. This is supposed to be a girls' weekend. Not Mommy and me."

Nely wilted like a cut flower left out of the vase. All the fun camaraderie they'd had vanished.

Aggie withered with shame. She hadn't meant that. Not really.

"You suck," Nely said before she could apologize, and then sat down.

The hilltop, with its hard-packed dirt and rocks circling the roaring fire, had been denuded of plant life. Sparks shot up into the great big bowl of a sky. The full moon, plump and golden, regally made its way from behind the mountains in the east, threatening to crash into earth.

"The guru will approach when he senses that our minds are silent and our spirit guides have settled among us," Nely's star sister announced. "I am Spring Calf."

Nely clenched her jaw rather than roll her eyes.

"The guru has asked that you begin thinking about what you want most. What your conscious mind craves to possess," Spring Calf instructed. "And then release it. Free your mind of desire, attachment, and self."

Another woman joined Spring Calf. They raised flutes to their lips and began a mysterious song.

Not only was it cold as hell out here, everyone was better dressed than her, Nely silently fumed.

Still smoldering after Aggie's verbal bitch slap, Nely fingered the minibottle of Cuervo in her pocket. She knew she should've stayed home, but Aggie had talked her into this and now they were both stuck up here with these wiggy chicks hopping up and down, blowing into flutes. On top of it, her butt had fallen asleep.

She wanted to go home. Aggie could deal with her stuff on her own if Nely's limited conversational skills were that annoying. But she stayed here. Why? She didn't know. Well, maybe she did. If she lost her mother the way Aggie had so suddenly, she might be willing to try something as nutty as this to get one chance to say good-bye.

Loyalty sucked.

Suddenly, the women stopped playing their flutes, and then there was just the snap and hiss of the fire. Out of the indigo night and the looming shadows of the trees, the guru approached the edge of the ring. His chiseled face, harsh in the light of the fire, radiated a leonine serenity. Compact but powerfully built with bronze skin, he appeared to step out of a painting of a Mayan warrior.

Abruptly, he shot his hands up and the buffalo hide he wore over his shoulders spread like hideous wings.

"I am the Guru Sauro."

"Greetings to our teacher," Spring Calf intoned, and Nely had to bear down to keep from rolling her eyes.

"Tonight we will transcend ourselves and begin walking the path of enlightenment and freedom," he said.

Spring Calf came forward and removed his cape. Bare-chested and wearing tight, deerskin pants, he stopped closer to the fire. He reached with his right hand, in which the other Star Sister placed a giant seashell. Putting one end at his lips, he sent a throaty echo down the four sides of the hill that flowed out into the shadowed valley.

The sound shot through the center of Nely and rippled out in shivers over her skin. The ominous gold moon now stood above the mountaintops, shining through the clouds smudged against the sky. Up here the sky overwhelmed her, deep and wide with layers upon layers of stars.

She glanced at Aggie out of the corner of her eye. Her friend tilted precariously to the left, destined for the lap of her neighbor, or a face plant in the dirt.

She reached over, tugging Aggie over until she lurched upright.

"Now I want everyone to imagine . . ." The guru dramatically paused, making Nely shrink back to her rock as if she'd been caught passing notes in class. ". . . you inhale, filling every cell with life-giving oxygen, and then breathe out, sinking deeper into the rock."

If she sank any deeper against this rock, it would be her first experience with taking it up the ass.

"We're about to take a cleansing breath, focusing only on the breath and letting all thoughts drift through our minds like clouds in the sky," the guru intoned. "All of our wants, our needs, fading by the powerful light of nothingness."

Casting another look at Aggie, who hadn't rolled down the hill, Nely exhaled a breath that sounded like a sixteen-wheeler releasing its air brakes. Okay, she was going to clear her mind of Simon, her need to be surgically attached to Audrey, La Cacuy . . .

The guru blew into the conch, and the vibrations blew a hole through her and in poured words she couldn't interpret that sought her most vulnerable places, her darkest of secrets and her most precious hopes. She resisted the crushing seduction, her spine bowing as if the guru himself had plunged his hand in and loosened her very soul. His voice circled her, surrounded her, and then without warning she swore that without moving from where he stood on the other side of the fire, he whispered into her ear.

Let go.

Like a leaf gently blown off a tree, her mind gradually fell into silence.

But when the silence went on for too long, Nely's eyes snapped open. Had she fallen asleep? Was the crowd laughing at her as if she were the kid in class who slobbered all over her desk?

She jerked her gaze around to see who was sniggering at her. But they weren't. Her vision had gone sepia, like an old photo.

Clutching at her throat with her hand, she expected to feel warm flesh and bones. But it was just warm air. She glanced down. Both hands still rested on either thigh, and yet, her hands were also up around her chest.

A gold nimbus outlined her whole body. Kind of like that *Aha!* video.

"What the hell are two up to now?" Helen demanded.

Nely's whole body stiffened like she'd been struck across the face. Helen, Aggie's mama, stood at the edge of the fire with her fists pressed on hips that were encased in skintight turquoise capris.

Thinking that it was the smoke from the fire, that they'd tossed some hallucinogenic weed into the bonfire, Nely rubbed her eyes. Even though it had been ages since she'd done any recreational drug use, she knew she wasn't trippin'.

"I asked what the hell you two are doing?" Helen repeated, the beaded tassel on her high-heeled wedge sandal dancing in time to her tapping foot.

"I—We—She—" Nely turned to Aggie, who was also outlined in the gold light. Her eyes were still closed. "She wanted to tell you that—"

Helen pointed her finger, which had a gold ring pierced through the tip of her violet-colored nail. "You tell that baby girl of mine that when it's her time, I'll come for her."

"But—" Nely wanted to shake Aggie awake, forgetting all about their tête-à-tête just a few moments earlier. "Aggie!"

But her voice sounded like she was shouting underwater, and Helen was fading back into the fire.

"Wait!" Nely begged. "She's been waiting for this! Hold on! Aggie!"

But Aggie didn't move.

"Nely, honey pie," Helen called her. A bittersweet ache throbbed in Nely's chest when she saw the way Helen was admiring her daughter. "You know there are times when no matter how hard a mother tries, she has to wait for her daughter to be able to hear her."

Helen smiled as if she were trying not to cry. "Tell her that I know."

Even though it was a sacred ceremony on a sacred site,

Nely lost all sense of propriety when she cried out, "Aggie, open your fucking eyes!" and lunged over, grabbing Aggie's right hand.

A warm tingle bubbled in Aggie's hand and heated as it climbed up her wrist and forearm. She had just managed to get Kevin and Saturday morning out of her head when Nely screamed the F-word.

"What is wrong with—" Just then, a kaleidoscope of images and sounds exploded around her, spinning faster and faster.

Aggie grasped helplessly for something, anything, to pull herself out of the swirling cacophony. She squeezed her eyes tight in an effort to block it out, and then abruptly was standing before Simon, his eyes brimming with tears as he slid a gold band onto her finger.

Before she could react, she was looking down at her pregnant belly, which visibly shuddered with a baby's movement, and then the image switched to gloved hands holding up a squirming newborn about to be laid on her stomach.

A beat ricocheted through Aggie, threatening to tear her away from that baby. Something switched inside her and a primal urge to hold onto that baby erupted in a terrifying force. She fought so hard that she almost forgot to breathe. And then she was yanked forward, hurtling through a screeching blur of sound and color. White pain erupted as if ripped from her very skin.

Nely screamed from a far distance.

Aggie tumbled in a blinding darkness.

"Aggie!"

Her eyes snapped open.

Still perched on the rock, Aggie caught herself from falling off. Her body felt too big for her, like she'd pulled herself out of the ocean in a ski suit. Her mouth felt stuffed with cotton, her breath forced out in tight sobs. An annoying whine persisted in her ears, making her want to smack the side of her head to loosen it.

She lifted her hand to wipe the sweat beading on her forehead, then saw that it wasn't her hand.

The shock was cold as it pierced her heart and radiated through her.

Somehow she was sitting outside her body, looking back at it. But then her face turned to her and asked, "What did you do?"

"Nothing! I—" And then she realized she was speaking with Nely's voice.

Aggie's eyes blinked back at her and then she dipped her chin down with both hands pressed against her stomach.

Wake up, she told herself. But she already was. "Nely?" she said.

Aggie watched her own face erupt with horror.

"It is you, isn't it?" Aggie asked. "But—"

The word caught in her throat. Nely was definitely in her body, which meant that—

Aggie looked down at her hands, which she held with palms up. They were Nely's hands, dried and peeling at the cuticles and whiter than her own. She rocked her hips from side to side, her lower back tight and achy. But Nely was also gushy and warm. Aggie never felt this soft in her own body.

She was about to say something to Nely—no, to herself—no, to Nely, who she knew was inside *her* body, just as she was inside Nely's.

But before she cracked her mouth to speak, Nely pressed

her fingertips to her Aggie's forehead and then brought her palms over her face, dragging them down her neck and chest, stopping at Aggie's boobs.

Aggie watched with an eerie fascination as her—no, Nely's—face pleated in a puzzled frown.

Aggie braced herself for a horrific outburst of revulsion and fear that would make everyone around them think they were insane, because this *was* insane . . . and yet, somehow, it was real.

Nely jerked her chin up in shock. "You bitch!"

Six

When the elevator doors came together and the floor hefted under her feet, Nely's fervent hope began to wear off that this was only a nightmare from which she couldn't wake up. This wasn't a parallel reality where she had ridden down the mountain with her real body sitting next to her.

Oh no, this was real-time, really happening right now while the Muzak version of Diana Ross's "Inside Out" played in the background. And then it occurred to her: How was she going to get home?

Aggie cleared her throat and shifted beside her, signaling that she had something to say about their circumstance. But Nely kept her gaze firmly on the light bar as they traveled up the floors.

Aggie would be devastated that she had seen her mother, Nely thought. But she had to tell her. The debate about it caused a weird sizzling feel under her skin that seemed to grow worse. She was certain that at any minute she'd burst through the seams of Aggie's several-sizes-too-small body.

"You didn't have to call me a bitch in front of everyone," Aggie said out of the blue.

"What happened to us?" Nely demanded. Horror surged as she heard her words through Aggie's voice. She slapped her hands over her mouth.

"I don't know," Aggie stammered, and then cleared her throat. "But maybe it's temporary—"

Aggie touched Nely's arm, and the contact with her former flesh sent a jolt of revulsion through Nely. Her knees unlocked, and if she hadn't been leaning against the wall, she'd have been a pile on the floor. Someone was gasping for breath . . . oh yes, that would be her.

But as she caught a glimpse of herself in the mirrored doors, her stomach was still flat even as she was bent over. Not bad, she thought in a moment of vanity.

"Nely? Nely, just breathe, okay?" she heard Aggie calling as if she fought to be heard through a roaring crowd. "We have to think."

Why did she have to think? Nely wondered. She'd just talked to a dead woman! She'd just switched bodies with her best friend!

"Nel—I swear, I didn't do it on purpose—"

"I know you didn't! Just stop. Just stop talking. I can't—"

"Okay, this is what we need to do," Aggie began, completely ignoring her pleas for silence so she could think this through. "First, we need to see each other naked."

Nely nearly choked. "Wha—hah . . ." She hadn't been naked in front of Aggie since August 2000, when they'd gone down to a spa in Rosarito for her bachelorette weekend. "Why?"

"Because."

Nely held out for a more thorough explanation.

"We have to shower, right? Pee," Aggie suggested. "Might as well get it out of the way."

Nely didn't care for that idea. If she were ten pounds lighter with better skin and a professional bikini wax, then she'd consider it. At least she'd shaved her underarms this morning.

"And then I'll talk to Guru Sauro about getting us back," Aggie said.

Aggie kept talking about how this couldn't have happened in a more perfect place and that the shamans and *curanderas* on staff would easily fix it. Her blabbering blurred into an incoherent buzz as Nely faced the part—the tiny part—of her that didn't want to switch back.

She didn't want to go back into a body with boobs that rattled around in her bra, hips that refused to go back to where they'd been, and a rusty vagina. And then there were those nights when Audrey refused to be comforted, when she had prayed for a reprieve from it all. Her life in the past year and a half felt like an endless blur of nursing, pumping, diapering, and shushing, all while smothering the guilt that her identity as an educated, accomplished woman had been swallowed by motherhood.

Overwhelmed, Nely pressed the heels of her hands against her eyes and curled her knees to her chest. She'd known something terrible would happen on this trip. Her gut instinct kept telling her to cancel, but she hadn't. Now look what happened.

"Nely, listen to me," Aggie implored. "We can switch back. No problem."

"How?" Nely managed in a watery voice. "We don't even

know how we did this in the first place. God! I can't believe we're even having this conversation!"

Aggie pressed her lips together, and Nely wondered what it was that she couldn't bring herself to say.

The elevator doors opened. Aggie stood up and offered her hand to Nely.

"Dude, I don't know about you, but I keep thinking I'm just really drunk and when we wake up everything will be normal."

Nely looked up. A shiver swept from the crown of her head down to her soles at the thought of what Helen had told her to say to Aggie.

She got to her feet on her own. "I don't think it's going to be that easy."

But it could. That's what Aggie kept telling herself as they walked to their room and lay in their beds. It might wear off while they slept. Who knew how these things worked?

She shut her eyes, waiting for sleep to take her, but her mind wouldn't stop whirring.

And then she bolted up into a sitting position.

If she could leave her body and end up in Nely's, then how come she didn't get to see Mama? Tears spilled out and a cold ache spread deep in her chest. Maybe Mama was *gone* gone. No trace left, vanished like a document deleted off a computer.

Maybe spirits didn't linger around like they did in the movies, waiting for their chance to talk to the ones they loved.

She didn't know how or when, but she must have cried herself to sleep.

Aggie woke up to a buzzing sound in her right ear and opened her eyes to the weak gray light creeping through the high windows. Memories of what happened last night stirred in her sleep-fogged mind.

She held her breath. If she peeked under the covers, what would she see? Was last night some alcohol-induced mania? Or had Spring Calf, or whatever her name was, put some wacky tobacky in the campfire?

"Oh God," came from the other bed.

The walls shook from a shotgun blast of thunder. Aggie pressed her hand against her chest, and when she didn't feel saline implants, she realized it hadn't been some alcohol-induced nightmare or hallucination. She really was in Nely's body. Thunder struck again, followed by a downpour that struck the windows like bullets.

"Are you— Did you sleep okay?" Aggie winced at the innocuous question.

Suddenly, Nely flounced off the bed and ran to her duffel bag. She began tearing through it, and then, with one shirt clutched in her hand, stopped.

"What the hell am I doing?" she asked herself.

"I don't know," Aggie said, sitting up with the fear that Nely would do something dangerous like cut off her hair or put on eighties style leg-warmers.

Nely threw down her shirt and marched over to Aggie's bag. Propelled by a ridiculous sense of possessiveness, Aggie started out of bed. Yes, she wanted her body back, but that was a monogrammed bag she'd bought at Neiman Marcus.

"I have to get dressed," Nely said as she unzipped Aggie's bag. "But you have to wear my old crap while I get to wear yours."

"Nely, now let's not be hasty," Aggie said. She was still dressed in Nely's yoga pants and sweatshirt.

Nely turned and eyed her. "You can't fit into these," she ground out. She held up Aggie's beloved pair of Bleu Jeans as if they were a bloodied trophy of war. "And I . . ."

"Fine," Aggie said to cover the excruciating silence. "I'm going to check out your ass."

"Aggie no!"

Aggie had her thumbs in the waistband of her pants, about to yank them down. She wanted to see what a body that had given birth to a new life looked like. So far it felt roomier, creakier, and warmer than her body had been.

Nely leapt over, and Aggie jumped out of the way.

"Stop!" Nely cried. "Don't!"

"Why not? You can check me out."

Nely scrunched her lips. "That's just . . . just wrong."

"Oh come on, admit it. You want to see what fake boobs look like."

Nely's eyes guiltily flicked away.

"And we have to see each other sooner or later," Aggie reminded her. "So it might as well as be now. It's not like we haven't seen any of this before."

Nely quirked the corner of her mouth, torn between curiosity and prudishness.

"We'll do this together," Aggie added. "On the count of three."

Nely reluctantly walked to her mirror and then brought her hands to the waistband of her pants. "I want you to know that I was planning to go on a diet. It's just that I never got around to it."

"On one," Aggie started, "two, three . . ."

Wow, was Aggie's first thought. She wouldn't call it ugly, just . . . different.

Nely's shape looked like a fertility goddess with the round

belly and breasts. Lightly, she pressed her hands against her middle, remembering when Nely had carried Audrey. This body had given life, nurtured it, fed it—

Aggie went cold to the bone. "Are you still breast-feeding Audrey?"

Nely was eyeing her butt in the mirror. "Would it gross you out if I said yes?"

Aggie didn't want to be judgmental, especially when she'd been such a bitch last night, but . . .

"What kind of bra is this?" Nely asked, admiring a black satin bra embroidered with wine-colored roses along the top and under wire.

A pang struck right in the center of Aggie's chest as she thought about Kevin and what he'd said when he saw her get out of bed. "It's a Lavit bra," she said wistfully.

She'd peeked into Nely's bag of mommy couture: granny panties and bras that were brawny enough to withstand machine washing.

"It feels like another lifetime since I've worn a bra like this," Nely said wistfully. "Not that you need one."

Nely turned around and clenched her butt muscles. They hardly moved, they were so hard with muscle. Aggie glanced down at her butt. The only way to save this ass was lipo.

"When I get my body back," Nely said, "I'm giving up mashed potatoes and chocolate."

Aggie reminded herself that Nely's body had had a purpose other than seduction and fashion. It had been a temple of life, a holy—

Dude, was that what stretch marks looked like?

Seven

"You can't just see Guru Sauro. You need to make an appointment."

Claudine sat posture perfect behind the antiseptically clean desk. Unlike Spring Calf and the rest of her star sister crew, Guru Sauro's chinless assistant was all taut lines and sharp angles. You wouldn't see her dancing around playing a flute.

"We don't have time for an appointment." Aggie stood strong against Claudine's unblinking stare.

"He's in seclusion. Till the new moon."

"Is he here on the grounds?" Aggie asked.

"There are many of Guru Sauro's specially trained shamans who can help you—"

"We cannot leave unless we see *him* personally."

"How much?" Nely demanded. "How much will it cost for us to get ten minutes of his time?"

"An acceptable offering is five hundred." In a fluid movement, she rotated to the computer monitor. A desk fountain trickled softly. There were no windows overlooking the grounds. No pictures. It was the kind of office that would drive Nely nuts.

"But he won't be open until—" She clicked the mouse rapid-fire. "June twenty-first at 3:45. Next year."

"Don't panic," Aggie cautioned as the doors clicked shut at their backs. "We will find him."

"How?" Nely nearly choked trying to speak past the cold fingers squeezing her throat. Simon had called her cell phone, wondering about her night. His deep, dusky voice suggested that he wished she'd spent it with him.

She should've stayed home!

"We go to the help," Aggie said, as it if would be so easy. "There's gotta be some bitter minimum wager who'll rat him out."

They found four. The first informant, who waited tables in the dining room, claimed that she once saw the guru walk through the wall connecting the kitchen to the main dining room.

The second claimed, as he mulched the moonlight garden, that he was the guru's illegitimate son and had come here to confront him. Except he hadn't seen or talked to him, and would they tell the guru that he was here?

The third cryptically whispered that these walls had ears. She then pushed her cleaning cart down the hall, stopping every few feet to turn around, point at the walls and bob her head up and down meaningfully.

Nely pressed her fist over her mouth and her face crumpled into sobs.

"We're not done yet," Aggie assured her. "We *will* find him."

Nely shook her head as she banked down her rising impatience with Aggie and the question of what the fuck they were going to do now. Didn't Aggie realize that she had a child to go home to? A husband? A home?

Oh God, what if they never found him?

Having to physically remove herself from the place where that thought occurred, she began walking with no direction in mind. She couldn't go home like this, face Simon like this. She would find him.

Aggie hurried to catch up.

Nely's breaths grew shallower the deeper she made her way through the rabbit warren of hallways. She prayed for something, anything, that would get them out of this mess. She prayed like she'd never prayed before.

"Nely, I know this is partly my fault—" Aggie started.

Nely ignored her.

"You didn't deserve for me to yell at you like I did, and now I'm—I'm so—"

"Are you lost?" a gentle voice asked from behind an ancient bougainvillea. A dusty boot appeared and then a long, dusty denim leg.

If this was a movie, Aggie thought, the guru would be walking around the resort disguised as a gardener.

But it wasn't. The man standing before them had the build of a basketball player, stooped-over shoulders from talking to shorter people and long thin arms. He told them his name was Javier.

"You can help us?" Nely asked.

"Of course," he said as if they were a shivering pair of rabbits.

"I know you can't tell us, but we really need to find Guru Sauro. Just point out where he is and I swear we won't tell anyone you told us."

His smile never wavered, which gave Aggie the creeps. "Why are you looking for him?"

"Because we—" Nely looked at Aggie for help.

"We had a, uh . . . a reaction to the meditation last night."

"Oh. That's very common, you know. What about your assigned shaman guide? Have you talked to him?"

Aggie took a deep breath and then said, "This is only something the guru can help us with."

Javier stared off into the distance, his nostrils flaring as he took in a deep breath.

Aggie couldn't take another psycho response. "Never mind. Thanks."

"I was going to say that he's that way."

"What way?" Nely and Aggie asked together.

He sent them back to the place where it all happened. Up the hill and to the guru's shack they went.

When they reached the top of the hill, an ugly black gash was all that remained from last night's bonfire. Surrounded by the hollow hush of the wind, sharp with the smell of wet earth and trees, Nely eyed the brooding clouds.

Javier had told them to look for a footpath about three-quarters up the hill. But there was no footpath. They'd been had.

Staring at the place where Helen had stood, Nely told herself that she'd waited too long to tell Aggie. Then again, there hadn't been a good time . . . like now.

"Fucking Javier," Aggie yelled at the sky, then pointed

at Nely, looking a lot like her mother. "Don't say it."

"Say what?"

"And don't cry."

"Okay."

"Just forget it," Aggie sobbed, coming apart at the seams. "We're going to die like this."

Like hell they would. Thinking of Simon and Audrey, Nelly resolved to crawl every inch of this damn forest to find Guru Sauro.

Mud squished into her Pumas, while the sky wept big blobs of rain on the top of her head that crept down her neck and into the collar of her water-logged hoodie.

When she went back to looking for the footpath, she spotted a cut in the wild grass that led to the deep dark of the trees.

"I found it," she cried.

"I don't see anything," Aggie said.

Nely started when she turned and saw her body standing beside her. Shuddering, she dug her hands deeper into the pockets of her form-fitted pink sweatshirt.

"Let's keep going," she managed past the teeny tiny hole her throat had become.

"What if we get lost?"

How much more lost could they get? Nely wondered as she headed toward the forest.

Spooky trees crowded in on them, narrowing their view of the sky. Without warning, the path suddenly ramped down.

Behind her, Aggie yelped, followed by a thud.

"Aggie, are you okay?" Nely asked, running back down to help her up.

"Jesus," Aggie heaved. "Don't you exercise?"

"Gee, I guess my vanity isn't a priority. You know, having dedicated my entire existence to my husband and baby."

"My life is important too, you know," Aggie shot back.

Nely clenched her teeth to keep down a flare of anger. "Aggie, no one ever said your life was unimportant. Now come on."

"Can't I rest for a minute? I haven't felt like this since Lauren Bruner called me 'Trailer Chunk' in seventh grade."

Nely almost burst from the anger building under her skin. She should leave the self-centered bitch behind. But then she stared back at her own face, framed with wet strands of hair and flushed with exertion.

Aggie blinked and understanding dawned in her eyes. "Nely, I didn't mean to say that—"

"It's going to rain again," Nely said coldly, and then started off before she retaliated with something nasty.

But the longer they hiked, the more lost they seemed to get. Nely closed her eyes and sucked in a breath to hold the tears at bay. They had no food, no shelter, no matches for a fire to keep warm. A fierce wind whipped through the treetops, pelting them with water. Thunder grumbled in the distance and the air thickened with that particular smell before rainfall and . . .

Nely sniffed harder. Chimney smoke.

"Hey!" Aggie called as Nely hurried toward the smell.

At the summit, she stopped. There, amidst the trees, stood a one-room adobe house. Hanging from under the rough hewn timbers that made up the porch were dried herbs and animal pelts.

The door opened and out stepped Guru Sauro.

"That's him, isn't it?" Aggie panted at her side.

"Looks like it." Nely stepped closer. Wait. She watched

him stop and hold his hands, palms up, to catch the rain. "What is he doing?"

Suddenly, he turned and stared straight at them.

Aggie gasped and fell to the ground, hiding under a log.

"What are you doing?" Nely asked. "Get up!"

"I-I thought we were sneaking up on him," Aggie said, feeling ridiculous.

He watched them steadily, even as the rain slid down the sides of his face and soaked his khaki shirt and gray dungarees.

"I thought I'd see you sooner or later," he said.

"You sensed we were coming?" Aggie asked expectantly.

He dug a Moto Razr out of the pocket of his pants. "My staff told me."

"I'm sorry to interrupt your, uh, quiet time but—"

He cut Nely off. "In the tradition of the healer and his alma, there must be an offering."

Nely exchanged a glance with Aggie. He was nothing like the all-powerful guru who cut through the night with his presence. His eyes were puffy and the watch on his wrist could be a down payment on a condo.

"We don't have any cash on us," Nely said. "But we have to speak with you."

"We could promise some," Aggie added.

At that, he paused and then sized them up. Nely tried to stare him straight in the eye, to show she meant business. But his eyes traveled all over her and Aggie.

"I'll take that," he said, pointing to the rhinestone pendant around Nely's neck.

"No," Aggie yelped. "Maybe you should hear our problem first."

"What do you do for a living?" he asked.

Aggie faltered, and then answered warily, "I'm an entre-
preneur."

"I am, too. How do you think I built all of this?" he spat,
as if he were referring to a disgusting joke. "I didn't do it by
selling cheap."

He pointed to the rhinestone star pendant Aggie had worn
ever since the seventh grade. "The offering, please."

"But it's not worth much," Aggie argued. "My mother
gave that to me."

He frowned. "Then why is *she* wearing it?"

Nely froze.

"Oh, I see," he said softly. "Did she die?"

"Nine months ago," Aggie answered softly.

"Will it bring her back from the dead?"

"That's enough," Nely snapped. "I have something I can
give you. I have—" She turned to Aggie before she lost her
nerve and asked, "Give me your left hand."

She snatched the watch and was about to give it to him
when Aggie yanked it back. "Nely, no. Simon gave this to
you. It's your push present."

"He and Audrey mean more to me than this," she said,
cutting a sneer at Guru Sauro as her numb, wet fingers fumbled with the clasp.

He just laughed at them.

Aggie grabbed the necklace around Nely's throat and
ripped it off. "Here," she said to the guru, throwing at him.
"You better be worth it."

Eight

Their shoes squished water on the Mexican paver tiles, while rain fell through the hole in the smoked-stained ceiling, making the fire hiss and spit. The cowhide swayed in the doorway.

After last night, Aggie expected a wise, grandfatherly man whose spiritual connections were so strong that he'd believe them and then immediately reassure them. But he was a shrewd, grumpy old fart who stole her necklace and then made them sit on the cold floor.

"Now what do you want?" he asked.

Aggie stumbled through their tale as if she were trying to make her way in a pitch-black room. The more she talked, the more the ridges in his forehead deepened. When she finished, he said nothing for a long moment as he stared at the fire. He startled them when he bounded out the door.

"What should we do?" Aggie hissed when it was certain he wasn't coming back anytime soon.

"He didn't tell us to leave." Nely rubbed her arms with her hands.

The fire radiated heat, but Aggie got chills from the spiritual power radiating off the walls. She wasn't sure if it was a good energy or a bad energy. Frankly, from the way Guru Sauro treated them, she wondered if leaving now would be a better idea.

"Thank you for trying to keep my necklace," Aggie whispered.

It took Nely a moment to coldly respond with, "You're welcome."

"I didn't mean to—" Aggie anxiously rocked from side to side on her bottom like a kid who had to go to the bathroom. "You've never been fat and ugly like I was back when they called me—"

"What are you doing?" Nely asked testily. "You're going to give me a hemorrhoid."

Aggie stopped. "Is that why you wear the granny panties?"

"They are not granny panties! They're a Lycra support system."

"They're really comfy. It's kinda nice having a little extra cushion."

"Are you always this hungry?"

"Oh. You get used to that."

"Aggie, I have something I have to tell you and I think it might upset you."

"You know, this whole thing is giving me perspective on what it means to have problems."

"The reason why I touched you was because I, uh, saw your mom."

Aggie went into pause mode.

"I was trying to get you to open your eyes so you could see her but—well, you know."

"What did she—" Her voice sounded like a creaky old rocking chair.

"She told me that she knows and she'll come to you when you're—"

The cowhide flapped open as Guru Sauro marched inside, carrying a shallow bronze bowl. With an impatient sigh, he knelt down to place the bowl between the two of them.

"I thought about having you both thrown off the property," he said. "But then I figured what the hell, there's one way to find out if you're telling the truth."

Nely shut her mouth, wishing he had stayed away a little longer.

Aggie cleared her throat, her face a mask of neutrality. "What the hell is this?"

"This is the smoky mirror, a tool of the *naguals* to see the reflection of the soul," he explained, as if she'd asked an obviously stupid question. "I'll create the sacred circle and then the spirits will part the curtain of our spiritual blindness so we can see your true selves."

"How long will it take?" Aggie asked.

"We'll see," he answered impatiently.

"Fuck, what kind of guru are you?" she demanded, her voice too large for the room. "I paid good money to stay at this place and now look what happened to us!"

Nely winced, thinking this was when he'd put a curse on them or toss their asses back out in the rain. Amazingly, a grin cracked his grim face.

"I'll be honest," he said, "I've never done this before. But things have been getting boring around here, so I figure, what the hell."

Before they could protest, he began to chant in an ancient language. He waved an eagle feather over a bowl of incense as he walked a circle around them.

Nely resisted following him with her eyes, and then the air swooshed out of the room and for a moment the fire banked before it roared to life, throwing gold heat over their faces.

"Look into the water and tell me who you see," he said.

"You go first," Nely said to Aggie.

"You're the one who started this," Aggie said. "You go."

Nely leaned forward. She opened her eyes, and her real reflection looked back at her. Aggie's reflection joined hers. But when they looked up from the bowl, they were still in each other's bodies.

The muscles around Nely's mouth danced as she fought back her despair. Aggie didn't make a sound.

Guru Sauro shook his head, dropping back onto his haunches and rubbing his chin. "Man, you two really screwed up," he sighed.

"Then do something!" Aggie demanded.

"You don't get it. If I can switch you back, it can only happen at the full moon." He waved his hand over the bowl and the water went clear again.

"When is that?" Nely asked, her pulse hammering against her throat.

"In twenty-eight days."

"Why not now?"

"Because the moon is dying. In this phase, a wise shaman does not attempt medicine of this magnitude. We
wait for the next moon to gather its strength, and only
when it is full can we do spirit medicine such as you two
nincompoops did."

Calling them nincompoops didn't seem very shamanly
to Nely.

"How did this happen?" she asked. "I was meditating and
then I saw, uh . . . Aggie's mother, and when I tried—"

"You saw your soul," he finished for her. "That's the point
of transcendental meditation. But most people who come
here never go that deep. They just want to be seen because
of those idiots who wrote those magazine articles about me.
They ruined my life's work and—"

The lines around his mouth deepened. "I don't know how
you two did it."

Nely and Aggie exchanged a guilty glance. Neither felt it
wise to mention how much they'd had to drink last night.

He rubbed his hands together and rolled back to sit cross-
legged. "I'm thinking you two needed to do this. You need
to walk in each other's shoes." He contemplated them both.
"Your paths have diverged and now they are coming together again."

"I have a daughter," Nely said, her voice wobbling. "She's
only eighteen months old and she needs me—"

"Yes, she does," he acknowledged gently. "But there
were times when you wished you didn't have the
responsibility."

Her skin prickled from the cold truth of his words. He
seemed to glow right before her eyes, like a candle that re-

gained its power after a fierce wind tried to blow it out.

"And you," he turned to Aggie, "you see what she has and you want it without knowing why. Life has given you many treasures and yet you ask for more, for better."

"I work hard and I deserve everything I have," Aggie argued. "I just paid three hundred a night for us to stay here at *your* resort. You're not exactly piss poor, either."

He waved Aggie off as if she were a mere child who would never see reason. "Come back in twenty-eight days. If you have learned the lessons you need to learn, your souls will return to their rightful places."

"And if we don't?" Nely dared to ask.

His gaze gave her a fresh bout of the chills. "Then nothing I can do will help you."

As the shadows thickened with oncoming night, Aggie sat alone with all of her uncertainties. Nely cried in the bathroom.

Aggie rested her forehead on the cold windowpane. If there was ever a time she needed Mama, this was it.

As much as she tried feeling sorry for herself, her mind began churning out plans for what they would do in the next twenty-eight days. There was so much she didn't want Nely to know about her life. Curdling with embarrassment, she imagined Nely's concern when she told her about the business.

Then again, maybe Nely would be too caught up in pining for Audrey to notice that the boutique wasn't doing well.

As Aggie traveled down the river of denial, she began to see the benefits of their predicament. All she had to do was babysit a kid and a husband; kind of like premarital training. Since she needed to stay away from Kevin for her own good, Nely would be a perfect stand-in. If anyone could keep from putting out, Nely was her woman.

The bathroom door clicked open and Nely emerged red-eyed and pale. Aggie tried not to flinch, seeing her body standing across the room.

"Should I order room service?" she asked faux brightly.

"I'm not hungry," Nely whispered in a watery voice.

"I think we should talk about what we need to do."

Nely didn't seem to hear her as she wandered to her duffel bag.

"I'll take care of them," Aggie plunged in. "You know how much I adore Audrey—"

"She can't stand you," Nely answered.

That hurt. "But she won't know the difference," Aggie said quietly.

Nely's eyes burned into hers. "What about Simon? What if he wants to have sex one night?"

A frying pan to the head was Aggie's first answer. But the tormented lines on Nely's face kept her mouth shut.

"I've never spent a night away from Audrey till now," Nely said, pressing her fingertips gently against the window. "And the times when I wished . . . God, I'd give anything to take those thoughts back."

Aggie didn't know what to say. Nely had seemed so earth motherly and happy to be a SAHM. All she could offer was, "You can trust me with Audrey. I know you've never let me babysit her, but I'd never hurt her, you know that."

"What do you know about taking care of a toddler?"

Nothing. But she was quick on her feet and she'd read some books. "I've had to close the store for celebrity clients. They're like children."

Nely laughed softly. "I know I can trust you with Audrey," she apologized. "Do you know what it means for a mother to give her child to someone else?"

Aggie was about to answer, then realized her friend didn't need empty reassurances. But she still owed her an apology for being so nasty.

"I'm so sorry, Nely, for the things I said. I'm just really jealous that you have a baby and husband to talk about and—" She waited a moment before continuing, "No matter what, I will not sleep with your husband." She then muttered, "Not that I'd want to."

"Excuse me?" Nely asked, all huffy. "Just what is wrong with my husband?"

"I mean he's definitely hot and if he wasn't married to you I'd—" She knew she'd ventured into dangerous waters. "Let's not go there."

"So you're serious?" Nely asked, watching her struggling to sit in the lotus position on the chair. "You really think we can pull this off?

"Yeah. You wear my clothes and—hang out. I play house and get you in shape."

Nely bit down on her knuckle.

"What other choice do we have?" Aggie asked.

Nely pulled her wet knuckle out of her mouth. "I could tell Simon."

"You think he'd really believe you?" Aggie had never seen two people as close as those two.

But expecting him to believe this was really pushing it. "Never. He's a cop. He only deals in facts. If he told me that he switched bodies, I'd lock him out of the house and hide with Audrey."

Aggie couldn't imagine telling Kevin, either.

"So how hard can it be?" she asked, trying to rally their morale. "I'm not scared."

But then she remembered that Audrey still wore a diaper and that Nely was kind of still breast-feeding and Audrey had those sharp little teeth and—

Nely skeptically hitched up the corner of her mouth. "Oh, you will be," she promised darkly. "You will be."

Nine

"One last thing," Nely said when they pulled up to her house.

"That was a nasty thing, making me think I had to breast-feed Audrey," Aggie pouted.

Nely kept her gaze steady when she said, "Do not sleep with my husband."

Seriously, what kind of friend did Nely think she was?

"Dude, you've told me a million times! I do not want to sleep with Simon."

"But he can be persuasive."

Aggie's shoulders hitched up to her ears as she made a face like she'd bit into a steak full of maggots. "Then I have one more request, too."

Nely waited.

"When you see Kevin—"

"Oh, Aggie," Nely sighed.

"Wait. Just hear me out." Aggie gulped in some air as her hands flew nervously from her hair to the imaginary lint on her shirt. "Be friendly but not too friendly."

"Got it."

"I couldn't ask you to cheat on Simon, but I think you could—I trust your judgment."

"Thank you." Nely started out of the car but Aggie stopped her.

"But he's my friend. I know how you think he is, and you're right to a certain extent but—" She struggled to make Nely understand. "He's my friend."

Nely took a fortifying breath. "All right."

"And another thing," she quickly added. "You have to take me in for a wax and detail."

"The car?" Nely asked.

"No, *me*." Aggie pointed to Nely's lap.

Nely's lips curled. "Sorry, but absolutely not."

"It won't hurt."

"Only my husband and my gynecologist see me down there."

"But it's not yours."

Nely shoved the door open.

"Consider it on loan!" Aggie yelled after her.

Of all people, it had to be La Cacuy who greeted them at the door.

Nely instinctively stiffened, but her mother-in-law's predatory eyes fastened on Aggie. "You're late," she pronounced.

Nely choked up, forgetting that she was in Aggie's body.

"What's it to you?" Aggie spat.

Nely's head bobbled on her neck. La Cacuy swept off to tattle to Simon, leaving them in a cloud of her signature perfume.

Aggie turned, her eyes sharp and snappish. "Does she always talk to you that way?" But with her blood up, she didn't wait for an answer. "'Cuz she isn't talking that way to me. I won't stand for it."

"But you're not you," Nely explained. "You're supposed to be me."

Chastened but unbroken, Aggie picked up Nely's duffel. "Then you need to stop letting her push you around," she said, and Nely could almost hear Helen saying those exact same words.

"Whatever," Nely muttered, following her into the lion's den. "I need to show you where I stored my milk."

"Oh my God, that is so wrong."

They snuck through the living room and into the kitchen. Aggie gasped when she saw the small mound of dirty pots and bowls in the sink. But that was nothing, Nely thought. Crumbs, sugar, and other unidentifiable substances littered every surface.

Nely opened the freezer, and a startled "Whoa!" shot out of Aggie's mouth.

"You made all that?" she hissed.

"It will only last you for the next two days, so try to use as much as you can."

Aggie stared in wonder. "You were like a walking dairy farm."

"Motherhood is not for the faint of heart," Nely informed her, then slammed the freezer door, only to see Simon holding Audrey in his arms.

Her heart swelled. He seemed tired and run-down but

happy to see her. Audrey's hair was pulled into a water spout on the top of her head and her diaper was so full, the tabs could spring free at any second. Normally Nely would've been irritated at that, but she was so happy to see them that it hurt.

"I missed you—" she began, but they didn't seem to hear her. Their smiles were for Aggie. They weren't even looking at her.

Audrey stretched her arms toward Aggie with an excited scream. Nely's heart shriveled.

Aggie gave Nely an uncertain glance before Simon pulled her close and murmured, "Hey there," before he kissed her.

Aggie stiffened as if she'd just been electrocuted.

Nely couldn't look, and yet she couldn't look away, her insides twisted with possessiveness. *That's not me!*

"Hey there, Aggie," Simon said to her, his eyes friendly but not warm, as they'd been when he thought he was kissing his wife. "You took good care of my woman, right?"

Nely's throat clamped tight with longing. She jerked her head up and down, ripping her eyes from him, to her Audrey.

"How did she do this weekend?" she asked automatically. "Did that rash go away?"

He blinked, and Nely realized that she'd slipped.

"Uh, Nely told me, and I was worried, so . . ."

She noticed then that Audrey was no longer reaching for Aggie. Her daughter arched her back like an angry cat, sizing Aggie up like a mean girl meeting fresh meat. Her chubby fingers tightened on Simon's shoulders as if to say, *Get your own man, bitch.*

Unaware of the simmering hostility wavering off his

daughter, Simon twisted to hand her off to Aggie, saying, "Why don't you go to Mommy? Daddy has to finish our dinner."

"You made dinner," fell out of Nely's mouth.

"Yes, he did," La Cacuy said from behind Simon.

Aggie looked from Nely to Audrey in a silent plea for help.

"Yeah," he answered, something flickering in his dark eyes. "All of Nel's favorites. Want to stay? We have plenty."

Suddenly all the walls seemed to close in on Nely. He'd done something special for her, and all the things she loved about him threatened to squeeze her to death.

She had to leave now, or she never would. She couldn't bear to see Aggie get all the appreciation and gratitude that she had craved so badly.

But there was a part of her that didn't mind so much that Aggie would have to deal with La Cacuy.

"I should go," Nely said.

"Aw, come on!" Simon teased. "We've got a special dinner and chocolate. You'll miss out."

She spun on her heel, making for the door, which seemed to stretch farther away.

"Don't leave!" Aggie desperately cried, then sputtered, "Uh . . . you should stay."

"I can't," Nely said without turning around. The longer she stayed, the harder it would be to leave.

"Are you sure?" Simon asked as Audrey wailed in protest.

"Stay with Mommy," Simon said to Audrey. "She missed you."

She shook her head vigorously.

"She's been asking for you all day," he said.

Nely trembled with the primal instinct to reclaim and comfort her daughter. She was just about to turn around when a whiff of perfume betrayed the presence of La Cacuy.

"So," La Cacuy said beside her. "You girls have a good time?"

"We did," Nely answered carefully.

She sighed. "You should've seen this place. It was a sty."

Alarmed, Nely glanced around her living room. Her stomach plummeted when she saw what this manipulative, controlling *suegra* bitch had done to her Pottery Barn sofas.

"Too bad you can't stay," La Cacuy chirped while holding the door open and gently pressing her hand against the small of Nely's back. "Oh, don't worry," she said when Nely glanced back at Aggie, who was awkwardly trying to get a firm hold on her baby. "I'll take care of Audrey."

The triumphant gleam in her eyes confirmed Nely's worst fear that La Cacuy had finally gotten what she'd always wanted: her family.

"But—"

But the door shut on her face with a *whump*.

Aggie watched Nely disappear and fear crawled up inside her.

Oh dear God, please tell me I'll wake up and this is not really happening.

A sticky hand shot out like a snake and yanked her hair. "*Yahhh!*" Aggie shouted, bending to the will of an angry, confused toddler.

"Here," Simona said smoothly. "Let me have her."

Pain bit into her scalp as Audrey tightened her grip.

"Get it off!" Aggie howled, bending over as Audrey took her hair with her. "Get her off!"

"Now now," Simona said, untangling Audrey's hand from Aggie's hair.

"Dude!" Aggie exploded when she saw the amount of hair clenched in Audrey's hand.

"What did you expect, dear?" Simona asked primly. "I knew she'd react this way."

"Oh yeah, right," Aggie said, wondering where Nely kept the alcohol and why the house looked so different.

"I noticed you hadn't done the laundry, so I did all of Audrey's and the linens," Simona said. "And that detergent you use doesn't get clothes truly clean, so I bought you the brand that I use."

"Okay," Aggie said without thinking. And then it hit her why this didn't feel like Nely's house: Except for the kitchen, it was spotless . . . eerily spotless. Typically it looked like SWAT did practice raids in the living room.

"I was wondering if you'd actually notice all that I've done," Simona purred. "I bought doubles of everything so we have the exact same living room."

Aggie didn't have the words to describe the horror her eyes beheld.

"Now don't worry about the cost. I got everything out of storage, and look at the upholstery . . ." Simona patted it with her hand. "I had it covered in plastic but you can remove it when company comes over."

"Wow," Aggie managed "It's—It's . . ."

So . . . so Nancy Reagan and the White House years.

Draped curtains in baby poop yellow fell over the windows, blocking out all natural light. Matching throw pillows, with some avocado green and brown ones, were tossed in, leaving two inches of sitting space.

Aggie heaved and coughed back the vomit as she saw that

Nely's stylish Pottery Barn sofa and club chair had been slipcovered in blue velour and then wrapped in plastic.

"It's so, uh, wow," was all she could come up with.

"Dinner is served," Simon announced. He leaned in for a kiss, and Aggie ducked out of the way just in time for him to kiss the air where her cheek had been.

"You hate it don't you?" he whispered, his hot breath tickling the baby hairs over her ear.

Aggie cleared her throat as Simona's lips thinned with disapproval. Those eyes didn't miss a thing, especially the way she had evaded his kiss.

She knew she had to act the part. She would not ruin Nely's marriage.

"Nely, don't you have anything to say about all I've done for you?" Simona asked. "I also told Leila that you and Audrey will be back in class tomorrow."

"Who?"

La Cacuy looked at her like she'd just yelled an obscenity. "Your friend, Leila," Simona answered, as if she was slow witted. "How could you forget her? You were so close."

Nely had a friend that she didn't know about?

But then Simon quickly jumped in. "So you want to tell us what you girls did over the weekend?"

Simona stepped into her field of vision and tipped her head in Simon's direction. "Yes, dear. Tell us *all* the things you did."

The door creaked open and Nely stood in the doorway of Aggie's Golden Hills bungalow apartment. She sucked in her breath, awed by the spotless, chic living room that greeted her.

Shafts of sunlight filtered through the sheer organdy curtains. Objets d'art were tastefully scattered on shelves and tables, rather than toys or discarded bottles.

Four club chairs upholstered in cream were arranged in the center of the living room. A teak tray, holding a set of Japanese tea cups, waited to serve guests on the vivid teal ottoman. Graceful orchids reposed from designer pots that stood on Victorian plant stands. Nely hadn't had a live plant in the house since the instructor in her baby care basics class told them tales of children who'd died from eating plants.

She took a careful step inside.

It's so clean, so civilized. Wiping her tears away with the back of her hand, she began to see the bright side of things. Even when she'd been single, she never had a place this stylish, this elegant, this . . . *quiet.*

Nely strained her ears for the sound of the TV, or a baby chattering or crying. All she heard was the curvy little 1950s style refrigerator humming in the kitchen and birds singing in the garden of the complex of refurbished bungalows.

She started to tear up, remembering how Audrey liked to yell and laugh at her Baby Einstein videos before her afternoon nap. How Simon had a secret tea fetish and kept his drawer of English and specialty green teas flawlessly organized. And then she thought how Simon had made her dinner tonight, which Aggie would get to have with *her* family.

Even if this hadn't happened, Nely knew she wouldn't have appreciated it. She had to lose her husband and daughter to know what she'd had. Shame oozed into her gut.

"No," she told herself. "No more tears. Aggie will take care of them."

BAM BAM BAM!

She leapt away as a heavy fist struck the door behind her.

"Is that you?" a man demanded. "Aggie? I saw your car, open up!"

Holy shit! Nely slapped her hands over her mouth.

"Aggie!" The door shuddered against the frame.

Cops . . . 911 . . . and a gun flashed through her mind as she frantically searched for the phone. Knocking candlesticks over a Chinese lacquered box, she couldn't find the phone.

"Aggie, I'm using my key!" he shouted. "We need to talk!"

This was a cozy two-bedroom apartment with nowhere to hide. The key crunched into the lock and the glass knob turned. Nely sprinted into Aggie's bedroom and glanced wildly around, realizing the bed was too low to hide under. He was now in the apartment, calling Aggie's name.

Nely ran into the bathroom and locked the door.

She panted so hard she had to cover her mouth with both hands. Turning, she caught a glimpse of herself in the mirror and for a moment froze with shock at seeing Aggie's face. She wasn't Nely anymore. She wasn't the wife whose cop husband told her too many awful stories about what happened to some women when strange men broke into their homes.

But he'd come in with a key, which meant that Aggie had given it to him. She must have felt safe with him. Then again, Aggie had dated some real psychos. *Okay,* she asked herself, *what would Aggie do?*

He called her name again, this time from the bedroom door.

Kevin. He was Kevin. The realization only made her feel like a sheltered, very uncool suburban mom.

She yanked open the door and yelped.

"Hey there, gorgeous," Kevin said with a predatory grin. His arm braced against the door frame and his body heat covered her from head to toe.

"What do you want?" she asked unsteadily, trying to act like Aggie.

"You read my e-mail," he said, not moving to let her by. "I said I'd be here."

"I, um, I . . ." Typical Aggie. She loved her secrets, and had failed to tell her exactly what his e-mail said. Aggie always created a mess that she had to pick up after. In college she'd stop dating guys without telling them, and then they would show up when Nely was alone in their shared apartment, begging for explanations or her intervention.

But this was worse, far *far* worse.

Men like Kevin intimidated her. They slept with too many women and then pushed them aside when they were through.

"The longer I know you, the less I can figure you out," he said. "I never pegged you as a hide-in-the-bathroom type."

"I wasn't hiding." But her blush gave her away.

He pushed himself off the door frame and stopped in the middle of her bedroom, arms arrogantly crossed over his chest. "So how was your weekend? Miss me?"

"Uh, well . . ." For God's sake, she was a thirty-two-year-old, married mother of one. Why was she so tongue-tied?

"Well, I just wanted to check in on you," he said with a tremor in his voice. "See if you needed anything."

She shook her head.

"Hey," he murmured, "what happened to your star?"

"My what?" she said, before remembering Aggie's pendant. "Oh. I gave it as an offering."

"For what? So they'd let you out of that loony bin?"

He had that right. But she answered, "Something like that."

He shifted his weight and then crossed his arms. "Why don't I make us dinner? We'll just put everything that happened Saturday morning to rest and hang out and stuff."

When she didn't answer right away, he unfolded his arms and pressed his fingers to his forehead.

"All right, then, we won't do this," he continued, as if he just wanted to get it over with as quickly as possible. "We've been friends for too long and— Yeah. Friends."

She couldn't bear this any longer. He was trying so hard, and yet, she didn't trust him with Aggie's fragile heart.

"I think you're right," she improvised, and when his hands fell to his sides, she quickly added, "I'm tired and we had a long ride back and . . ."

Just go, she pleaded, and then he did.

Without looking at her, he pulled something out of his back pocket and slapped it on a tiny table standing by the door.

After he strode out, she realized it was a key to the apartment. She listened to the thumping footsteps down the hall. He unlocked a door and then slammed it shut.

It was then that she realized he lived in the other apartment. Cursing Aggie for not telling her, Nely slumped against the door frame.

Ten

All of his efforts were for nothing. Simon could see it in Nely's eyes, the way she held herself away from him, and her deadly silence, which screamed boiling fury at what his mother had done to the living room.

But he'd done his best. He had cleaned. He'd washed most of Audrey's laundry and changed their bed sheets. He'd even vacuumed, but his one fatal error had been letting his mother watch Audrey so he could make a special dinner for his wife.

But Nely said nothing, not even "Wow" much less a tepid "Thanks," even when he served her favorite *pasilla* chile chocolate cake.

Unable to take the suspense, he asked the one fatal question that all husbands knew better than to ask. "Are you mad at me?"

She just stared at him.

It was the delayed anger, he realized. That was the worst kind of anger because it was the kind that was born of no logical origin.

"You're mad about the living room and my mom being here," he prodded. "If you have something to say, say it."

"Uh . . . I, uh—"

"I know this wasn't a fancy weekend away with your friend, but I'll clean all of this after dinner," he snapped. "Or do you want to wait and watch in case I miss a spot?"

"Why are yelling at me?" she asked. "I liked the dinner. It was really— What are you doing?"

One moment he stood safely on the other side of the kitchen. Now he pressed right up against his wife, like he had when she was about to leave for the weekend. That flowery scent of hers radiated around him, making him want to touch her, to hold her close.

"I had to think about what we didn't get to finish every night you were gone," he murmured. "I want to do everything I was going to do."

Nely remained stiff and cold against him. Just a few days ago she melted like ice cream left in the sun, and now the worst insecurity bared its teeth at him: Maybe the reason she'd stayed away from him was that he wasn't doing it for her anymore. Her excuses that she was too fat—because she wasn't—could have been a cover.

Doubt slithered into his head. He wondered if she'd gone off with Aggie as a cover to meet someone this weekend. Was that why she'd snubbed his kiss and now walked around him like she wasn't sure what she was doing back?

He had to stop listening to his mother.

"Nel, are we—" He almost couldn't bring himself to ask. "Are we okay?"

"No," she practically yelled, and then stammered. "Sorry, I mean yes. We're fine."

A fake smile he'd never seen on her face flashed on and off. Panic lit up her eyes and then she stepped back, catching her jeans on the drawer pull.

Call him crazy but something about the way she was acting reminded him of suspects who tried to pull off a lie, even when they knew they were caught.

"You'll be okay—I mean, we'll be okay," Nel said.

He caught the slip and it fed the doubts he didn't want to think.

"Let's give it a couple of weeks before we do anything like, uh, you know," she said dismissively. She then opened the cabinet to the glasses and shut it, glancing around the room as if lost.

He reached over and opened the cabinet where they kept the plates. "Looking for these?"

She briefly met his eyes and slipped the clean plates inside, careful not to make physical contact with him.

When he reached out and tangled his fingers in her hair, she stiffened and held her breath as if his touch physically repulsed her.

Nel wouldn't cheat on him, he reminded himself. She wouldn't even let him see her naked, much less some other guy.

"Sorry," she said. "I'm tired and . . . I'm really, really tired."

Torn between angry pride and stark fear, wanting to know what went wrong with them and yet not, he backed off.

"Do you want to go upstairs and unpack?" he asked, giving her an out.

She was gone so fast that he couldn't help but wonder if he'd ever see his wife again.

Kevin barely saw the guy walking toward him until his shoulder slammed into the other guy's.

"Hey!" the guy called out.

When Kevin spun to face him, the guy held his hands up in surrender. "Sorry. I didn't see you."

If he'd been twenty years younger, he would've beat the crap out of the guy. Nice to know he'd grown out of some impulses, he thought.

Kevin mumbled an apology and then opened the garden gate, heading up the street to his car. He pushed down the sleeves of his shirt and then pushed them back up, remembering that guys were supposed to be impervious to things like chilly morning air.

What would Aggie have said if he told her everything that had pent up inside him over the weekend?

Her imaginary laughter cackled in his head. Kevin had only told four women that he loved them: his grandmother, his mother, and his sister, Sandra. He only spent one summer with his grandmother, but his mother hated the male species so much she never seemed to accept her son's love as genuine. No matter that he took care of her; even when he could barely afford to care for himself, he made sure she had everything she needed. But even that wasn't enough.

As for the fourth woman, Colleen, said she needed to think about it while spending a weekend with her ex.

Falling in love after sleeping with someone was only supposed to happen to women; it was a hormone thing he'd read about somewhere. But somehow, science screwed with him and he'd spent the whole weekend with his sister Sandra analyzing Aggie's every word, gesture, and nuance.

Sandra loved it; he had to medicate himself with his best bottle of Herradura Anejo to get through it alive.

You didn't sleep with her. Get over yourself.

But if he'd woken up first, he would have.

That morning it took twenty minutes to worm his way back to the Gaslamp Quarter and his restaurant, Sazón. He parked the BMW M6 in a garage two blocks away and stalked his way up Sixth Avenue.

A huddle of tourists moved in front of him, barking about how they'd never seen a homeless person before. Kevin exchanged an eye roll with Rockin' Roll George, who was currently working his side of Fifth Avenue between Harbor Drive and J Street.

"Should we take a picture with him?" a girl with a mouthful of braces asked.

"No," Kevin snapped.

Their heads whipped around, eyes rounded with fear, and someone muttered, "I think we should cross at the other street."

"Yeah, you should," he said.

As the huddle inched away, his cell phone trilled. It was Sandra.

"What?" he asked, stopping short as a taxi sped around the corner.

"You blew it, didn't you?" Before he could ask how she knew, Sandra launched into her attack, "If you were still there, you wouldn't be picking up. So what did you do? You didn't say any of the things I told you to say didn't you? I told you—"

He snapped it shut and stuck it into his back pocket.

He'd miss Aggie's friendship; or, the way it had been before they woke up in bed together. Bitterness riddled his forehead. He never missed the others. He had cared about them while seeing them, but once it was over, their faces joined a sea of forgotten women. Even though Sandra called him heartless, he was pretty sure that the women he dated were smart enough to know what to expect from him.

But it was not that simple with Aggie. She had been his friend, one of the guys who happened to be a woman. Even though the most he'd done was kiss her on the cheek at her mother's funeral, she was the hardest to walk away from.

"Don't you hang up on me!" Sandra yelled at him, standing in the mouth of the alley behind their building. "I'm the only family you've got!"

Kevin practically growled with exasperation. Even though she was a major pain in the ass, there was no one else whom he loved and trusted more. Except Aggie.

When he walked by her and the trash, Sandra followed him with a litany of all the things he'd done wrong.

She lapsed into silence when the noise of the kitchen smacked them. He had personally trained each and every member of his kitchen staff, from the dishwasher to his assistant chef. They looked up to say good morning as he made his way into the small office and then went right back to work like he taught them to do.

Sandra shut the door behind her.

"I don't play word games," he said in his defense. "Aggie made it clear what she thinks of me."

Sandra heaved a conspiratorial sigh that women shared when despairing of men. "I was perfectly fine being an only child," she told their mom's *quinceañera* photo. "But you thought I looked lonely.

"He's got nothing to say for himself," she tattled to Mom. "I did what you would've wanted me to do, but he still went off an acted like a typical man!"

She swung her blue-eyed gaze at him. "Aggie is protecting herself. I've told you over and over again—"

"She could've been honest with me," he said, jerking off his leather jacket.

"You're too judgmental. You have to see this from her point of view. She's in love with you."

Kevin's heart gave a sharp kick but he told it to knock it off. He should just find himself a cute little twenty-one-year-old college girl to get his head back on track. Eventually the idea would hold the appeal it once had.

"Are you even listening to me?"

"Trying not to."

Kevin tossed his jacket on his office chair. The hangers danced when he yanked one of his chef's coats out of the closet. They had plenty of staff for tonight's private party but there was no way he was staying in his apartment when Aggie's door was just down the hallway. When he heard her leave last night, he'd stood at his door, forcing himself not to confront her.

"You can't give up on her this easily," Sandra said. She eyed the jacket he'd tossed, trying to fight her obsessive compulsive tendencies. With a delicate snort, she huffed, "Why can't you ever hang up your clothes?"

She picked up his discarded jacket and stalked to the closet.

"Remember Pierce?" he asked, hoping she'd bite and let him change the subject.

"Is he leaving P.F. Chang's?" she asked hopefully.

"No. He's proposing to his girlfriend next week. Here."

"Oh?"

"And he's reserving five tables throughout the restaurant for family. When he pops the question, they all get together for a toast."

"How romantic!"

He braced himself for her to say something like, *You could do the same thing when you propose to Aggie.*

But she didn't.

Then why was he ever so faintly disappointed?

"You want to call him and arrange it all?" he asked.

"I will."

He buttoned his chef's jacket, still waiting. But she went to her computer.

Okay, he was safe. That was good.

"Helen sent you to her," she said when he opened the door. "Don't give up."

He knew she didn't say it to hurt him, but it did. "Well, Aggie sent me back."

Eleven

Aggie skimmed the surface of sleep at the sound of rain tapping the metal roof of her double wide trailer.

The weekend was over, which meant today was Monday, and Monday meant school and having to face Lauren Bruner all over again.

She pressed her face deeper into her pillow to block out those bad thoughts. But it was too late. Lauren, with her pink highlighted hair and the jean jacket Aggie had helped her make with band logos, would be there to taunt her.

"Look at her ass. It's clapping!"

Tears squeezed out the corners of her eyes. She didn't want to open them and see the rolls of fat where her waist should've been or her greasy face with pimples breeding more pimples. She wanted to wake up and see someone so beautiful she'd be dangerous. Because that kind of woman would have the best comebacks for Lauren Bruner, who had once been her very best friend, until she got tall and pretty while Aggie stayed short and fat.

Aggie snuck her hand under the pillow, feeling for the necklace Mama gave her.

"I know what that little bitch is sayin' to you," Mama had said when she gave it to her out of the blue. It was a rhinestone star on a thin silver chain. "But you can't let Lauren see you cry, baby. She sees you cry and she knows she has you. So when you feel like you're gonna cry, I'll be right there with you, ready to kick her snotty little ass."

Suddenly, Aggie was walking by Lauren's desk in fourth period English and Lauren looked up and said loud enough for everyone to hear, "Hey, Trailer Chunk, did your mom buy that necklace with her food stamps?"

Lauren's new friend, Michelle, snickered and delightedly said, "That is so cold!"

"Shut up," Aggie whined.

"Shut up," Lauren mocked.

Aggie stopped short, staring down at the floor as her throat constricted with tears. Her fingers instinctively curled around her star and she knew her mama would be disappointed if she let Lauren see her cry.

Mama's hand clamped down on her shoulder and rattled her out of sleep.

"Your weekend's over," she said. "Audrey's crying."

Aggie's mind scrambled with confusion. Part of her was still in the seventh grade, wondering where her rhinestone star went.

"Nely! Wake up! I have to go to work!" This time it was Simon's voice, not Mama's.

She peeled back her eyelids. This wasn't her pillow. Where was the jacaranda tree outside her window?

"Where am I?" she asked, her throat painfully dry.

"Home. Now get up. Audrey's awake."

It all rushed back at her. She was in Nely's bed. She'd spent most of the night trying to get Audrey to sleep. But she thought she had fallen asleep in the rocker in Audrey's room. Wait. She had, but then she woke up and walked into the wall when she tried to go to the bedroom.

"Can't you take care of her?" Aggie begged him.

"I'm going to be late. Get up."

"I was up all night. This isn't fair!"

"Life's not always fair, is it?"

Over the baby monitor, she could hear Audrey beating on something as she screamed at an impossibly high octave, "Mama!" Through puffy eyes, Aggie watched Simon's legs disappear out the door.

This couldn't be happening to her. But it was. Guru Sauro had her rhinestone star. Nely was at her apartment. How had Nely put up with this? The drudgery alone could kill a person.

"Nely!" Simon shouted down the hall and over the monitor.

Aggie tried to sit up, but her stomach muscles were shot. She grabbed the edge of the mattress and, with the strength of will she never knew she possessed, pulled herself out of bed.

"Stop crying," she whimpered, reaching for her robe in the tangled bed sheets. "For the love of God, stop crying."

The search was futile. She reached for the closet door. Unprepared, she gasped with horror at what she saw.

The wheels groaned like ghosts as she rolled the door open all the way. It was jammed packed with mom-wear—Gypsy skirts, jeans, standard issue sweatpants, and oversized T-shirts—competing for space with Simon's clothes. The beaten-up shoes, including—she gulped in revulsion—Birkenstocks, weakened her knees as she sank to the edge of the bed.

"Nel! I have to go, will you please get out of bed! Audrey's screaming her head off!" Simon shouted from the kitchen.

Aggie whispered, " I can't do this."

He slammed a door downstairs. Panic choked off her breath as she looked down at Nely's chapped, reddened knuckles and uneven cuticles. The walls seemed to contract and the ceiling felt like it would crush her into the floor as Audrey's screams ripped her eardrums to shreds.

She was alone with ugly clothes, uglier shoes, and a kid that hated her. Polka dots floated before her eyes.

But the look on Nely's face after Guru Sauro told them that he couldn't switch them flashed in her mind. She'd never had much experience thinking of others before she thought of herself. It wasn't as satisfying.

The dots faded and the walls and ceiling went back to their normal places. Audrey still cried for her mama, and while she was anything but, she'd damn well try to be.

Zipped into a housecoat and somewhat more coherent, Aggie reached down into the crib to haul Audrey out. "I know that you know I'm not your mommy, but—"

Audrey hissed and bared her front teeth. Aggie snatched her hands back. "Kid, the only way you're getting out of here is through me." She sniffed. Was that the smell of . . . She sniffed again.

Pooh?

She glanced down at Audrey's suspiciously thick diaper. Saliva swelled in her mouth at the thought of what waited for her.

But she'd read the magazines and even watched an episode or two of *Nanny 911*. How hard could it be? She wiped the sweat off her upper lip.

"I have to get you bathed and dressed," she said bravely. "And unless she's been partying the night before, a girl needs to be dressed."

Apparently, Audrey didn't agree, and opened her mouth to release a scream at operatic levels. The window over her crib rattled.

Aggie planted her feet firmly into the floor. She pulled up her sleeves and said a quick *oración* to whoever happened to be listening. She was going in. "Here we go, Audrey!"

Her shoulder and back muscles screamed as fire ripped through them. Audrey stiffened her body until her spine bowed. They made it kicking and cursing and screaming onto the changing table.

Aggie rattled the toy monkeys above Audrey's face and instantly ended the assault. Steeling herself for what lay within, she undid the snaps of Audrey's footed jammies. *It's only a diaper*, she coached herself.

The tabs ripped. The legs went up, and when the folds parted, the smell took on a life of its own. Audrey's hand clamped down over her privates, her fingers squishing into the mess.

"Oh my Go—" Aggie staggered back.

With one hand over her mouth and nose, she armed herself with a baby wipe and shuffled her feet into a guarded stance. Audrey let out a battle cry as she stomped one foot into the green, sticky mass, and then flung it. A pooh missile flew straight at Aggie. She dove, the projectile whistling by her ear. She grabbed the water bottle, aimed, and shot at Audrey. Wielding a washcloth, she lunged forward to wipe Audrey when she could get in without being hit, bit, or attacked.

When she finally could see Audrey's skin through the mess, Aggie reached down for another wipe. Without hesitation, Audrey tangled her poopy fist in her hair and Aggie froze as she realized, *Pooh. In Hair.*

"Haaaaah!" Audrey cried and yanked harder. Aggie whimpered and broke down.

"Eh?" Audrey tugged again, looking at Aggie curiously.

Aggie cried harder, defeated by a toddler who was one quarter of her body weight.

"When I get my body back," she sobbed, "I'm getting myself fixed."

Audrey screwed up her little mouth into what resembled a squiggly line between her plump cheeks.

"Will you let me try? Please?" Aggie begged.

Audrey stopped mid-scream, the word "please" holding her attention. Aggie pushed her hair behind her ear and realized she now had crap on her hand.

Taking a deep breath and then gagging, Aggie told herself she could do this.

"We don't have a choice, Audrey," she said. "We can make this work if we work together."

Audrey stared at her, waiting for her to name her terms of surrender.

"I know I'm not your mama but—" Aggie told herself not to appear frightened. "But I'll let you watch TV and cuss and do whatever you want if—"

Audrey narrowed her eyes.

"If you just pretend to put up with me until the next full moon, you'll get your mama back."

And probably never see me again.

Aggie waited Audrey's decision.

Audrey sucked in her lower lip, rolling the terms around in her baby brain. She then uttered her agreement. "Heh."

Aggie felt just a bit ridiculous for negotiating with someone who still crapped her pants.

"Okay, then," she said with a brave nod. "Let's get started."

Twelve

Dawn smiled gently upon her street as Nely, slumped down in the driver's seat, watched her house. Gold light burned through the fog left over by night. A mother pushed her jogger stroller. Two pink-socked feet stuck out of the blanket, relaxed in sleep.

She had tried to sleep in Aggie's bed, but every time she drifted off, the silence jolted her from a sound sleep. She could do whatever she wanted, go anywhere she wanted, and yet, there was no place she'd rather be than back home with Audrey and Simon.

She wasn't sure what time it had been when she finally grabbed Aggie's car keys and ended up here, parked three doors down from her own house. Nely glanced at her left hand. Even though it was dangerous, she wanted her rings, those tiny pieces of her old life, to get her through the next twenty-six days.

The front door opened and Simon walked out in black workout pants, tight T-shirt, and his stuff in a red backpack. She ducked down, her knees bumping against the steering wheel. His pants clung to his tight buns and that shirt stretched across his back . . . God, it was like the old days when they were first dating and hadn't slept together yet.

The red taillights of his green SUV blinked and then he backed down the driveway. She could almost smell the tang of his skin and feel his hair scratching her cheek. Even though he headed the other way, she went completely out of view in case he checked his rearview mirror.

She waited till he disappeared around the corner. Peeking over the dash, she grabbed her empty travel mug and then heaved the door open.

With a furtive look over her shoulder—not that anyone would recognize her—she slipped across the lawn toward the tall side gate leading to the backyard.

She reached over the top of the gate for the latch and then remembered that Aggie was a good four inches shorter than she was. Rising on the tips of her toes, she felt for the latch with her fingers and grabbed it. Wincing from the burn in her calves, she tried wiggling the latch free. She almost had it but her legs gave out.

Giving it one more try, she jumped up and missed the latch. Man, she'd been so much better at this sort of thing in high school.

"What are you doing on my son's property!" Simona barked. Nely fell against the gate.

She couldn't face La Cacuy. But she had to. There was nowhere to run.

"Hello La Simona," she said, clutching her hands behind her back.

Simona probably thought she'd caught Nely's no-good friend drunk on the front lawn.

"I asked," La Cacuy said, "what are you doing on my son's property?"

Excuse me but this is my damn house, too, she thought.

Simona raised her hand and dialed three numbers into her portable phone.

"Nely accidentally took something of mine," Nely hastily explained. "She told me to come in around the back."

"You're wearing the same clothes you wore yesterday," La Cacuy observed, her finger switching off the phone. "Have you been drinking?"

"No."

"I should call my son to clear this with him."

"Excuse me?" Nely shot back. Now that she was in Aggie's body, she didn't have to be the obedient, respectful daughter-in-law. "I don't have to explain myself to you or your son."

"I'll follow you in. Go."

Nely considered slipping through the gate and then locking La Cacuy out. But then she'd call Simon, and the last person Nely wanted to deal with was her husband.

Choking on her resentment, she walked around to the sliding glass doors. But then she stopped short when she saw herself—Aggie—through the window over the sink. Seeing her body like that, separate from her; God, it was as if she was a ghost that realized it was dead and life had gone on without her.

But the house still stood and Audrey wasn't running naked and starving on the front lawn. From the looks of it,

Aggie had walked effortlessly in her place and taken over her family.

If La Cacuy wasn't making her way to the doors, Nely would've run away.

Aggie looked up when La Cacuy rapped on the glass.

"Open up, Nely," she said. "Your friend said you invited her over."

Aggie froze when she saw Nely standing at the edge of the grass.

Nely held up her hand in greeting and crossed over to the doors.

"What are you doing here?" Aggie asked Nely as La Cacuy pushed by her into the house.

La Cacuy debated whether to listen to them or go to Audrey. She chose Audrey.

"I had to see Audrey," Nely murmured. "Where is she?"

"Watching the Thomas video you told me she likes."

"Why isn't she watching the one I told you to show her?" La Cacuy's voice came across the room. "Leila has been showing it to her daughter, and that little girl has been talking for months. Audrey is very behind."

"No, she isn't," Nely snapped. "She doesn't like that video."

La Cacuy swung around, astonished that she'd spoken. Nely remembered that La Cacuy thought she was Aggie. But standing outside her body and watching the scene—literally—made her realize how patronizing her mother-in-law was.

Nely's arms trembled from the effort to keep them at her sides, when she really wanted to use them to rip La Cacuy's head off. But then the top of Audrey's head popped up from behind the sofa and Nely's heart sobbed, *My baby.*

La Cacuy swooped Audrey off the rug, holding her protectively as she glared at Aggie and Nely.

Nely's maternal instincts howled to take back her baby.

"She should've been bathed already," La Cacuy told Aggie.

Aggie's head swung from La Cacuy to Nely and then back. "I was waiting."

"And she shouldn't be on the floor. It's dirty."

"Dude, does she look like I'm abusing her?"

La Cacuy's mouth dropped open, unaccustomed to so much defiance this early in the morning.

"Go get Audrey," Nely hissed to Aggie. "I just needed to hold her."

Aggie hesitated but then went over. La Cacuy sang to Audrey in Spanish, pausing when Aggie held out her arms.

"I've got her," she told Aggie.

Nely growled.

"Didn't you just say she needed a bath?" Aggie retorted.

La Cacuy stepped out of Aggie's reach. "I'll take care of her. You should visit with your friend."

Audrey looked over La Cacuy's shoulder straight into Nely's eyes. Her eyebrows wrinkled while her pink lips thinned just like Simon's did when he was trying to figure something out. Recognition blossomed on her face. Audrey planted both hands on her grandmother's chest, pushing away and mewing, "Mama! Mama!"

La Cacuy locked her hold tighter. "I'll bring you back," she teased. "Mama wants to talk to her friend right now."

But Audrey shook her head, now using her legs to push away.

Suddenly, Aggie took Audrey and swung her out of La Cacuy's grip. Nely watched Aggie fly Audrey in circles, both of them giggling and laughing as if she wasn't there.

"Nely! You're going to hurt her," La Cacuy scolded.

Even though Aggie did it for her, Nely didn't want Audrey to have fun with anyone but her. As selfish and awful as that sounded, she wanted her daughter to need her and only her.

"You want to visit your Tía Aggie?" Aggie asked Audrey, walking her over to Nely. "Here you go."

Nely hoped Aggie could read the thank-you in her eyes.

"Hi there, baby," she cooed to her daughter. She held Audrey tight, hoping to imprint her daughter against her skin and carry it with her when she had to leave again.

"See, she's okay," Aggie said. "You can trust me."

"I know but—" Nely's eyes watered. "I thought you might need my help."

"Nely," La Cacuy said, calling for Aggie's attention.

They both whirled around, remembering that she stood within listening distance.

"Apparently you don't want me here," she said with injured dignity. "I'll see myself out."

Aggie exhaled until her lungs went flat. So close. If Nely and La Cacuy had shown up ten minutes earlier and seen her covered in Audrey pooh, she would've been kicked to the curb so hard, she'd wear the footprint on her ass for a year.

But Audrey kept her end of the bargain and together they not only fooled Nely, but also the evil Cacuy.

Aggie had everything under control. She needed to prove to herself that she was mom material. Even though she'd thought about tossing the kid out the window and letting her fend for herself.

"Maybe you should go," Aggie said, forcing her spine straight and her eyes level. "That was too close."

Nely stared at Audrey with such longing that Aggie almost faltered.

"Where?" Nely asked.

I am the lowest of the low, Aggie told herself, *the worst of the worst.* But she was doing this for Nely's sake. They had a month to go and she didn't want Nely to suffer, thinking that she would accidentally kill her daughter.

"She misses you, too," Aggie conceded, and bingo, Nely brightened. "But she's okay. Look at her."

"I know but—"

"You're supposed to be me and I'm supposed to be you." Aggie swallowed her pride and it left a bitter film on her tongue. "Go micromanage my life. You know you've been wanting to."

Nely pressed a kiss against Audrey's cheek.

"I mean, someone has to run Lola's, and it might as well be you." And then Aggie realized she probably shouldn't have said it like that. If Nely ran Lola's, her friend would discover that she was deep in the hole without even a shovel to dig her way out.

"Then again, just hang out," she suggested breezily, even though she'd already slipped the noose over her head. "Relax."

"Wait," Nely said. "Who was running Lola's this weekend?"

"I closed it."

"And you want to keep it closed for a month? How would you make any money?"

"I'll be all right," Aggie lied. She didn't want anyone to fight her battles, or worse, pity her.

"I trust you with my daughter and my husband," Nely argued. "The least you could do is trust me with Lola's."

"It's not that I don't trust you, it's just—" Aggie shut her mouth, realizing how patronizing she'd sounded. "It's just that things are complicated right now."

Nely handed Audrey off, into Aggie's arms. Audrey whined and twisted back toward Nely.

Aggie knew she faced a woman on a mission. "Where are you going?" she asked in alarm, following Nely out of the kitchen. She should've let Nely stay and be the mommy. "What are you going to do?"

"I'm going to micromanage your life," Nely spat, yanking the front door open. "Oh, and if you can handle it, Audrey has Miss Cheryl's Toddler Time in an hour today."

"Then you should stay here with Audrey and—" The walls shuddered from the door slamming.

"Dude, she's going to rip me a new one, isn't she?" Aggie said aloud when she returned to the family room.

Audrey paid her no attention, staring at the trains crashing on TV.

Aggie set her on the floor, trembling at the thought of Nely uncovering all of her secrets.

Thirteen

Her pride stung so badly that Nely forgot all about her wedding rings.

But she was already at the golf course, waiting for the left turn signal. Aggie had been so patronizing, as if she was just a little happy homemaker who couldn't handle running a business.

The more she replayed it in her head, the more Nely wondered what Aggie had been trying to hide. As she continued toward the freeway, on her way downtown, she realized that not once during their weekend did Aggie talk about the business. That wasn't like Aggie. She was always going on about the exclusive new designer she sold and stuff like that.

An hour later, having fought through traffic like a salmon swimming upstream, Nely unlocked the front door to

Whatever Lola Wants. She entered the boutique designed to evoke the boudoir of a 1950s femme fatale. Through Lola, Aggie had created a ferocious, feline man-eating ambience with no traces of Audrey Hepburn's gawky serenity or Grace Kelly's patrician reserve. The dressing rooms were named after Ava Gardner, Rita Hayworth, Sophia Loren, Katy Jurado, and then there was the one called Lola, which was the largest, draped in gold velvet.

The fictional image of Lola was a dame who knew her worth and never sold cheap. Like her cinematic girlfriends, she smoked, drank, cursed, and conducted affairs like a man, while draped in silks and glittering in diamonds.

Aggie had built Whatever Lola Wants out of the trunk of her battered Toyota Corolla, selling T-shirts imprinted with old Mexican movie posters. Nely had been proud of Aggie, but secretly a tiny bit jealous. She played it safe, going to business school while Aggie dropped out and started her own business. She had taken the corporate path, lured by a generous salary, excellent benefits. and a 401(k) plan. But then the grind of her job wore her out with its sameness. If it had been possible to die of boredom, her job could've done the trick.

She marched straight to the light switches, and flicking them on, the glass chandeliers came to life. She'd never worked retail except to fold jeans at the Gap in high school, and had only the faintest idea how Aggie ordered clothes, much less how to turn on the cash register.

But all businesses were the same, Nely assured herself as she stared at the controls mounted under the counter. She could wing it. It would be like when she was kid and would play fashion model with her friends, except this time she'd have real clothes to play with.

The phone rang. Nely reached for it and then stopped.

How should she answer it?

Oh, for God's sake.

"Are you planning to work today?" a man demanded before she could utter a word.

"Uh, who is this?"

"It's me, Kevin. The man you slept with Friday night." He slapped his hand over his end of the phone and talked to someone. Then he returned with, "Where did you go last night?"

"Nowhere," she answered, and then after a long pause wondered if he was still there.

"Huh," he snapped. "Well, then . . ."

His voice faded off into uncertainty. Something tickled at her intuition. She pressed to see what he'd do. "Well then, *what?*" she asked.

"Nothing," he stammered. "I'm busy."

He hung up.

Interesting. If she hadn't caught him in the ladies' room with that barely legal girl, she would almost have thought that—

The phone trilled again.

"This is Giada from Sugar, is this Aggie?"

It took Nely a moment to reply, "Yes, this is her."

"Oh, cool." She cleared her throat. "I received your order, and when I brought it up to my manager, she . . . well, she . . . Aggie, I'm really sorry. We can't."

"Can't what?"

"Your sales aren't what they used to be, and I really hate doing this to you but my manager wants us to take our line to another store."

Nely didn't know what to say.

"I'm sure things will turn around for you. If there's anything I can do, just let me know."

Nely's scalp tingled.

"Aggie, this isn't personal. You're one of the best people I worked with and—"

"I'm fine," Nely forced through the shock. "Just surprised and—"

Well, surprised was one way of saying it.

She went on autopilot to end the call. With one quick glance at the door, she saw that no crowd threatened to beat it down, then went into the back office. She clicked through the computer files, and when she saw the financials, fell back against the chair, her heart throbbing from the bloodbath.

Whatever Lola Wants hadn't posted a profit in six months. Aggie had let her staff go. There were periods of days when the store posted no sales receipts at all. Two large infusions of cash told Nely what had happened to Aggie's sexy Nissan 350Z.

"Why didn't you tell me?" she asked the screen.

She happened to glance up at the hundreds of photos plastered on the wall above Aggie's desk. There was a picture of them at nineteen when she had scored free tickets to Maui. Suddenly, the memory of the car they rented in Hawaii replayed in her head.

"Fuck, dude," Aggie had screamed. "These roaches should be chipping in for gas!"

They took that picture at one of the waterfalls on the way to Hana. Damn, they were young. And poor. But back then they shared everything. Now it seemed like they kept secrets from each other.

But if she could find out where the hemorrhaging took place, maybe she could save Lola's.

The phone rang again, and Nely seriously considering shutting it off and using Aggie's Sidekick to save money.

After Nely left, Audrey welshed on their surrender. Aggie tried shushing and holding, bribery and threats. She would remember Audrey's cries for the rest of her life, and at one point, seriously considered calling La Cacuy to take over while she hid under the bed.

Helpless, she left the baby howling on the family room floor. Tears sprayed out of the corners of her little eyes and she choked on her own sobs. Desperate for alcohol, Aggie raided the cabinets until she found the next best thing: a bag of Hershey's Pot of Gold truffles behind Jenny Craig Chocolate Caramel Peanut Bars.

"There is a God!" she shouted.

Truffles exploded over the counter when she ripped open the bag.

Almost panting, she grabbed one and her fingers fumbled with the foil, mere moments away from bliss.

Her teeth sank into the sweet ganache. Chocolate oozed onto her tongue, delighting all the pleasure centers in her brain and silencing the horrible screaming.

By her fifth chocolate Aggie felt a tiny finger tapping her leg.

Audrey stretched her fingers up. "Eh?"

"You want this?" Aggie asked.

Audrey reached up, standing on her tiny toes, all but wagging her tongue.

"How bad?"

"Ning ning ning!"

That was good enough for Aggie.

She ruthlessly exploited Audrey's weakness to get her

dressed, in the car, and then out of the minivan to—she shuddered with distaste—Miss Cheryl's Toddler Time.

At least the dark gray minivan had a Bose sound system and red leather upholstery.

Pulling up to the recreation center, Aggie told herself to stop being such a snob. This was hands-on training. If she could survive Nely's offspring, than she would survive her own.

Not even thirty seconds later, as she nearly lost the tip of her middle finger from wrestling the stroller out of the back, she realized that her promise was easier made than kept. Wheeling the stroller to the side door, she begged and bartered with Audrey who squirmed as Aggie tried to un-buckle the car seat.

"Chocolate!" she yelled, like a trainer commanding a dog.

Audrey immediately stopped squirming and complied.

If it wasn't for Hershey's, and she were the last ovulat-ing woman on this earth, the human species would die with her.

She reached into the only stylish accessory Nely owned: an Asian brocade Petunia Pickle Bottom backpack. Her hand dug for her stash.

They couldn't be gone. She yanked the bag open, shov-ing diapers and all kinds of crap out of her way. No . . . *no* . . . *NO!*

Desperation sent her blood pounding through her veins. Audrey started panting with frustration, flapping her arms like a pissed-off goose.

Anxiety gained on them, but then Aggie spied a Host-ess cupcake under the front passenger seat. She dared not hope as she crammed her hand under the seat and plucked it free.

Relief flooded through her like the first gulp of cold water in the desert.

A lawn mower burred in the distance and the occasional car swooshed by. Aggie pushed Audrey up the sidewalk, longing for her normal life, when she'd stop in at Pannikan Coffee & Tea on G Street for a large black French roast for Kevin and a nonfat, decaf latte for herself.

God, she missed her old life, her old clothes, and—

A sigh escaped her lips. She missed *him*, too. She missed the way he pointed at her to make sure she heard every word he was saying. She missed that he was so protective of Sandra and his employees. She missed that sly sideways glance he'd give her and only her.

Aggie screwed her face into a look of disgust at the way Audrey had mashed most of the cupcake into her face and hair. She molded it like it was edible play dough.

"Dude, that is sick," she said.

Audrey glanced up from her cupcake sculpture and opened her mouth, which was black with chocolate.

"Hey, Nel," an Indian woman greeted as if she'd thought she'd never see her again. "Hi there, Audrey! Look, Naveen," the woman said to her curly-haired boy, "it's your girl-friend."

She winked at Audrey, and Aggie wondered if this was Leila, Nely's new best friend.

"We haven't seen you in a long time," the stranger said.

"Yeah, I uh . . . you know, got busy and stuff."

Aggie followed her into the squat building. An armada of Bugaboo strollers was parked outside. Mommies holding Starbucks cups chatted while toddlers played with the toys on a giant blue mat that covered the floor.

Scanning the huddle, she immediately spotted the queen

bee, a perky ponytailed mama with a not-so-nice plastic smile on her face.

Sure enough when they joined the swarm, Perky Ponytail's bloodletting gaze traced over her and then Audrey's chocolate-encrusted outfit. Aggie's confidence sagged when Perky ever so subtly nudged her minion and inclined her head in her direction. It was like Lauren Bruner and her gang all over again; all sparkly and perfect. Even Perky's shiny baby girl scowled at them before pounding a doll's head with a plastic hammer.

But then Aggie thought if she was back in her real body and Audrey was her kid—with an au pair, of course—they'd make Perky and her offspring look like five-dollar skanks who worked the Chevron station on Friday nights.

"Nely, is that you?" Perky Ponytail gushed, as if they were long lost friends. "It's me, Leila! We *need* to talk!"

Don't make eye contact, Aggie told herself, then remembered that she wasn't a loser anymore. She had a business, fabulous friends, an enviable apartment, and any man—even Leila's husband, if she felt like being a real bitch—she wanted. Her hand drifted up to her rhinestone star, and when she didn't feel it, her heart gave a jolt of alarm.

The huddle parted, allowing just enough space for Aggie and Audrey to enter. They quickly closed around them, keeping Naveen's mom on the perimeter.

"So how is Annie?" Leila trilled, smiling down at Audrey.

"Annie who?"

"I'm sorry, what's your daughter's name?"

"Audrey."

"So is she saying real words yet?"

"Of course."

"Like what?" one of Leila's minions asked.

Aggie shrugged and answered, "I don't know. Words."

"You don't know?" Leila asked accusingly. "Emerson has been chattering away for months," she gushed, her little blue eyes as cold as a serial killer's. "But trust me, when Audrey starts talking, you'll wish she shuts up."

On cue, the huddle tittered in agreement.

Was Audrey the only kid who wasn't talking? Had La Cacuy been right that she was behind the other kids? Panic built up in Aggie's chest. Not only did she have the dirty kid, she also had the slow one!

Leila then tapped her hand, and she yanked it away, expecting to see the Death Eater's mark burned into the skin.

"Could we talk for just a second?" Leila asked, and the huddle tensed with envy as she pulled Aggie closer to the ladies' room.

"I don't want to create a *situation*," Leila hinted, her eyes quickly cutting to Naveen's mom. "But you need to talk to her."

"Why?" Aggie asked.

Audrey screamed from across the room. Aggie turned and caught Emerson standing over her, probably sucking the life force out of her victim.

"Pema doesn't fit in, and her little boy is too disruptive," Leila hissed.

"She doesn't?" Aggie asked, edging away to rescue Audre.

Naveen quietly chewed on some bright blue plastic thingy, while his mom, Pema, laughed with two other mommies who had been left out of the huddle.

"And he's the only boy," Leila complained.

"You talk to her," Aggie snapped back.

Leila's mouth dropped open in shock. "I can't do that! I hardly know her, but you talked to her all the time at the last class."

Oh my God. She'd been sent back to high school. But this time with high-octane estrogen.

"Leila," one of the moms called. From her white zippered hoodie to her Nikes, she was perfectly coordinated with her daughter's blue and gray ensemble. "Kaylie's here!"

Aggie jerked back. This was Leila? Nely made friends with her?

"We're good then?" Leila confirmed, then turned to the huddle that awaited her attention.

Aggie walked over to where Audrey and Naveen were playing. Emerson had toddled off in search of fresh meat.

"What happened?" Pema asked. "Are you okay? What did they say to you?"

Aggie shook her head. She couldn't look at Pema, ashamed of what had just taken place. She couldn't imagine Nely falling in with this crew. Never. Then again, Nely had been meeting with them once a week for the past few months. Could that be one of the reasons why they hadn't been as close?

"Nely?" Pema asked.

"Sorry," Aggie said, checking Audrey for marks. "They're really foul."

"Nely, we're really glad you came back but—" Pema looked at two other moms, who nodded. "You should've stayed away."

"Then why are you here?"

Pema shrugged with a crooked smile. "We were hoping to run into you."

Aggie was humbled by Pema's honesty. Without even

thinking, she turned to the other moms and asked, "Now, what're your names?"

Their faces stiffened with shock, and Aggie remembered they thought she was Nely, who met with them once a week.

"Kidding," she trilled. They blinked and then they forced smiles that suspected it wouldn't be long before she dumped them for Leila and the rest of the Evil Mommy Brigade.

Well, she wasn't that kind of girl. But she wondered if deep down Nely was.

Fourteen

Not one soul walked through those doors. It was six o'clock, hunger pulled at her innards, and her eyes burned from reading through the last two years of financials.

Nely flipped the Closed sign and stepped out into the canyonlike streets of downtown. Squealing car brakes and impatient horns echoed down the corridors of buildings. Signs sparkled to life as the sun sank out of the sky.

She knew she was free to stay out as long as she wanted, go wherever she wanted; but the only place she wanted to be was home.

If this hadn't happened, she'd be feeding Audrey when Simon walked through the door. He'd then set the table or fold the laundry she hadn't had time to take out of the dryer. She might have been tired and sore from carrying and picking up a twenty-five pound toddler. She might have had a moment when she thought about doing it all again tomorrow and feeling so overwhelmed that she'd want to cry.

Turning up G Street, she found her way into the Borders bookstore. Her eyes wandered over the books on the front tables.

"Excuse me, Aggie?" a man behind her said.

Nely turned and had to tilt her chin up to see who had tapped her shoulder.

He had the posture of a military man, and unlike most office workers off the clock, he still wore his tie and coat.

"Um, hi," she said hesitantly, then he smiled.

"I saw you walk in and thought I'd ask if you wanted a drink."

Who the hell was this guy? Nely sized him up, beginning with the dark hair that swept up from his high forehead. He had gray eyes that sparkled with interest, and his lush lower lip reminded her of a more serious Brad Pitt. All in all, not bad. She could do without the tiny patch of hair under his lip. She'd gotten used to a clean-shaven husband *and* she hadn't had been on a date since . . .

"I'm Jeff," he said, pointing to himself. "I manage your lease on the store."

"Oh. I'm sorry I didn't recognize you."

"Would you like to get a drink?" He suddenly held his hands up. "No pressure."

Something about him felt off. She couldn't say what or why . . . Then again, it had been ages since she'd been on a first date. He was a business colleague, so Aggie probably trusted him. Maybe it would be fun to see if she still had some of her old mojo.

"I'd love to," she finally said.

His smile flashed on, twitching ever so slightly at the

corners. Nely hesitated, and then told herself to stop being such an old lady.

"Great," he said. "I know a place and--"

She stepped forward and he did at the same time. His cheeks tinted pink as he laughed at himself. "How about I go after you?"

With him at her back, Nely rolled her eyes at herself.

They ended up at a sexy, contemporary restaurant with a wall of rippled glass separating the bar from the dining room. Beautiful people draped themselves over curvaceous red leather sofas arranged around black tables set with white pillar candles on silver chargers. Glass stars in yellow, orange, green, and blue hung from the twenty-foot ceiling. The sleek bar changed colors as it glowed red, then orange, then yellow, and back, running the length of the bare brick wall.

Her stomach begged for food. But she noticed that no one was eating.

"Aggie, what can I get for you?" Jeff asked.

"A rude cosmopolitan," she said, remembering she'd read about it in a magazine.

He flagged a waitress dressed all in form-fitting black that made Nely wonder if she doubled as a superhero.

When he finished their order, he coughed into his fist and then rechecked the cell phone clipped to his belt. She smiled when he just stared at her, expecting him to say something.

"This is the first time I've been in here," she said, to cover the awkwardness hovering over them. "Are you a regular?"

"Am I what?"

"A regular. To this bar?"

"No, but my mother recommended it."

Alarms pealed in her ears as if a nuclear reactor had been breached.

"Look, Aggie, I've been meaning to call you and—"

Nely clenched her jaw, waiting for what he'd say next.

"The management company wants to raise your rent when your lease is up."

Where the hell was her drink?

"Oh, okay," she answered carefully.

"But I think you and I could . . ." He paused as his eyes lingered at her chest. ". . . talk about this. Just the two of us."

His knee began jumping and his hands trembled as he rubbed them on his thighs. Suddenly, his lush lip wasn't so cute and his gray eyes sparkled like a predator's.

She shifted her bag onto her lap like a shield, her mind scrounging around for a reply.

But his phone rang and saved her. "Excuse me a moment," he told her.

She wondered if she should just pretend to go to the ladies' room and then run like hell for her car. But if he worked for the building owner, she'd have to explain herself.

"Mom, I'm at the bar . . . Yes, it's quite nice . . . But that's out of my way . . . I know but . . . No, don't take a cab . . . Yes, I'm on my way."

He snapped his phone shut and sighed. "Mother just needs to use my house key. She locked herself out of the house. She does it all the time whenever I go out."

"Well, nice chatting with you," she said, relieved it ended before it even began.

"But you're coming with me," he said.

Shocked, she blinked several times before replying, "I don't think so."

"Why not? You said you'd have a drink with me."

"Yes but—" *Come on, say something. Anything.* "But I should review my lease agreement before we talk any further. I'll make an appointment with your assistant."

She got to her feet, the table edge biting into her shins. Out of the corner of her eye she saw him accessing her like a car he wasn't sure about purchasing.

"Wait a second," Jeff said, grabbing her arm just when she reached the door.

She should've hid in the girls' room.

"Don't blow me off," he threatened. "I could make things easy." She tried to pull her arm free, but his grip tightened. "Or very difficult."

Her back stiffened as her fight instinct kicked in.

His smile flashed on. He thought he had her scared, that he had her right where he wanted. Well, he did. But she wouldn't show it.

Instead she smiled back at him, the kind of smile Lola would give to a little man.

"I already did," she said. "Good night."

Kevin watched Aggie's date disappear into the moving stream of people.

He thanked God that Sandra was in the office and not here to witness him pathetically watching Aggie bring dates in his restaurant. He should've thrown them out on the street and washed his hands of Aggie completely. She was a picky eater, for one. He had no business even thinking of swapping his DNA with a picky eater.

But he wanted to know why. Why was she meeting guys *here*, of all places, right under his nose? Did she think he wouldn't know what was happening in his place?

The Aggie he knew would never pull crap like this.

But then, he'd watched her change since Helen died. When his mother died, at least he had Sandra. Aggie seemed convinced she had no one.

He'd tried to pull her back, to keep her from falling. Helen would have kicked his ass for letting Aggie slip out of his hold. She'd made no bones about wanting them together.

What really got him was he could swear that person who came out of her bathroom yesterday wasn't the same woman who had booted him out just a few days earlier.

Just then, a female body stepped into his view. He tilted his chin down to a blonde in a polka-dot top and black pants.

"Excuse me?" she said, bending closer to make herself heard over the growing crowd. "Are you the chef?"

Annoyed that in his chef's jacket, it was obvious he was. He replied, "I am."

"Your food is amazing," she gushed, her hand landing on his arm. "It's the best sex I've never had."

She laughed at her own joke, and he was polite enough to smile.

"Thanks. Dessert is on me."

"Wait."

He reluctantly stayed where he was.

"I'm Bianca."

He glanced away from Aggie still standing by the front door. "Kevin."

"What exactly would you recommend for dessert, Kevin?"

He repressed a sigh, still caught up in the puzzle of Aggie. Something about the way she moved wasn't quite right. Usually Aggie moved like a pixie on speed. She had the bruises on her elbows and knees to prove it.

And her fire had dimmed. Aggie usually sucked in a

room's energy, drawing everyone's attention. She stood there like she was trying to stay out of everyone's way.

Bianca lightly touched his hand, bringing his attention back to her. Her smile was worth several thousand in dental work, but her eyes were determined to keep his attention.

"Sorry. I got sidetracked," he apologized. "We're breaking in a new bartender."

"I was wondering if you have a chef's table," she paused. "For intimate parties."

Nely happened to see Kevin canoodling—she'd always wanted to use that word—with a blonde whose halter top bared her tanned, toned back.

She'd been right about him. He'd take any woman who threw herself at him.

An elbow jabbed her in the side. The elbow's owner gave her a cursory glance over his shoulder by way of apology. If she were here with Simon, he'd use his stocky build to protect her from the growing crowd. How had she become so dependent on him?

Squaring her shoulders, Nely made her own way through. She shuffled around loud-mouthed executives, who had stuffed their ties into their breast pockets, and bored-looking girls holding martini glasses. There was something so desperately high school about the singles' scene.

Free to breathe the night air, she thought enough time had passed since Jeff left to take care of his mother. Slipping her hands in the pockets of her coat, she began walking toward the parking lot where she'd left Aggie's car. The Gaslamp came to life as restaurants that had been empty not that long ago now spilled out onto the sidewalks.

Meeting that creep unsettled her, and she kept looking

over her shoulder in case he lurked around. She'd met Simon when she was twenty-three, which made her dating history pretty much nil. Uh, she felt so 1950s. But how did women do this? Did they end up packing guns?

"What did you think you were doing? My brother is impossible because of you."

Nely hadn't seen the tiny woman coming, and she now practically stood on her toes. "I'm sorry, what?"

"The entire line is threatening to quit," she went on. "He's bad enough when everything is normal, but now—"

Sandra, Nely realized. This was the sister, Sandra. Aggie had mentioned her several times. Nely was certain they'd even met at Helen's memorial.

"Sorry," was the only thing Nely could think to say. *Please don't kill me.*

"He has feelings, too," Sandra said, her Veronica Lake waves not budging an inch in the sudden swoosh of a bus passing by. "How could you meet some guy in our restaurant?"

Nely's mouth gaped open as she scrambled to come up with something to say. She'd been so caught up that she forgot Sazón was Kevin's restaurant.

If it weren't for the burgundy velvet platforms, Sandra wouldn't have been staring down at Nely. In her high-waisted pants and crisp white blouse, she looked like a Mexican Katharine Hepburn. "So what, you've got nothing to say? I thought we were friends, Aggie."

"We are," Nely managed. "It's just that I—I'm going through a thing right now and . . ."

She wished she'd gone straight from Lola's to Aggie's apartment and hid in the closet.

Sandra's glossy red lips twisted with disdain, thinking that Aggie was giving her the brush-off. "A thing, huh?"

Well, yes, that was one way of putting it.

Sandra deliberately shoved against her shoulder as she flounced off. Nely wanted to chase after her and apologize. She didn't want to mess up Aggie's friendships, but then again, what would she say?

Fifteen

Aggie had a window of uninterrupted time and a wireless connection to do what she had to do. Nely wouldn't approve, but she had to communicate with Kevin.

The little junkie crashed under the coffee table after Aggie put on that video La Cacuy had gotten her panties in a twist over. Aggie did a quick check in case ants were devouring Audrey alive.

She launched Explorer and then tapped into her Yahoo e-mail account. No e-mails from Kevin since Saturday.

She opened a new message and began to type, disturbed that she couldn't get the "Wheels on the Bus" out of her head.

I don't know what really happened the other morning. And right now I'm not ready to go into it with you. I need time . . .

Time to what? Think? He'd never buy it.

She deleted it all and tried again.

I don't know what's happening with us right now. Waking up next to you was . . .

What? She wished she had a thesaurus.

. . . was scary and intense and honest, in a way. I think we've been dancing around this for a while and I don't know . . .

Yes, she knew. Or she was pretty sure she did.

Either way, she just wasn't ready to admit it. And even if she was ready, she couldn't exactly show up at his doorstep and yell, "Surprise!"

She went back to *dancing around this for a while*, then wrote:

. . . and I need time to figure out what I want.

She almost told him the rest. But she held back.

I know you hate games, and this isn't a game. I swear! It is what it is. For now. Aggie.

She hit Send before she lost the nerve.

Fingernails tapped on the glass door behind her. La Cacuy gestured for her to open up.

"Hi," Aggie said through the crack in the doorway. "Can I help you?"

La Cacuy muscled her way in, pushing Aggie back as she entered the house. "It's been quiet over here," she said, her eyes fastening on the computer screen.

Aggie skipped over and closed the Explorer window. "We're having a good day." She didn't know how else to ask. "So what do you want?"

La Cacuy gasped when she saw Audrey. *"Mija!"* She rushed over.

"Quiet! She's just sleeping," Aggie hissed.

"Look at her," La Cacuy exclaimed. "Look at the state she's in."

She was a little messy, but when Simon came home, he could shower her off.

"She's a kid," Aggie said. "Aren't they all like that?"

La Cacuy's nose sniffed like a rat's. "Is that pee pee I smell? When did you change her diaper?"

Oh. She'd forgotten about that. "An hour ago," Aggie lied.

"And what about these scratches? What did you do to her?"

"I didn't do that! Leila's kid did it."

"What? Why would you say something like that?"

"Because I saw her do it." Actually, she hadn't, but after witnessing Emerson toss a beach ball in Naveen's face and then use another kid's head as a drum, she knew her first instinct had been right.

"I don't believe it," La Cacuy argued. "Leila is a wonderful mother. And you should try to be friends with her. It helps to be around the right people."

"Is there a reason why you're here?"

La Cacuy's thin lips pressed into a taut line. "I have my concerns," she said. "I've hinted that you should bring someone in."

"To do what?"

"To help you with Audrey. I can't be here every second, and it seems that . . . well, that motherhood doesn't come natural to you."

If flames had burst out of her eyes, she wouldn't have been surprised.

"Your daughter is miserable," La Cacuy added, "and my son is beside himself."

Aggie knew *she* was a bad mother, but *no one* accused Nely of that. Especially some dried-up, frigid, frozen-assed bitch—

"I will stay until Simon comes home," La Cacuy decided, and then dismissed her like she was the help. "Go get dinner started."

Startled, Aggie watched as La Cacuy gathered a still-sleeping Audrey in her arms and carried her up the stairs.

Aggie tried to tell herself that this was cool. Someone else would take care of the kid. Someone who knew what she was doing.

But it didn't feel right as she stood there in the living room, the sunlight reflecting off the plastic couches. It felt like she'd let Nely down.

"What are you doing here?" Simon asked his mother when he walked in.

"Taking care of my granddaughter," she replied. "Your wife was on the computer and then she left. When I came over, Audrey was caked in filth, asleep under the table."

He shouldn't have come home, even though his bones were exhausted after chasing a drug-dealing suspect over a chain-link fence and through Mount Hope Cemetery.

"I'll go change," he said, suppressing a wince when he moved too suddenly where the suspect's elbow connected with his ribs. "Did Nely say where she was going?"

"She's acting suspiciously . . . if you know what I mean."

He glanced at his watch. "It's seven. She should be putting Audrey to bed."

"Exactly my point. You should go out and look for her."

Even if he could, even if he wanted to—which he did—

Simon had to show trust in his wife. Especially in front of his mother. "She's my wife, Mama," he said. "Not my daughter."

"*El hombre en la plaza y la mujer en la casa,*" she intoned, emphasizing each word with a tap of her fingernail on the counter. Men in the plaza and the women in the house. "Wives have no business running around when there is a family to take care of. When I came over, she was on that Internet and she didn't want me to see what she was doing."

"It's my turn to put Audrey to bed anyway," he lied. He started toward the stairs before she could press on. It wasn't like Nely to run off, leaving his mother with Audrey. Usually she made arrangements that put the military to shame. Also, she had a thing about one of them tucking Audrey in bed every night.

An interview he had with a guy who ran over his wife's boyfriend snuck into his head.

"She was on the fucking Internet all the time," he had said, pausing to wipe his nose with the back of his bare hand. "All like, secretive and shit. She's just as guilty as I am for settin' that asshole up."

"Are you saying she worked with you to run him over with your car?" he asked, fighting the urge to show the disgust and amusement he'd felt at the time.

"Naw, man. I'm sayin' if she'd stayed her ass at home, I wouldna had to run the motherfucker over."

He'd gotten a lot of laughs out of that one. But now he was starting to understand how the guy felt.

Shaking his head at himself, there was no way she'd stray from him. No way. But he called Nely's cell phone anyway, to see what was up. Not that he needed to . . . more than likely, she'd run out to get something for the mom group she hung out with.

But she didn't pick up, and he pictured her with some guy, maybe sitting in a booth at some restaurant far from the house.

He tried again. This time the picture in his head changed to her, naked on a motel room bed.

His fingers clamped down on his cell phone as he told himself this was stupid . . . crazy. But when he called Nely's cell phone a third time, he left her a voice mail: "Call me as soon as you get this."

When Aggie walked into the house, the front room was dimly illuminated by the porch light behind her, and she had to struggle with her bags to find the lights.

"What's going on here?" she asked, finding La Cacuy sitting at the dining room table in the half-dark room.

"Do you know how long you've been gone?"

"I did some shopping while I was out," Aggie said, then caught herself. She wasn't beholden to this woman.

"Your daughter would've starved if I hadn't fed her," La Cacuy accused, and then muttered under her breath, "*Es una papa enterrada.*"

She's a buried potato. Her mama used that expression when she didn't want someone to know she was calling them stupid.

"*Eres el reflejo de tus pensamientos,*" Aggie returned as she walked to the light switch and flipped on the chandelier. You are what you think.

La Cacuy dropped her smug frown and just stared at her, her cheeks burning red.

Crap. She remembered that Nely didn't speak Spanish.

"What?" Aggie demanded when La Cacuy continued to stare at her.

"Nothing," she said briskly. "If you think your behavior is appropriate, then—" She stood up. "Well, let me just say that I know what you're up to."

Aggie flashed hot and then cold.

"And it won't be long before my son sees you for who you really are."

What the hell was she talking about? There was no way La Cacuy could know.

"Where's Audrey?" Aggie asked.

La Cacuy stared long and hard without blinking. Aggie's eyes began watering, and she told herself it was beneath her to engage in staring contests.

"It is almost eight," La Cacuy answered slowly. "Simon is putting her to bed."

No it wasn't. But then Aggie glanced at the clock and realized that it was.

If La Cacuy had figured out what had happened, would she use it against Nely? Of course she would.

But no. There was no way she knew. She chuckled to herself, thinking she was silly for even entertaining the idea.

When La Cacuy swept out of the house, shutting the door behind her, Aggie switched off the porch light. If that old woman fell in the dark, it was no concern of hers.

As ridiculous as the idea was—there was no way La Cacuy could've figured out their charade—it burrowed into her head. Leaving her bags by the couch, she hurried to the computer.

Quickly logging in, she listened for Simon upstairs. The

refrigerator hummed in the kitchen. When she read Kevin's name, her heart lurched and then pounded in triple time. He had replied:

I don't know what any of this means. Is it the truth, or just some excuse? Write back when you have something real to say.

Aggie recoiled, immediately shutting down the computer. She was trying, damn it. But would he believe the truth? Hell, she had a hard enough time believing what had happened to her!

"Where've you been?" Simon asked.

Her knee slammed up against the desk and she whirled around. He'd snuck right up behind her.

"Shopping," she squeaked.

"Where?"

"At the mall. I wasn't gone very long."

"Why didn't you call me back?"

Without thinking, she started, "Because I gave my—I mean, I left my phone off. Sorry."

Now would be the best time to escape, she thought. "I should get all my bags taken care of," she said, hoping he'd step back.

"Did my mom give you a hard time?"

He still wouldn't move. But luckily, she was quite accomplished at maneuvering her way out of uncomfortable situations. Or so she thought. "Oh, you know . . . the usual."

"What did she say?"

"She said I was a bad mother."

His hands fell at his sides. "She what?"

"This actually surprises you?"

"You mean that she actually said those words?"

"More like she insinuated it. Strongly."

"You want me to talk to her?"

Did she have to answer that question? If so, she should do Nely a favor and move. "I'm going upstairs. You can figure it out on your own."

He didn't move to stop her, nor did he back off. She squeezed out from between the chair and the desk.

Relieved she'd escaped, Aggie didn't see him pick her purse up off the floor and look inside.

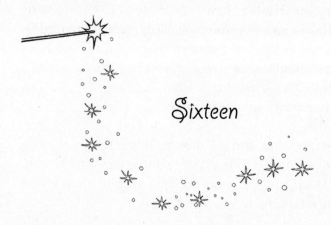

Sixteen

The searing pain in her neck woke Aggie up. Her eyes felt lined with grit as she hovered between wakefulness and sleep. Pale dawn light filtered through the window blinds, and it took her a moment to realize she'd fallen asleep in the chair by Audrey's crib.

After leaving Audrey with La Cacuy, it had felt wrong to let Nely's baby sleep alone when Nely was out there by herself. Aggie squeezed her hand through the bars and laid her hand on Audrey's back. She held her breath until she felt the gentle rise and fall of the baby's breathing.

She swung her legs down, and the room tilted as pain shot up from the soles of her feet. But sleep in a warm bed with a pillow gave her the will to move on.

She leaned on the wall to keep from falling as she stumbled down the hallway. A pillow never felt so good as this one when she sank into the bed. Sleep quickly closed in on her.

"I was just about to go in there and wake you up," a man's voice rumbled in her ear.

"What time is it?" she murmured.

"Five-thirty."

Sleep confused her, and she thought it was Kevin's lips on the back of her neck. His hand stole under her shirt, ticking her belly. Thick, rough fingers brushed the plush underside of her breast. His breath warmed her neck.

She turned toward him and he brought her against his chest, his chin nesting in her hair.

"Will you be there for me when I come back?" she asked.

"You bet," he whispered in that gravelly voice.

"It didn't sound like you would."

"What do you mean?"

"Your e-mail, Kevin," she answered as she fell completely away.

His breath froze into a jagged clump of ice.

Who the fuck was Kevin? Was that the face she saw in her sleep? Is that who she thought was laying beside her?

Simon pushed away from her. Nely rolled onto her back, conked out from exhaustion. He noticed she wasn't wearing her wedding rings. And that thing about her cell phone. It had been in her purse. He'd checked her call history. Nothing out of the ordinary.

His heart tripping over itself, he got out of bed and went downstairs to the family room, where they had the computer. It sat there, holding all of her secrets.

He knew he should trust her; all good marriages were built on trust. But he hit the power button anyway. He had a name, a fucking name!

Never in a million years did he think he'd be the guy whose wife cheated on him. Not with Nely. She'd always been straight with him, even when his mother tried to work them against each other.

His breath exhaled in a long hiss. What was he doing? He was playing right into his mother's hands with her insinuations that Nely would commit the worst betrayal a wife could commit.

Suddenly, in his mind, he was looking into Nely's eyes the morning after Audrey was born. Nely refused to sleep after fighting to bring their daughter into the world. He'd never seen that kind of strength in another person, and in spite of the pain and the blood, she'd found the energy to nurse their daughter.

"I want to tell you something," she had said as Audrey's cheeks worked sporadically, nursing at her breast.

"What?" he'd whispered, mesmerized by every detail of his daughter.

"This little girl is a new commitment to each other," Nely said. "No matter what, I'm staying married to you, so don't get any ideas."

His hand had slid under Audrey's body and found Nely's. They'd threaded their fingers together and held on.

Now, standing in the weak, gray light of the early morning, Simon rubbed his chest, trying to ease the emptiness that spread. He had no armor against this kind of thing. Not when it came to his wife, whom he thought he knew best of all.

If he was going to get to the bottom of this, then he'd get Nely to admit it.

Or, he realized, he'd get Aggie to tell him.

Nely snapped awake, patting the floor for her baby.

A moment ago she'd held Audrey in her arms. The downy dark hair tickled her nose and little feet rested in the crease of her thighs. Every breath brought in that particular smell that was her baby.

The nap of the rug burned her cheek as she realized she had fallen asleep on the floor between the couch and the coffee table.

Her throat begged for water but all she had was a cup of melted ice water and essence of diet Sprite. She drank it anyway.

Last night she had closed the blinds and sat down to work. She had no idea whether she'd slept five minutes or five hours. Wiggling the pad, the laptop blinked awake. The clock read 7:28.

They would be awake right now, she thought. Simon would have breakfast made. It was his day off, and they would hit the grocery store and run errands. She would be able to catch a catnap while he watched the baby downstairs.

Her fingers wrapped around the vintage-looking phone. The click as the phone left the cradle seemed to ricochet off the walls. She shouldn't be doing this. It was dangerous to Aggie, but especially to herself. But knowing they were together without her, being alone in this quiet apartment rode right over all of her common sense.

The call went through, and she told herself to hang up with each ring, until Simon answered.

"Simon!" she said, then realized it was the answering machine.

She slammed the receiver down and snatched her hand away as if bitten.

Even though business at the store wouldn't be different from yesterday, she should get ready for work. As she walked through the shadowy apartment, she played with the idea of moving some of the displays around and redoing the front window

Then again, she didn't have an eye for putting together complete ensembles; not the way Aggie did.

She pushed open what she thought was the bathroom door, and when the lights came to life, her eyes widened as angels sang and the hand of God parted the clouds to reveal Aggie's closet.

Aggie always did love Italians, Nely thought wistfully. Rows upon rows held curvaceous Ferragamos, glittery Cavallis, and a pair of vintage, peep-toed pumps that looked like they were never taken out of the box. There wasn't a flat sole in sight.

Excitement trickled into her blood as her eyes ate up the seemingly endless collection of tops, skirts, pants, and coats. It was like that warehouse where the government hid the ark in *Raiders of the Lost Ark*.

At home, Nely only owned two coats, one camel and one black, while Aggie possessed everything from a simple Gap jean jacket to a Trina Turk peacock print trench lined in faux fur.

Guru Sauro was right. She *should* walk in these shoes.

Eventually, she settled on a double-breasted pantsuit in eggplant with pink pinstripes, along with tricolored suede Ferragamo pumps and a Mayla clutch. Looking in the mirror, she felt confident and decisive, ready to take on anything that came her way.

Striding into the sun-washed kitchen, she sighed at the blessed cleanliness before her. Nothing out of place. The floor didn't stick, and a collection of baby blue milk glass plates were demurely displayed behind glass cabinets. She smiled lovingly at the sleek coffeemaker because the timer had done the work and freshly brewed coffee waited just for her.

She searched for a mug and froze when she found a cabinet full of foodstuffs. Other than coffee and champagne, the most Aggie kept in her kitchen was olives for cocktails. Nely peered at the note tacked to the inside cabinet door. It was a man's handwriting, telling Aggie to pick up condensed milk.

Kevin?

The breeze from shutting the cabinet raised the hair off her shoulders. She eventually found the mugs, pausing mid-reach when Audrey's cry sounded from the bedroom. Her gaze swung around the apartment and the crying stopped.

Nely dismissed it as her imagination. As she filled her cup, her morning began to lose some of its shimmer when her ears itched to hear a frustrated husband or child.

There it was again. Audrey's crying was coming out of the walls.

She called her house, and when Simon said Hello, his voice slammed into her like a fist. "Who's this?" he demanded when she didn't answer.

"Me—I mean, Aggie."

"Oh hey, Aggie. Nel's asleep."

At eight? Worries assaulted her from every direction. Why? Had Audrey been up all night? Was she sick? New teeth?

Her baby needed her and she was stuck far across town.

"Tough night, huh?" she managed to say.

"Not really. I'll have her call you back."

"Is Audrey okay?"

He hesitated. "She's right here with me, eating her Cheerios."

Nely rolled her eyes. He was always feeding their child Cheerios and throwing her off routine. She didn't mean to, but it just came out of her mouth. "You aren't giving her too many, are you?"

"No," he said slowly, irritated but trying not to show it. "I'll have Nel call you later."

"Wait! Could you put Audrey to the phone?"

Nely knew she shouldn't have asked.

"I don't want to come between you and Nely," Simon said, startling her after a heavy pause. "And what you guys did on your weekend isn't any of my business, but . . . where did you go again?"

"Ventana de Oro."

"Have you noticed anything different about Nely?" he asked.

Nely slapped her hand over her mouth in case she said something she shouldn't, like *Yes*. If she was going to tell him, now would be the best time. But then what would he do to Aggie if he didn't believe her?

She put a lid on the screaming in her head and calmly replied, "Well, maybe she's just overwhelmed."

"Yeah, but—"

"And then with her mother-in-law living next door, I think there's some added pressure."

She could see him trying to rub the tension off his forehead. The thing that got her was that he wouldn't be listening if he knew she was on the other end of the line. Every time she made so much as a peep about La Cacuy, he started in with that tired, old line about how she imagined things.

The more she thought about it, the more miffed she got. As soon they ended this call, he'd better do two loads of laundry and clean the kitchen floor.

"But is all that enough to make her see someone else?" Simon asked, and her miffiness collapsed like a bad soufflé.

"See who?"

"Never mind," he snapped. "I'll get Audrey for you."

"Wait!"

But he already held the phone away from his ear. She heard him say to Audrey, "Guess who's on the phone? Say hi."

Audrey's breath rumbled through the earpiece.

"Hello there, baby girl," Nely said, her eyes burning with tears. "I miss you so much. But I'll see you when I come—" She almost said "home," then remembered that Simon might be able to hear her. "When I come over again. Are you being a good girl for Daddy?"

"Maa?" Audrey asked, and then whined as Simon took the phone away.

"Take care," he said and hung up as Audrey yelled, "Maa!"

It happened so fast that Nely didn't know how to feel, much less think. He thought she was seeing someone . . . like a shrink?

Oh no. Oh God. He would actually think she was having an affair! What an idiot! Then again, it served him right.

If she'd had to put up with La Cacuy butting into their lives, then he could put up with some imaginary boyfriend. Let him stew in it a while and learn to appreciate her, she thought as she slammed the phone down.

Seventeen

He did not need this right now.

Two of his line cooks called in sick, they were missing sixteen forks, and one of the waiters quit with no notice. Even better, the newbie forgot to pack the tomatillo sauce in ice before stowing it in the walk-in, which meant it all went into the trash.

"Apology accepted," Kevin reprimanded. "But if this happens again, it comes out of your pay. Understand?"

She nodded so hard her eyeballs could've fallen out of her head. "It will never happen again," she stammered, her voice quivering with tears.

"This is the kind of mistake we can't afford to make," he lectured, hoping to drill it so hard in her that she wouldn't forget. "People could've gotten sick from eating that."

"I know, I know."

He should've left it at that, but he was getting soft in his old age. "Hey, I've made mistakes, too. We all do. Now get to work."

Nicole sucked it up and did what he told her. Her mistake wasn't only costing them money, but time.

"Wow, did my ears fool me?" his sister said, all wide-eyed and astonished. "Did you actually say you've made mistakes?"

"I can acknowledge that I've learned a thing or two."

"Really? When?"

"Our meat delivery is late," he said, retreating into business. "Again."

She sighed. "I don't have it in me for another fight."

Could've fooled him. "I wasn't asking you to. But I'm thinking we might need to look around for another supplier."

She threw her head back. "Oh God," she groaned. "Two waiters asked for a raise and now you want to look for another supplier?"

"Who's poaching on our staff now?"

He was impressed when she named the restaurant. Well, that meant they were doing something right.

"What do you need? I'm in the middle of my rounds."

Sazón hadn't become and then stayed the city's best haute Mexican cuisine restaurant for three years for nothing. He spent more time on his feet taste-testing, checking every single delivery that came through the back door, and making sure the kitchen would pass a random Health Department visit.

"Just checking in with you. Are you okay after last night?"

He'd managed to put Aggie and her date and that infuriating e-mail out of his head. But then Sandra let it all roar back in. "Why wouldn't I be?" he answered smoothly.

Sandra shrugged as if giving up. "I'll look into—"

"Stay out of it."

Her grin spread slow and thick, and he realized he'd been had. "I was talking about the delivery," she said. "But since you brought it up, I've been thinking—"

He told himself to tune her out, to replay a song in his head so she would think he was listening and then leave him alone when she finished.

But her voice penetrated his brain.

"You should play hard to get. A woman wants a little challenge, too. If you keep appearing desperate for her, she'll think you're weak and never respect you."

He didn't admit it, but he'd kinda done that by replying to Aggie's e-mail.

"Women want a man who is confident and not all afraid," she lectured.

"I'm not afraid."

"Yeah but—" She clamped her lips shut and her eyes drifted to the floor. "Well, it's just something I heard."

She walked off, and he resisted the urge to yell back, *I'm not afraid!*

He was a lot of things, most of which were unpleasant. But he wasn't a liar or a coward . . . until now.

Mausoleums saw more action than this place. Two Japanese tourists walked in and politely asked Nely when Urban Outfitters would open. There hadn't been one sale this whole week, and according to the books, the last sale of $456 took place thirteen days ago.

The door opened and Nely put down her duster, smiling

her best customer service smile. Until she realized who had just walked in.

"Remember me?" Jeff asked.

Well, at least he hadn't brought his mother with him.

Nely's smile collapsed. She replaced it with what she hoped was a cold, commanding stare.

His spooky eyes were fixed on her as he stepped across the empty boutique to the counter. "I thought I'd come to apologize."

In the light of day, when there was not a single person nearby, waves of creepiness radiated off him.

Abruptly, he thrust out his hand. She flicked her eyes to it and then back into his eyes, resisting a lifetime of conditioning to be a polite girl and make nice. He slipped it into the pocket of his suit.

"What can I do for you?" she asked, and winced inside.

He looked around, one eyebrow curved up. "I would like you to come to dinner with me so I can make up for what I said to you last night."

"No thanks."

"And why not?"

"I called your office and asked to be reassigned to another representative." That was a lie. She'd searched and couldn't find the lease agreement. But she would as soon as he left.

"Hmm. Well . . ." He made her feel as if she'd just been slid under a microscope. Her gut told her if she showed any weakness, he'd pounce. "Would a cappuccino tempt you?"

"No. I have lots of work to do."

He glanced around the empty store and the corners of his smug mouth tightened. "I can see that."

He stepped forward, and she instantly regretted all the times she'd blown off Simon when he offered to teach her self-defense. He stood between her and the doors. She held a feather duster in her hand. It occurred to her that she could brain him with the stapler if he jumped her. But to reach the stapler she'd have to run behind the corner, and then she'd really be cornered.

The door opened and she saw Kevin standing in the doorway. Gratitude washed like liquid gold through her.

"You've got a visitor," Kevin said, abruptly pivoting and heading back out the door.

"Wait!" She didn't care how desperate she sounded as she hurried over to him.

Kevin didn't even glance over his shoulder.

"I need to talk to you," she tried again, which finally got him to stop. "Please don't leave me," she whispered.

Kevin turned. He took another look at her visitor and his eyes flared.

"What's going on?" he murmured, not looking down at her.

"Just stay here until—"

"Excuse me, Aggie," Jeff said as if he owned her. "I don't think we finished our conversation."

"You did," Kevin barked, making her weak in the knees. "The door's right there."

"Who are you?"

The air heated with two angry, proud males ready to go mano a mano. Nely watched their chests puff up ever so slightly, waiting for the other to make the first move.

She never imagined she'd be the damsel in distress. If her mind wasn't swirling with panic, she'd have been ashamed that an ever so tiny part of her kind of liked it.

Jeff tugged at his coat lapels and then marched toward

them. Her eyes flicked to the glass table, hoping if they did start pummeling each other, they'd go in the other direction.

But he walked toward the door. When he realized there wasn't enough room for him to walk by—Kevin didn't appear like he'd step aside—Jeff sidestepped his way out of the store.

"If I didn't—" Kevin cleared his throat, then shoved his hands into his back pockets. "If I wasn't the nice guy I am," he told her, "I would've let you deal with that alone."

"Thank you," she said, hating that her voice trembled. "He didn't do anything but he just—" She told herself to pull it together.

"God, Aggie, how the hell do you get yourself into these situations?"

It was such a typical male thing to make it her fault.

"I don't get myself into these situations," she snapped. "He approached me."

"And dragged you to my restaurant?"

Her stomach clenched. "I was careless."

"Damn right you were."

They stared at one another, and she was the first to look away when it dawned on her that Kevin's eyes lingered on her lips. Tension wavered off him. His blood was up from the stand-off and his frustration that Aggie—well, Nely—hadn't fallen into his bed at the snap of his fingers. Simon had once come home in a similar condition, and while that ended up as some of their best sex, she wouldn't go there with Kevin.

She backed away. "Well, like I said, I'm sorry for last night and—"

For each step she took back, he took one forward.

"I have to get back to work," she continued, bringing her feather duster in front of her.

"You're sending me off after I saved your ass?" His face tightened, his eyes narrowing in on her.

She cleared her throat. "No."

The corner of his mouth hitched into a grin. He was enjoying her holding him off, stretching the moment until he caught her. Perhaps she could do this if she closed her eyes and imagined her husband. If he kissed her, it wouldn't count as cheating because—

Nely nearly jumped out of her skin when a figure moved out of the corner of her eye. The figure turned out to be two young women who ventured in through the door.

She pasted on a smile and greeted them. They mumbled shy "Heys" as they wandered around, probably trying not to be obvious about checking the price tags.

"Okay," he said, stopping within an arm's reach. "I really came here to tell you that—"

He reached out and then hesitated, not knowing what to do. She didn't either. "I'm cool with us as friends," he said. "The more I think about it, the worse an idea it is."

"What idea?"

"Us."

She couldn't help but wonder, *Why?*

"See you around," he said, and then left her staring at his broad, proud shoulders that painfully reminded her of Simon's.

"Who fits into a petite size two?" one of her customers whispered loud enough for Nely to hear.

She pretended to dust, hoping it would settle the sparks

erupting under her skin, while she edged closer to her customers. As she got a better look, it seemed that the taller of the two had just had a baby, maybe eight months ago.

The cute one turned from the mannequin wearing a chartreuse dress with a deep V neckline and bronze beading on a ruched waist.

"This would look gorgeous on you," she gushed to her friend. "What's your size?"

"It's too expensive."

"But you can wear it to the rehearsal dinner," she pleaded, her eyes catching Nely's.

"And then it'll stay in my closet."

"Take it out when you go to dinner."

"Like Alex and I ever go out."

"You will on your honeymoon."

"What size may I get for you?" Nely asked.

"No, Tamara," the bride-to-be said to her friend, then turned to Nely, surprising her with a pair of deep blue eyes. "No, thank you."

"I think you should try it," Nely urged.

"See?" Tamara said.

"But it's—" She reached for the tag and then threw it away from her. "No, definitely not."

"Isa," Tamara hissed. She turned to Nely. "I think she's a size ten."

"We have that in a ten," Nely piped in. "It's in the back."

"Eight," Isa corrected with a glare at Tamara.

"I'll get both."

"Oh, they have shoes. Did you see these?"

"Why do you keep the larger sizes in the back?" Isa asked.

Nely didn't know. "We have limited floor space and we
. . . I'm not really sure."

She caught the glance Isa slid to Tamara, the kind of glance
that said, *Let's get out of here.* But Nely wanted to say that she
was the last person to discriminate against size tens.

"My treat," Tamara announced, ignoring Isa. "Now that
you've had the baby, we need to clean you up."

"Did you have a boy or girl?" Nely asked.

"A boy," Isa said with a proud but shy smile.

"Congratulations," Nely gushed, always happy to meet
another mom. She turned to Tamara. "And you?"

Tamara ran her hand down the sleeve of a gauzy blouse,
her smile collapsing.

The silence that fell on them made Nely realize she'd
stepped on a land mine. Isa approached Tamara and said
softly, "Let's come back another time, okay?"

She gave Nely a weak grin as they walked out the door.
Nely's heart sank at having practically chased the closest
sale the store had seen out the door.

She took a moment to stare at the people strolling down
the streets, suddenly dark from the clouds that coated the
sky. They all carried shopping bags from stores other than
Lola's. In five minutes she counted only one potential size
four. The only female who came close to a size two looked
like she was seven.

If the majority of women were regular bodied with arms
that would make a model scout faint and little poufy tum-
mies, why was Lola's window populated with size twos?
When she'd been her old self, she never walked into these
boutiques for exactly that reason.

Nely's eyes opened to an idea. Friday was only two

days away, which in Lola's dubious past was its most profitable day.

She could try this one teeny tiny experiment. If it didn't work, she'd put the window display back the way it had been.

But if her idea did work, then maybe, just a tiny maybe, she would be on to something.

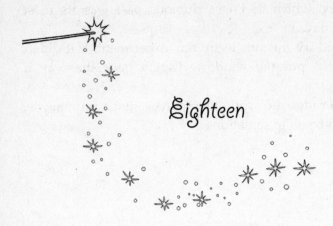

Eighteen

The only reason Aggie was back in the van on her way to Miss Cheryl's Toddler Time was so Pema and the girls wouldn't be left alone with Leila and her slobbering minions.

That, and she wanted those bitches to eat crow when they saw her in Bare Escentuals makeup and a black and pink swirly skirt with a simple black top that, together with the body contouring bra, deemphasized Nely's rolls. This time, she swore, she would not shrivel up into some deer-in-the-headlights yes-girl.

"This is my chance to impart knowledge to you, Audrey," she said, glancing in the rearview mirror.

Audrey rolled her head to stare at Aggie. With a few days under their belts, Audrey seemed calmer and less pensive. Simon had been putting in overtime, which suited Aggie fine. He'd been watching her, like she was a rabbit and he was the fox waiting for her to pop out of her hole.

Rubbing the back of her neck, she hadn't quite settled in Nely's skin but the days had passed without incident.

"When you hit preschool," Aggie said, resuming her lecture, "you're going to meet some girls who will do everything they can to tear you down. You have to hit hard and fast, or else you're chum."

Unimpressed, Audrey began yelling, "Dee dee dee dee!"

Aggie sighed. One day, not only would Audrey respect her, but she'd actually use real words.

"Nely," Leila yelled across the parking lot when Aggie strolled up with Audrey. "We have a job for you!"

The huddle ceased chattering to watch the alpha female gut her prey. Playing Gwen Stefani's "Rich Girl" in her head, Aggie took her time approaching them—she'd never steered a stroller in heeled sandals before—which gave those bitches plenty of time to check her out.

"Nely? Nely!"

Giving Leila her best *Oh, were you talking to me?* glance, Aggie shrugged her shoulders. "Oh hi, um . . . Leila."

Leila paused in sipping her Starbucks. Aggie told herself not to break eye contact or go fumbling for her rhinestone star. Unlike high school, she had to set an example for Audrey.

"We decided to have a Halloween party," Leila informed her. "And we want you to organize it unless, of course, you can't."

She knew she would be back to her own life by Halloween. But by the time she was through with this crew, Nely probably shouldn't come around.

"I can't," she answered pertly.

"What? Why not, Nely?" a voice asked out of nowhere.

Aggie shuddered from the sudden temperature drop. She turned, and there was La Cacuy, looking poised and fabulous in a black running suit with a pink stripe that emphasized her long legs.

Aggie hated it when nasty people happened to great clothes.

"Señora Mendoza," Leila gushed, and ran to her with arms flung open. *"Siéntese por favor con nosotros."*

Please come and sit with us. She had said it with great deference. La Cacuy ate that shit up. Leila and the huddle couldn't hide their delight that their prey's mother-in-law had showed up.

Apparently, this wouldn't be the first time La Cacuy had humiliated her daughter-in-law in front of them.

"But tell me, what do you need from Nely? Maybe I can help and—"

La Cacuy quickly switched to Spanish, and Aggie didn't quite catch what she said. Leila's glare indicated that she agreed with whatever insult La Cacuy had flung her way.

"We want to do something nice for the children," Leila explained, "and Nely says she can't help us. We were really counting on her."

"But why, Nely?" La Cacuy turned to her. "You have to do it."

Aggie's internal temperature shot up with her pounding pulse. She wasn't just angry for herself, but for Nely as well.

"Nely? Did you hear me?" La Cacuy clarified, waiting for an appropriately humble response from her.

"But if it's too much trouble or expensive . . ." Leila added, clearly relishing what she thought was Aggie's humiliation.

"Oh, I'll make it worth the trouble," Aggie promised in a strained voice.

La Cacuy patted Leila's arm affectionately. Aggie could almost see the cartoon bubble over her head that read: *If only Simon had married a nice girl like Leila instead.*

"Now don't you worry," she told Leila. "I'll have Nely do the invitations but I'll take care of everything else so it will be perfect."

"We'd hate to put you out—"

"I insist. Nely is . . ." La Cacuy paused just long enough to insinuate the depths of her daughter-in-law's incompetence. ". . . so *busy* these days."

They strolled away from Aggie as if she were an inconveniently placed trash can.

"*Un momento,*" La Cacuy said, then dipped down, undoing Audrey's buckles. "Come with Nana, *Mijita.*"

"That's okay," Aggie intervened as a fierce maternal instinct took over. If she allowed La Cacuy to take Audrey to sit with Leila and her minions, Nely would never regain face. But what really made her sick was that La Cacuy would actually use her granddaughter, someone she would never have had if not for Nely, as a pawn in her little game.

"She'll stay with me," Aggie insisted. They locked eyes. But then La Cacuy went right back to freeing Audrey from the stroller.

Aggie locked her hand around La Cacuy's wrist. "I said, she stays with me," she murmured through a gritty smile.

The air around them sparked and hissed with the declaration of war. La Cacuy rose up, her lips pinched into a straight line and her eyes promising retribution.

Not exactly flush with victory, Aggie found Pema bouncing Naveen on her thighs.

"Poor you," Pema said with a surreptitious glance over her shoulder. "I'm so lucky my mother-in-law has other grandchildren."

"You have no idea."

"We're more than willing to help," Pema volunteered, and the other moms, Jessie and Moni, nodded loyally.

Shame reddened her cheeks as she remembered how Leila wanted her to get rid of them. She'd miss her if—no, when—it was time for her to return to her old self. Now it was imperative that she bring down Leila's reign of terror.

"What are you planning?" Pema asked.

"I don't know just yet," Aggie answered. "But I'd love to drag that bitch's face in the mud."

Glances shot between Jessie, Moni, and Pema.

"Well, she's not all that she seems," Pema said, and then Naveen cried to be released so he could play with the toys on the mat.

Aggie glanced around the room. A coordinated mommy and baby wore green and pink with matching headbands. Aggie foresaw the future for that kid, and her mother would be there every step of the way, trying to relive her youth through her daughter.

Then there was Kaylie, the athletic mom who coached her daughter through a plastic tunnel tube, and Michaela, the flash card mom who was constantly reinforcing colors and shapes to her drooling eight-month-old.

Dude, why couldn't they just let their babies be babies? she wondered. God knows, adulthood had its perks, but nothing beat snack and nap times.

"Hey, Emerson. That's not nice," Pema said, having followed Naveen back to where Aggie was sitting.

Aggie glanced down and saw that Emerson had slithered

over to swipe a red plastic phone out of Audrey's grip. Emerson then held it just beyond Audrey's reach.

"What do I do?" Aggie asked, ready to smack the kid with the phone.

"Call her mother over," Pema suggested.

Leila met Aggie's gaze and then turned away, pretending not to have seen the incident.

"Audrey," Aggie said, the heat of battle scorching her insides. "What did I tell you in the car?"

Audrey twisted around in her stroller, her eyes wet and desperate for her to do something. But Aggie knew better than anyone that Audrey had to handle this . . . with just a tiny bit of help.

Aggie pulled out a sippy cup, gave the lid a twist, then handed it to Audrey.

"Dude," she said with the solemnity of a kung fu master nudging his student onto the mat. "You have my permission and blessing."

In a matter of fact manner, Audrey took the sippy cup and threw it at Emerson. The red phone hit the ground. With fruit punch dripping off her perky white bow onto her pink and white sailor blouse, Emerson froze with shock. Aggie resisted the urge to high-five Audrey.

Leila screeched, "What the— Why did you let her do that?" Emerson squeezed her eyes tight and opened her mouth in a soundless scream.

"Do what?" Aggie asked, then pretended she just noticed what Audrey had done. She was so proud that she could have farted glitter. "Audrey, did you do that?"

Audrey sat with her hands primly clasped in front of her, spine-ruler-straight. Even at her best, Aggie knew she couldn't pull off that kind of innocence.

"You know that little—" Leila swept her dripping daughter into her arms.

"Nely, how could you let Audrey do such a thing?" La Cacuy asked. "Go get some more napkins."

"Emerson took Audrey's phone," Pema intervened.

"She must've knocked over Audrey's cup," Moni said, backing her up.

Aggie didn't dare exchange a loyalty glance with her co-madres or else she would have busted up laughing. Leila wanted to say something nasty—Aggie could see it on her tight, reddening face—but didn't dare with La Cacuy watching.

But as Leila whisked Emerson away and Aggie saw the big-assed stain on her D&G tank top, she bent down to pick up the red phone to give Audrey a smile; a special smile that acknowledged the student was on her way to becoming the master.

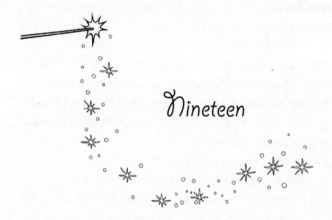

Nineteen

Nely watched Aggie flop down in front of the TV, poking at her dinner. After talking to Simon the other morning, she'd managed to stay away. She'd buried herself in work and in devising her plan to help pull Lola's out of the red.

When she saw that Simon's car was nowhere to be seen and La Cacuy's upstairs bedroom light was on, she made her move.

The sharp October wind rushed past her ears as she ran across the lawn. She avoided the angled square of light from the house. Hoping not to scare Aggie, she knocked on the glass door.

Aggie didn't look away from the TV.

Nely knocked harder.

Aggie stiffened and swung around, gripping her fork like a weapon.

Nely waved at her.

Aggie threw down the fork, pissed off that she'd been scared.

"Simon shouldn't be home for another two hours," Nely explained when her friend let her in. "I need to talk to you."

"Doesn't your mother-in-law have a job?" popped out of Aggie's mouth. "Or a boyfriend? Or something to occupy her time other than torturing you?"

"She has a job at that real estate office."

"Then why does she hate you so much?"

Did she really have to ask? "Remember when Simon and I broke up?" Nely reminded her. "In the end, he chose me over her. She'll never forgive me for that."

"Oh." Aggie's reply was loaded, no doubt remembering that period in history. "But that was her fault."

Nely had been dating Simon for less than a year when he applied to the San Diego PD. Simona took her to lunch and begged her to talk Simon out of his decision. When Nely said she couldn't, Simona went to her son and told him that Nely would never marry a police officer.

What she had said to Simona, not knowing she was a La Cacuy at the time, was that she never *imagined* marrying a police officer. But she would stand behind him because she loved him.

But Simon broke up with her, believing what his mother had told him. Unable to bear the permanent, physical ache when he left her, Nely rushed right into another relationship. Simon found her with the guy and—

Well, somehow they'd made it. Nely made Simon work for her trust, and when he proposed, she never hesitated to say yes. But they never spoke of it again.

Thinking about it made this separation all the more painful. But, she reminded herself, she came here tonight to deal with Lola's. That would make the time until the next full moon go faster.

"Aggie, there's something important I need to talk about," Nely announced as if psyching herself up to jump off a bridge. "I know about the store."

Aggie's head vibrated like a gong.

"I want to help you figure a way out," she continued. "And I think I have a plan—"

Aggie's possessive streak lit on fire. "You don't know anything about retail!"

"Let me remind you that I once got paid a lot of money to analyze businesses of all kinds. But if you want everything you've worked for to go down the toilet, fine with me."

Aggie took a deep breath. "Can I think about it?"

"You better think fast." With a sigh, Nely asked, "Is that *The Ghost and Mrs. Muir?*"

Aggie nodded. Nely glanced at the stairs, then sat down in front of the TV. "I'll go up when the next commercial comes on."

She sat down cross-legged and picked at Aggie's dinner. "Ever since you made me watch it in college, it's been my favorite movie."

"I didn't know that," Aggie said, wondering how she could ask about Kevin and not be obvious.

"There's a lot we don't know about each other anymore," Nely said quietly. "I know you can take care of yourself. But it's not weakness to ask for help when you really need it. I could've helped a long time ago."

It wasn't that Aggie thought Nely couldn't help her. She was so scared about looking stupid, and she knew she had been stupid—and careless and arrogant by expanding the boutique too fast. She'd seen the iceberg but refused to steer from her course. And now she was on the ship, watching the one thing she had given birth to, the one thing she'd nurtured like a mother, sink into the icy sea.

They both watched as Gene Tierney, who played Mrs. Muir, discovered that the man she'd fallen for was married with three daughters, by meeting his wife.

"This isn't the first time something like this has happened," the wife said, which was followed by a bombastic symphonic score.

Aggie slowly released the tension in her back, sinking against the couch. If she didn't look over at her own body sitting there, this was the way things were meant to be: her best friend at her side, watching an old movie.

Perhaps if she had jumped in Kevin's arms rather than hide in the bathroom, if she'd just told him what had happened and that she was in someone else's body . . .

"You know what I don't understand about this movie?" she asked. "How come Lucy never finds another man?"

"She was burned by her illusions of love," Nely replied after a thoughtful moment. "Maybe she got scared and couldn't trust herself anymore."

"You know what just struck me? Even dead, the captain was a typical man. Once he was scorned, he used his pride to punish her. Shouldn't he have given her the benefit of the doubt?"

"Aggie, he's dead," Nely explained patiently. "They could never have a real life. Until she died, of course."

They watched Lucy Muir walk the sands of the beach as the years swept by, dulling her delicate beauty.

"Do you think if you hadn't gotten married that we'd be like Lucy and Martha?" Aggie asked out of the blue.

"I want to be Lucy," Nely insisted.

"No, I'm Lucy."

"I'm married, and if Simon died, I'd be just like Lucy."

Aggie rolled her eyes. She knew the captain would pick her, whether she was Lucy or not. "Anyway, when we're two old *viejitas,* should we live in a seaside cottage?"

"I don't think so. You were so anal about keeping things clean. Remember how you divided our dorm room with tape on the carpet?"

"You never vacuumed," Aggie argued. "And wiping down the microwave after you use it is sanitary."

"Maybe we'd be better off as neighbors," Nely suggested diplomatically.

"Seriously, how do you think Lucy and Martha spent all those years being so close, and we—" She hated being so honest and touchy feely. "We haven't been that close in a long time," she finally admitted.

"They needed each other," Nely said quietly. "You and I drifted apart because we— I don't know. We just valued different things and you were so mad when I didn't accept that new position because I wanted to get pregnant."

But Nely knew it went back much longer than that. When she fell in love with Simon, it marked the beginning of the changes between them. It felt more like she had joined a different group, become one of the grown-up girls. And she knew that Aggie lost a lot of respect for her when she took Simon back, that Aggie disdained her happy housewifery as stale and boring.

Kevin's face popped into her head, and Nely wondered how long Aggie would wait before she was back in bed with him, thinking he'd give her the security she now craved.

But then she remembered the way he'd been ready to go

all OK Corral on the asshole at the store that day, on her behalf.

Nely sighed. "Well, we definitely need each other now, don't we?"

"I miss this," Aggie admitted. "I didn't even know I missed it until now."

"Me, too."

"Oh wait, here's the part."

Locked together in expectant silence, they watched as the now frail Lucy Muir took her last sip of warm milk. The camera followed her hand as she meant to set it on the table beside her chair. For a moment she held the glass with her arm resting on the chair. But then her fingers released the glass, letting it fall with a quiet crash on the floor. The music swelled as the ruggedly handsome Rex Harrison stepped into the frame.

Aggie and Nely simultaneously repeated his line: "'Stand up, Lucia, and never be cold again.'"

Nely's throat swelled as Lucy Muir, young and beautiful again, rose up from the chair with her hands in his and walked out of her bedroom with her beloved captain. All those years of longing, of loneliness, were over for Lucy Muir. She'd spent an entire life without her true love and now they'd be together forever.

Aggie pressed her fingers to her quivering lips as tears seemed to erupt from her eyes.

"Are you crying?" Nely asked in disbelief. Aggie never cried in front of her. Never. Not when she'd rushed to the hospital to see her after her mother had died, nor in the days afterward. Aggie always kept her tears to herself.

"No," Aggie whined in a strained voice. "You need to dust your living room!"

"Aggie," Nely said, all maternal tenderness.

"It's just that . . . will anyone come for me when I'm dead?"

"I will."

"It's not the same."

"Okay, fine," Nely joked. "I'll leave your ass behind and you can find your own way to heaven."

The laugh escaped before Aggie could contain it. "Stop trying to make me laugh. It's not helping."

She wiped away her tears as a Cialis commercial flashed on and Nely went upstairs.

Aggie knew she should be grateful that she had a friend who loved her enough to put up with her crap. And she was. With a deep breath, she tamped down the rising possessiveness in her chest.

If anyone could find that crumb of chance that would save her business while tidying up the messy men from her life, it would be Nely.

But she couldn't keep Kevin out of her head. Everything rolled around in there: his sexiness and the way he discarded women; his passion for his work and the way he treated his staff like they were his family.

Maybe he did want something more from her *right now*. But could she let herself fall into something with him wondering when he'd show her the door?

Rather than just sit there and allow thoughts of him to latch onto her brain like the tentacles of a B-movie squid, she marched upstairs. She meant to use all the new facial products she'd bought as part of her plan to upgrade Nely. But Nely's lullaby wafted out from Audrey's room, stopping Aggie in her tracks. She was just about to peek through the sliver-wide opening when she thought she should give

Nely and Audrey this moment. But the sweet sound drew her close. Stealing a tiny peek, Aggie's throat tightened.

Nely sat in the rocker holding Audrey, the nightlight casting a golden glow over them. Aggie choked up, feeling like Timothy Mouse as he watched Dumbo's mom cradle him through the bars of her jail with her trunk.

She, who'd once scorned everything that Nely was, had taken her friend away from everything she loved most.

Nely had never been selfish or kept secrets. Had never judged her. She always put everyone else first.

Aggie's shoulders slumped as all the selfish things she had done poured in on her.

Nely finished her song, nuzzling Audrey's head. Aggie thought she should walk away and hide with her shame. But at the same time, she wanted what Nely had so badly that she almost forgot to breathe.

"Is he here yet?" Nely whispered when she shut the door behind her.

It took Aggie a second to remember Simon and their situation. She shook her head no, unable to speak.

"I don't want to go," Nely said brokenly.

Aggie hated reminding her that Simon would walk in at any minute. But Nely seemed to pull it together, and after she left, Aggie crept back into Audrey's room.

"I miss my mama, too," she whispered into the crib, Audrey's black fuzzy head peeking out from under her blanket. "But yours will be back soon. And I'll take good care of you till she does."

Audrey moved her chunky arm, and Aggie ducked down, not wanting to wake her up. The blanket whispered from Audrey kicking her legs, and a cranky groan sounded from her lips. And then, as if a switch had been thrown, all went silent.

Peeking through the slats of the crib, Aggie sent up a prayer of gratitude that she hadn't woken the baby.

With the care of the bomb squad moving around a suspicious briefcase, she slithered up to the rocking chair and wrapped a blanket over her shoulders. Now, she decided, and for as long as Nely was away from her baby, she would watch over her.

Twenty

Kevin never should've agreed to this.

Pierce had picked Thursday night to propose to Marcel, and the place was hopping. Orders spit out of the system, pushing back the table wait time another three minutes. Everyone fed off each others' adrenaline, communicating in the particular shorthand they'd developed as a team.

Kevin looked up from the *nopales* he was sautéing. Faces were tight with concentration as meat hissed when it hit the pan and flare-ups spewed off the gas burners, all to the steady hum of conversation spilling out from the house. If he was working the line at a quarter to seven, God only knew how intense it would get when they hit the peak hour.

So far no one had stepped on anyone else's toes. Everyone worked at the same rat-tat-tat rhythm. With no walls hiding the kitchen from the tables, the crew was part of the show. They had to keep it clean.

"Lookin' tight," he called out to his team. "Stay that way."

"Thanks, Chef," the line intoned.

He plated the *nopales,* grabbed the squeeze bottle of sauce and did a garnish. Without breaking his rhythm, he looked for the next order when he heard his kitchen manager barking.

"Excuse me, sir, we need you on the other side of the window, please."

Kevin glanced over his shoulder. Pierce looked like he'd barely survived a street fight. His hair stood straight up off his head, his shirt misbuttoned and his pants wrinkled.

"It doesn't taste anything like her grandmother's!" he shouted. "Anything! It's not right."

Kevin handed off his plate to the finishing chef.

"Pierce," he said, his voice cutting through the din. "What's going on, man?"

"I tasted the soup and it's nothing like it was the last time we were here."

Pierce stood in the middle of the walkway, waiters zooming around him as they raced in and out of the beverage station.

If he touched him, Pierce seemed keyed up enough to take a swing at him. Kevin held his hands out, maneuvering him out of the way.

"What's not tasting right?" he asked.

"The soup!" Pierce screeched, pressing his hands against the sides of his head. "Everyone'll be here and nothing's turning out right and . . ."

As he railed on, Kevin glanced around for Sandra. She

was so much better at this sort of thing. But a customer held her hostage at his table.

"It always tastes the same," Kevin said, his ego boiling that someone would dare to question his culinary skills. "I didn't change the recipe."

"No it doesn't. She'll be here any second and— This is so fucked up—"

"Okay, settle down."

"Don't tell me to settle down, you screwed me!"

The kitchen paused and looked straight at them.

"How much have you had to drink, you idiot?" Kevin shot back. He'd spent weeks planning a special menu for this asshole, and look how he showed up, yelling and drunk, ruining everything.

"Hardly anything!"

"I can smell it over here!"

Sandra having freed herself from the customer, banged on a stock pot with a ladle. "In the back," she demanded. "Come on, both of you. Now."

She herded them into the office and shut the door. "The whole damn place can hear you." Waving her hand in front of her nose, she asked, "How much have you had to drink, Pierce?"

"I—" He shook his head. Kevin's arm shot out, catching him as he swayed. "I don't know."

"You of all people know what happens when you drink too much, don't you?"

"I just wanted to take the edge off," Pierce said from behind his hands.

"Kevin, taste the soup again." The look in her eye threatened that she'd smack him over the head with the ladle in her hand if he didn't. She then turned to Pierce, cooing like a mother dove. "I'm going to make you drink some coffee while I iron your clothes."

"What?" shot out of Kevin's mouth. She never ironed *his* clothes.

"You want to iron his clothes?" she asked.

"I'll check the soup."

"And bring back some coffee." She reached over and gave Pierce a hug, then guided him into a chair, patting his shoulder and making nonsense about how everything would be all right.

She never treated Kevin that way.

When he came back with the coffee, Pierce babbled while sitting in his boxers and socks. "I can't screw this up. She's been talking about her sister and how that asshole doctor proposed. Do you know what he did? He had his frat brothers write 'Will you marry me' in the sand at the Ritz Carlton. Guys like that screw everything up for the rest of us, and if this isn't perfect, she'll never marry me."

"Now that's not true," Sandra assured him, and rolled her eyes at Kevin as she ironed the shirt.

If a guy had to try this hard to get a girl, maybe she wasn't worth it, Kevin thought.

"I'm going to work some onion and garlic into the broth," he lied. The soup tasted just as it always did.

Pierce nodded, his eyes wide and unseeing as he drank his coffee.

"We'll do it very carefully, all right?" Sandra said, pretending to instruct Kevin, which still made him clench his jaw with resentment. "Now you and I are going to stay here until you finish that coffee. You'll give away the surprise if she sees you all sweaty and nervous, okay? There we go."

Kevin went back out to the kitchen.

"I didn't touch it," Chris, his soup chef, said.

"I know you didn't. He's a wreck."

"Are you going to change it?"

Kevin shook his head.

"That poor jerk," Chris sighed. "This is the only thing he gets to do until the honeymoon."

Sandra rushed in almost half an hour later.

"She just walked in and I put the drink order in myself. How's everything?"

"I told everyone that I'll take the ticket," Kevin said. When she just stared at him, he barked, "What?"

"You're so sweet sometimes," she said.

He rolled his eyes. "Who's serving them?"

"I put Jesse on it."

Kevin nodded his approval. Jesse was their best server. He had sharp instincts and a friendly way about him. He knew when to visit with guests and when to blend into the scenery.

"You'll keep an eye on them?" Kevin asked her, reaching for the shrimp that would be Pierce and Marcel's appetizer.

The line adapted to him dropping out to personally prepare Pierce's meal. He brushed shelled, deveined shrimp with a spicy chipotle salsa. Pierce had told him that his first date with Marcel had been a surfing lesson, so Kevin took an element of the sea and coupled it with the spice that came with new passion.

He told himself it wasn't out of sentiment; he liked a challenge.

He plated the shrimp on a beige platter splattered with a guava sauce and garnished with a salad of wild greens, cucumber, and jicama dressed in a lime vinaigrette. In a ballet of movement, he placed it on the window with a bowl of the reserved salsa, and Jesse swept it off to their table.

Kevin picked up the slack on the line and five minutes later ladled the *asado de bodas*. He'd learned the recipe in his teens when his mother sent him to his grandparents' ranch in Jalisco, hoping they'd straighten him up. At fourteen his Spanish had been limited to taco and "hasta la vista, baby," but his grandfather, the chef of the home, found a way to speak to him by sharing all of his culinary secrets.

"Make this for your bride on her wedding day," his grand-father had said. "And the soup has all the flavors of marriage. Spice for fire, tortilla from the earth, and broth to bind it together."

Kevin ladled the broth, thick and glossy with blended corn tortillas, roasted garlic, ancho chiles, Mexican choco-late, and succulent pieces of pork bobbing under the sur-face. Remembering his grandfather's thick, strong fingers, he watched his own fingers deftly create a small garnish plate of *crema*, *queso fresco*, and pungent Mexican oregano. That made it to the window, and he went back to begin work on the main course, a trio of sopitos using chicken, meat, and pork.

Kevin kept the courses small, remembering how his grand-father had said if he wanted to seduce a woman, never fill up her stomach.

"Chef," Jesse called over the clamor. "He's gonna do it."

Kevin looked up from the small cakes of corn masa he had just finished. "He said not till after dessert."

Jesse shrugged, his hands dangling over the window. "He's on his knees."

The kitchen looked at one another. "Go," Chris said.

Pulling off his gloves, Kevin stepped away, and Chris moved into his place to finish preparing the sopitos.

The hubbub of conversation ebbed away as every table in the place became aware that a proposal was about to take place.

Car lights and people passing by the windows seemed to belong to another world. The entire restaurant seemed to stand still, capturing Marcel's wide eyes and Pierce on bended knee, offering her a ring and a new life as husband and wife. Kevin crossed his arms, determined not to let any of this sappy stuff get to him.

Pierce's voice then carried to every corner of the restaurant. "Will you marry me in front of all these people?"

She seemed frozen permanently to the seat. Even Kevin leaned ever so slightly forward, waiting for her answer.

"Hey," Pierce murmured gently.

Her answer was a barely audible murmur, and when they held onto each other like they were the last people left on earth, the whole place erupted in cheers.

"Did he get a yes?" an older man yelled, craning his neck to get a better look.

Pierce jumped up, thrusting both arms up in victory. "I got a yes!"

"He'd better," someone grumbled behind Kevin. "That ring was from Tiffany's."

Kevin applauded with the crowd, meanwhile closing himself against the gaiety and the hope that swirled in the air. The only other person in the room whose lips twisted with cynicism was the jazz pianist, Sela Orihuela. She leaned on her piano, twirling one of her curls around a finger. She met Kevin's eyes and then put a reluctant grin on her face.

"Drinks on me," Pierce cried. "Drinks on me!"

Glasses were thrust up the air in an eruption of joy. Sandra wiped her eyes.

"Nothin' like it, boss," Jesse exclaimed, slapping Kevin on the shoulder. "Nothin' like it."

That poor idiot, Kevin thought, turning away from the scene. He was going to spend his whole life trying to make everything perfect for that woman. Little did Pierce know, nothing was good enough, much less perfect, when it came to pleasing women.

But still, he signaled the bartenders. They nodded in understanding.

Fifty on the house; fifty for the idiot who almost killed himself for a yes.

Twenty-one

Nothing would dampen her enthusiasm. Today was the day. Nely could feel it. Nothing could go wrong when a woman felt like a Hitchcock heroine in linen and brown alligator spectator pumps. Nothing would get in her—

She stopped when she saw the broken bottles littering the front of Lola's. Not the window, she begged, not the window!

Some unidentifiable substance stuck to the front window, but it hadn't broken.

Picking her way around the shards that glittered like pieces of amber, she wondered how she'd clean this up wearing a cigarette skirt in time for the store to open.

Unease crept under her skin as she reached for the paper rolled between the door handle.

The ink bled from the overnight mist that still lingered

in the air. In a childish scrawl it read, "This is what I do to bitches."

Black clouds of anger snuffed out fear. Fumbling with her keys, she opened the door and then locked herself in. She carried the note at arm's length, knowing that Jeff's fingers had touched it.

She called the police and then the management office. A voice mail answered, and she fought to control the trembling in her voice.

Grabbing a bottle of glass cleaner and a handful of paper towels, Nely went out onto the main floor and waged war with fingerprints and dust off the shelves while waiting for the police to arrive. But when she finished and it was time to open the store, the police still hadn't arrived.

She left her shoes somewhere safe and changed into some tennis shoes Aggie kept in one of the desk drawers. She then copied the note for her own records. Grabbing a broom and the Sidekick, she took photos of the damage outside and then began to clean up.

The skirt locked her legs together, but she balanced on the balls of her feet as she swept the last of the glass into the dustpan.

"You called about a vandalism?" an officer asked, pulling up on a bicycle.

"I did," she growled, struggling to get up without spilling the glass or falling on her knees in the mess. "An hour and a half ago."

He took a report and told her she was lucky that it happened today because the city would be power-washing the sidewalks next week.

Still no call from the management company, and the stuff had dried to a frothy crust on her window.

Undecided between showing up at the management office with a tire iron and opening up the store for business, Nely took the officer's card. He pedaled away, down the street.

She marched into the store and hoped customers would think the vandalism done to her window was a deliberate attempt to create an Urban Outfitters, postmodern edgy look.

The first hour remained quiet. The second hour was much the same. And then at noon she had to swallow her heart when she realized she'd failed. How could she be so stupid and expect that by changing the front window and rearranging the store she'd miraculously save Lola's? Even though it wasn't her fault that the store was dying and that she'd gotten herself a stalker, Nely couldn't help but choke on tears of defeat.

But then a familiar voice exclaimed, "You changed the front window."

The two women who'd come in the other day, Tamara and Isa, walked back in.

"I love this," Tamara said. "What a great idea!"

Isa stared longingly at the dress she'd admired a few days ago. Nely had moved it, in a size ten, to the center of her window display.

She had also taken the four mannequins, plumped them up with some padding she found in the back, to sizes six, eight, ten, and twelve. Then she'd arranged them so they looked like they were girls out on the town, walking arm in arm, like a stylish chorus line.

"Do you want to try that on?" Nely asked, finally recovering from the surprise of seeing them. "I moved all the sizes up front."

Isa ripped her eyes off the dress.

"This is for your rehearsal dinner, right?" Nely asked.

"Yes," Tamara answered, and turned to Isa. "But you should also get some things for the honeymoon."

"Congratulations," Nely interjected.

"Thank you," Isa said politely. "But I really want this."

"Oh, Isa they have so many cute things," Tamara insisted. "What about this? Or no, wait, this?"

"We're uh—I'm kind of on a budget," Isa said.

"I have things on sale." Nely sprung into action. "What's your budget?"

"Come on, Isa. We made this special trip down here," Tamara urged. "You've almost lost all of your baby weight. You deserve it."

"But then they won't fit after I lose the rest."

"You could always have everything taken in after you lose the weight," Nely suggested helpfully, so close to making a sale that she could almost feel the money in her hands.

"This will go perfect with these shoes," Tamara insisted. "Come on, try them on, please? Mom gave me extra money to treat you."

"Tamara, you're such a liar."

"Not when it comes to spending my mother's money. Now stop being such an old lady."

Nely happened to glance out the window when a woman slowed her stride as she came upon the boutique, pushing a jogging stroller. She smiled at the jogging mother, encouraging her to come in and take a closer look. Sure enough, the woman pushed her sleeping baby through the door.

She pointed to the middle mannequin, her oversized shirt drooping off her shoulders. "Do you have this in a smaller size? Like a ten?"

Tamara and Isa froze like lions who sensed competition over their kill.

"Let me check," Nely said, hoping blood wouldn't be shed. "I think it might already be spoken for."

Violence was averted when she found two.

She wasn't sure when the fourth customer walked in and then the next. Suddenly, she found herself greeting customers while running from the dressing area to the racks. Not only that, every single one of them actually bought something, rather than just browsed or ask to use the bathrooms. Not all of them bought the clothes; a few tourist types indulged in the pricey La Regazza di Firenze body care products and Seda candles.

"Are you open on weekends?" the jogging mama asked as Nely rang up her $400 purchase.

"We are."

"My sister's coming down from L.A. and we need to find her something for her first job interview. Would you hold that suit for me?"

"Absolutely."

"I'm so glad the dress was still here," Tamara later said as she waited for her credit card to clear.

Nely smiled, dying to log into the sales system to see the tally. But she'd wait until closing and then rush home to tell Aggie and see Audrey . . . She was getting ahead of herself and replied, "Thank you for coming back."

"She was dying for that dress," Tamara said. "And God, it's impossible to get her into a store! But Alex told me to *make* sure she got it."

"Alex is her fiancé?"

"Uh-huh. Really great guy."

Nely eyed the simple diamond on Tamara's finger. "Are

you next?" she asked, wishing she knew her well enough to pry a little deeper.

"I am," she said in a way that had Nely suspecting it wasn't only marriage Tamara was talking about. "We can't wait."

Nely plucked two Seda quince candles off the display behind the counter and stuck them in Tamara's bag.

"What are you doing?" Tamara asked.

"A gift."

"But—"

"Take it," Nely insisted.

There was a lull after Tamara and Isa hauled out their bags, with promises they'd send pictures of themselves in their dresses.

Nely straightened up the tables, brushed nonexistent dust off the glass displays, and returned clothes back to their respective racks. Finally, she couldn't take it anymore. She had to find out how much she'd made.

She typed furiously, and, miraculously, the screen flashed numbers that spoke plain English.

She had rung up $5,000 in merchandise in three hours.

Pride thrilled through her. She'd done it.

She closed her eyes, letting herself accept it. For once she wasn't going to downplay it or give credit to everyone else. She allowed herself this victory.

"Oh. Papi, ven mira!"

Nely opened her eyes when she heard the new customer. It was like God had personally answered her prayers when she beheld the blessing of shopkeepers around the world: the faux-blond Mexicana. Wearing a blue, tiger-print *Thriller* jacket and matching second-skin pants, the woman quivered with excitement.

An older, almost grandfatherly man chuckled indulgently at her ecstatic exclamations over the Santi beaded clutch bags. Nely took in the small mountain of shopping bags by the stone-faced bodyguard keeping watch in the doorway and dollar signs danced in her head. If cartel mistresses had a patron saint, she had just thanked her.

Twenty-two

With Audrey banging on her rainbow-colored piano and Paula Deen talking about crab soup on TV, Aggie folded Nely's old clothes, piling them on the plastic-covered couch.

Audrey walked over and threw down the pile of maternity jeans with a mighty swing of her arm.

"Dude, come on," Aggie said, pulling her away from the clothes. "Go do something educational."

Audrey whined, opening and closing her little hand. To stem a meltdown, Aggie grabbed a bag of goldfish and dumped them on the floor. Audrey pounced like a starving animal.

Aggie snapped the wrinkles out of a coral beaded tunic. Nely had worn it at her baby shower. Feeling quite domestic, Aggie folded it over her arm, placing it on the pile she would pack up and save in the garage.

They had one more week to go. Nely was raking in huge numbers at the store and had gotten Jeff, who managed their lease, fired from his job. Aggie grinned, wishing she'd been the one to do that ass kicking.

But having lived Nely's life for the last month, she understood why her friend needed those victories. Even stranger, Aggie understood why she needed to be in Nely's place. She liked the permanence, the belonging and the routine. Even though Audrey would never really be hers, she had become something of a mom to her.

Maybe not a perfect one, but a damn good one who was fun and bought her a bitchin' pair of red glittery Mary Jane's on sale at Target. Every girl needed a pair of ruby slippers.

The shirt gave a satisfying snap, and then Aggie held it up against herself, imagining a round, tight belly filling it out.

This had been a second chance, and when it was time for Aggie to go back, she promised herself that she wouldn't screw it up. Kevin momentarily cast a shadow over her sunny enthusiasm, but then she'd manage him as well.

"Why is Audrey eating off the floor?" Simon said, startling her.

"I, uh, gave her the bag and she must have spilt them," Aggie lied. Audrey was cute, she could fend for herself.

"Isn't the floor kind of dirty?"

Was that a comment on her housekeeping skills?

But then he whipped out a bouquet of Nely's favorite, sunflowers. "I saw these and thought you'd like them."

The corner of his mouth hitched into a grin when she stared at them with her mouth hanging open.

"Has it been that long since I last gave you flowers?" The tissue paper crinkled as he held them out to her.

Aggie struggled with the thought that Nely should've been here to receive these. Not her.

But she took them anyway.

"Nely, I don't want to lose you because of something outside us," he said.

"Like your mother?" she prompted. "If Nely hasn't left you yet—" She coughed, pretending something caught in her throat. "I mean if I—uh, never mind."

"Say what you were going to say," he replied quietly.

She made herself smile. "You wouldn't lose me because of her."

"So what would I lose you over?"

She realized she was gripping the flowers too tight. "Nothing," she said, an uncomfortable laugh burbling out of her. She needed to lighten the mood real quick and looked around the living room as if it might be written on a wall somewhere.

"I know," she said. "Those couches. They would eventually drive me to the brink."

He looked from her to the couches, not quite buying her joke. "Fine," he said. "I'll take the plastic off."

"You will?"

"My ass got stuck to it the other night."

Making sure Nely was busy upstairs, Simon went to the computer. He clicked into Local Settings, then Today's History, and scanned the list of websites she'd visited. Frowning, he noticed she had logged into Yahoo! Mail. Clicking into the file, he saw that Nely had logged in repeatedly throughout the day as she'd done every day that he'd checked this month.

Every time he got worked up to confront her, he chickened out. He really didn't want to know. He just wanted it to go away.

But he'd been checking her cell phone, credit card balance, and the mileage on the van. Nothing out of the ordinary except for the distance he couldn't cross to get to her.

Audrey tapped her headless Barbie doll on his shoe. "Hey there, stinky," he said, reaching down to pick her up. "Did mama clean you at all today?"

This paranoia was his mother's doing. He would trust his wife, and he was going to stick to it. Otherwise, what else would they have?

After dusting off the crumbs stuck to her face, he asked, "Wanna help me take off the plastic?"

She poked the end of his nose with her finger. "Eh."

"I need your opinion," Nely suddenly announced.

He looked up. "Okay."

"Aggie wants to get married."

"And?" He groaned, putting Audrey back on the floor.

"Anyway, because you're a man—"

"Thanks for noticing."

"You're welcome. Because you're a man, what kind of guy do you think would be perfect for Aggie? And be honest."

"There's no way I'm answering that question. I'm not stupid."

"It's just an innocent question."

"I'll answer and then you'll go tell your friend and you'll both get mad at me."

"Come on. We really need your help."

"I don't know! I never dated her, so I can't say."

"But you know her. What was your first impression when you met her?"

"I already told you."

Curious, Aggie pressed on. "Tell me again."

"I thought she was a major pain in the ass. There. See. You're going to get mad like the first time."

"Why is she a major pain in the ass? Is it because she's a strong, savvy woman?"

"No. It's because she's a pain in the ass. All she talks about are her problems in minute details with men, her period, how she looks or how much money she made. A guy doesn't want to hear that crap over and over again, and the guys who pretend they do are just waiting till they can get laid. Sorry, but you asked."

"But you like her, don't you?"

"Yeah. But I wouldn't marry her."

"So what kind of man do you think would marry her?"

He sighed as he stared out the window. "Someone who isn't afraid to call her on her bullshit. But then she'd have to start thinking of someone other than herself if she really wants a man that—"

Oh crap. Fighting with Nely was the last thing he wanted. He held up the plastic coating like the skin of a shedding snake and realized he should've said nothing. Nely just stared at the floor, her eyes wide with an expression that he could swear was defeat.

"But she dresses really well," he offered.

"Right," she answered softly, then started back toward the stairs.

"I knew it," he said.

"Knew what?"

"That you'd get mad at me."

She faced him again, her face stiff and pale. "You're just telling me the truth, and—and you're right . . . about the selfish part."

Simon felt rotten about saying things he would never have said to Aggie's face. "So, uh, do you want spaghetti for dinner?"

"No thanks. I'm not hungry."

Aggie went up into Audrey's room. She had piled all the clean laundry on the dresser, and now began putting everything away.

The sun pierced through the slats of the window shades, nearly blinding her. Blinking back tears, she went over to close them completely but stopped when she caught a view of the most dramatic sunset she had ever seen.

Pulling the blinds up, she shielded her eyes from the intense light. Violent purples clashed with ripe gold and pink through a haze of filmy clouds.

Sunset had always been Mama's favorite time of the day. She couldn't count the number of times they'd driven up to Cabrillo Point to see the green flash of light that occurred just when the sun disappeared over the horizon.

Why didn't you come to me? What do I have to do to be ready for you to visit me like you promised?

Her breath sent raw aches through her chest, which radiated out through the palms of her hands. "I still need you," she whispered.

Then she fell into a quivering mouth and hitching sobs kind of cry. She cried because she hadn't loved her mother the way she should have when her mama had been alive. She cried because she could only remember the terrible things she'd said. Mama had just loved her, while she criticized and sometimes hated her mama.

Helen had tried her whole life to tell her that selfishness would be her undoing. Then again, Mama's generosity had been her downfall. She always put everyone before herself: her boss, her coworkers, her men . . . and, Aggie. She never got ahead, never was more than a beauty supply store manager and an unmarried mother who never got a dime of support, because she was always so busy taking care of everyone else.

But then she remembered Kevin when he'd nudged his way into her bathroom and tried to get her to talk to him. He wanted to look out for her. He knew her inside and out and if he'd been her friend all this time in spite of what Simon said, then . . .

Her heart tripped over itself as it began jumping in her chest. Kevin was the one and when she got back, she'd—

Aggie wiped her cheeks dry. It wouldn't do to let Audrey see her like this. Her lips quivered but she kept that smile on when Audrey peered inside, giggled, then disappeared.

"Hey there, sweetie," Aggie said. "You want to play peek-aboo?"

Audrey ran in and then she let out a delighted scream. "Due!" she yelled, reaching up with her hands. "Due, due, due, due."

Aggie picked her up. Nothing felt as good as holding a baby.

Audrey slapped the tops of Aggie's shoulders. "Due, due, due."

"You want to try on your new ruby slippers?" Aggie asked. "Now you have to promise not to let anyone make you wear yellow. It's not your color."

"Due! You due!"

Aggie was so startled that she nearly let go of Audrey's tush. Audrey spoke! A word, a real word! Okay, so it was "dude," but it counted. It wasn't mama; not that it should have been. But Audrey had finally acknowledged her without the enticement of a cookie or chocolate.

She leaned away so she could look her in the eye.

Audrey smiled, showing off all seven teeth. She touched the tip of Aggie's nose with a pointed finger. "You due."

"Thank you, Audrey," she whispered, pressing kisses anywhere she could find. Settling her into a cradle hold, she played a little game of kissing Audrey's nose.

"Oogie oogie, pwee," Audrey said, reaching up and skimming her fingers along Aggie's chin.

"You want a cookie?"

"Pwee."

"After dinner."

Audrey chuckled and drawled, "Due."

Aggie's eyes went glassy with happy tears. "That's right, kid. I'm your dude."

"We were just talking about you," Simon said when he opened the front door.

"What? I mean, hi," Nely stammered. Nerves burst in her stomach and she nervously brushed her hair over her shoulder. She didn't remember being this flustered when they'd first been dating.

She'd managed not to run into him all this time, and the impact was—

"Hi," he said, then stepped back, holding the door wider. "She's upstairs doing stuff."

Did her husband make everyone feel as if he could see exactly what they were trying to hide? She crossed her ankles to keep from jumping on him and wrapping her legs around his waist.

She should've gone back to Aggie's apartment or worked in the boutique. But she was afraid of the quiet . . . not to mention thoughts of Jeff ripping the shower curtain open wearing his mother's dress with a knife in his hand.

She squeezed by Simon and his scent, the faded cologne she always bought for him—and just him—sent her insides topsy-turvy.

"I know you're up to something," he said, leaning forward, stopping her right where she stood.

She swung to look at him and nearly brushed the tip of his nose with hers. "How?" she asked, and cringed, wishing she could take it back.

But then that little voice in her head told her to tell him it was her. Maybe if she willed it into her eyes, Simon would recognize her, and then she could come home and have sex with him.

But then she remembered this wasn't her body, and there was no way she was sleeping with Simon in Aggie's body. Still, if he believed her, she could come back home.

"Who is Kevin?" was the last thing she imagined he would ask. But he did, and it took her a second to catch up.

"Who?"

He just stared at her, using silence to slowly slice open her secrets. She could sense the seams ripping from the cloth, but then snapped out of it.

She was his wife. Not some criminal or smart-mouthed witness he could push around.

"Are you serious?" she shot back. "He's Aggie's friend."

He flinched back but then snapped back into cop mode. "Aggie's friend?"

She realized she'd slipped and referred to Aggie in the third person.

"If you're helping my wife, I could ask you to leave," he threatened softly, looming over her, "and make sure that you never come back."

The intense yet hushed way he threatened her made her mouth go dry. A sudden thirst consumed her and it hurt to breathe. She involuntarily leaned closer, taking on the role of the aggressor.

"Let's see you do it," she threw back, and the heat made her skin break out in a fine sweat. She forgot that if he made good on that threat, she wouldn't get to see Audrey.

When Simon's eyes narrowed like that while his breath seethed between his clenched teeth, she knew he'd do it.

But he looked so delicious all worked up and angry. She wanted to lick his neck.

Simon meant to run and hide the minute he realized Aggie stood in their doorway. He knew Nely would blab all the things he'd said about Aggie.

But then the thought of them whispering together brought back his suspicions about his wife rattling in the back of his head. So he decided to shake her up a little, to see if she'd spill. He hadn't meant to provoke this.

He rolled his lips back, rather than moisten them with the tip of his tongue. His breath scraped his dry throat and he was growing harder with each passing moment they stared one another down.

There was something too surreal about this whole thing.

It was like fighting with his wife. She had that glitter in her eyes, the burning color up her neck that ended at her hairline. *Just like Nely.*

But this was Aggie, his wife's best friend.

Without a word, he stalked out the open door, not knowing why he was heading for his SUV or where he'd go once he got inside.

He didn't care that he'd been in the middle of taking off those plastic sofa covers, or that Aggie had been so close to spilling her guts. He had to put physical space between the two of them before they set the house on fire.

The key trembled in his shaking hand as he tried to jam it into the ignition. Disgust roiled in his stomach when his hard-on ached under the constriction of his pants.

It was Aggie, *Aggie*, who'd done this to him. Only Nely had had the power to do it, and, with a raging boner in his pants, he felt like he'd cheated on her. He shuddered.

"Mijo! Mijo!"

"Oh shit," he muttered. His mother hurried toward him. No man wanted his mother within a twenty-mile radius of him when he was in this condition.

"What?" he barked out the window, pulling the gear into reverse and releasing the brake.

"Where are you going? It's dinnertime."

He couldn't lie. "I'm just going out for a minute."

"Did Nely pick a fight with you? What did she say? Where's the baby?"

He held up his hand as if he could deflect all of the poisoned darts flying his way. "We're not fighting." He regained some composure to lie, "We're ordering a pizza for dinner."

"If you need dinner, I'll make it for you."

Nely would slit his throat in the middle of the night.

"That's okay. We already called it in."

His mother shook her head. "Doesn't Nely realize how much money you're wasting when you eat out?"

"I gotta run, Mom."

"Wait! What is that friend of hers doing here? She's been sneaking in through the back door almost every night."

Twenty-three

"You cleaned out my closet?" Nely demanded, slightly breathless when she burst into Audrey's room.

Aggie and Audrey looked over. Audrey arched her back, reaching for her mama.

Aggie wiped her tears away. "Guess what Audrey just called me?" she asked. "Dude. She says it 'due,' but she has a name for me."

When Nely didn't immediately congratulate her, Aggie quickly assured her, "I would never let her call me Mama, Nel."

Nely didn't say anything as she took Audrey into her arms. "I have to talk to you about something."

Disappointed that Nely could not seem to grasp the importance of this breakthrough, Aggie told her, "Go for it."

"I think we should start out small," Nely started. "Pick three or four designs that will work for maternity and then bring in the right lingerie so the customer will buy the dress, the slip, panties, and bra in one sale rather than go from one place to another for each item."

Nely put Audrey on the floor. "Has she had dinner yet?"

"Hold on a second," Aggie begged. "Okay, slow down. What are you talking about?"

"A partnership. I want to become partners in the boutique."

White noise erupted between her ears.

"I can bring in a hundred and twenty-five thousand to start us—"

"Where the hell did you get that kind of money?"

"It's my secret stash. I sold before the stock market crash and then invested in some real estate."

"Does Simon know?"

"Well, no, not really."

Aggie saw her friend anew, ashamed of how she'd looked down on Nely for leaving work to be a full-time mom. She had thought that being a homemaker was what women who were too dumb to work did.

"You need this investment. I've seen the books, and Aggie, you can't stay open much longer."

But Lola's was hers. It had started out as a dream when she was a fat, ugly seventh grader who carried a copy of Barbara Taylor Bradford's *A Woman of Substance* in her backpack. She'd built it from nothing, taken all the risk and—

And then she remembered how Nely and Simon had been there with Mama when she'd put it together. They spent days unpacking boxes, installing shelves, screwing lightbulbs into the refurbished chandeliers. She had taken all of them for granted. In fact, she wasn't sure if she'd thanked them.

Nely had invested her sweat and two fingernails, and now, when Aggie needed her more than ever, her friend was here to help. Also, Nely had given her full reign over her home, her husband, and her daughter. Nely trusted her, and she should trust her back.

"Let's do it."

"But we need a formal arrangement. That way there's no misunderstanding."

"What's there to misunderstand? We're partners fifty-fifty."

Aggie was all ready to go, but Nely insisted on bringing up every single detail of their business right then and there. It wasn't until Aggie realized they were nearly standing in the dark that she asked, "Where's Simon?"

Nely paused mid-sentence.
"He left."

"Where?"

"I don't know. Did you order out?"

"No." Aggie cleared her throat, suddenly unable to bear not knowing what was happening with Kevin. "So, uh, have you heard from Kevin at all?"

"Sorry, Ag. He called to tell me he's been real busy and . . ." She took her sweet time to finish. "I haven't really seen him around."

"Why? What did you say?"

"Nothing! I mean, he just came into the store one day and said it was best for us—I mean you—to stay friends. So I just agreed and . . ."

Aggie told herself to be strong. If she had to put up with Simon, the least Nely could do was keep up her weekly routine.

"So," Aggie said, pulling her shoulders back, putting on her brave face. "Did you go to my appointment?"

"What appointment?"

"My wax! Please tell me you didn't forget."

Nely avoided looking directly at her. "I didn't forget."

"Do you know what it'll be like if you don't keep up the routine?"

"You can do it when we switch back."

"You just made a real mess of things, didn't you?" Aggie raged, unable to stop herself.

Nely flinched. "Aggie, it's just a wax job."

"I have to make dinner," she said, still angry that Nely had lost Kevin and forgotten to get her waxed. And yet, she knew Nely didn't deserve that. But she couldn't bring herself to apologize and mean it.

Later that night, after Nely left and she and Simon suffered through a strained silence, Aggie waited for him to finish up in the bathroom.

What was he doing in there that took *this* long? What if she'd had to go to the bathroom?

But then she realized that if she were Nely, she'd probably just walk in and take her seat on the can. Aggie shuddered that any woman could pee in the presence of a man.

Finally, she knocked on the door.

"What're you doing that for?" he asked.

"Common courtesy. Are you done?"

"Come on."

The door squeaked open and she peeked through the sliver-sized opening to make sure he was at least in a towel. Well, she thought, when it came to looks, Nely had chosen wisely.

Wearing boxers and no shirt, he had his face an inch away from the mirror with a tweezer in one hand. "Do you think they look even?"

She glanced at his ass and then realized he was talking about his eyebrows. The only men she had known who plucked their eyebrows did not date women, much less marry them. Apparently, she'd been mistaken.

But knowing that he wouldn't want her to know some of his idiosyncrasies lessened the sting of what he'd said about her earlier.

"They look great. So have you thought about what we discussed at dinner?"

"No."

She took a deep breath before diving in. Nely had left without an apology from her, and she hated herself for being so stuffed with pride. She'd wanted to but just couldn't. Not yet.

But she would win Simon over. "I want to go into business with Aggie," she said, "in her boutique. Not because Aggie needs me but because I—" She wanted to roll her eyes at her Hallmark movie of the week dialogue.

"But I don't understand," he said, not waiting for her to finish. "I thought you were happy here."

"I am. But I need more. I love this other part of me that I wasn't using."

He set the tweezers down and turned to give her his full attention. "What part?"

"The part of me that needs to be part of—" She thought carefully about her answer, about what Nely needed from this whole thing. "I want Audrey to see her mother as someone she could be proud of."

"Nel—"

"No, you don't understand. Daughters don't always respect their mothers. We judge them harshly. I don't want to be a mom that Audrey will spend her whole life trying not to become."

"What I don't like is you're the one who would be taking all the risk."

"Aggie is. If we fail, she loses everything."

"What about Audrey? My mother will want to take care of her. How do you feel about that?"

Aggie improvised. "I was thinking of asking a friend to watch Audrey. Why don't you want me to do this?"

"I do, but—" Simon seemed to think about what he was going to say. "I'm trying to understand who you are now."

Her skin prickled hot then cold. *He knew.*

"When we got married," he said, "you said how you wanted to be a full-time mom till our kids were in school, and now you're changing everything on me."

Okay, he didn't know. Of course he didn't know. Aggie deflated with relief and tried to pull herself back together.

But he mistook her silence for resentment. "You're just going to do what you want, aren't you? Do you know what you're doing?"

"Of course, I do. I'm a—" Was Nely a CPA? She couldn't remember.

"I'm not talking about the business," he said, and the gravity of his tone made her realize that everything hinged on this one answer.

"I'm just going into business with a friend," she said. "She would do the same thing for me, and this will be good for us. For you and me."

"I hope so," he said quietly.

Twenty-four

Nely knew it was a dream when she breathed in his scent. She walked from room to empty room, led by a trail of heat that would lead her to him.

She might as well have been blindfolded in her search. He was a ghost, an impossible wish, waiting just within reach and then vanishing when she opened the door.

Suddenly the heat of his hand stroked her shoulder. She turned but she was alone. And then his breath heated her temple, leaving a trace of moisture that went cold as it evaporated off her skin.

"Where are you?" she whispered, then heard that appreciative hum he'd make when she'd touch him in just the right spot.

Her nerves prickled and heated with anticipation for him, all of him.

Turning a corner and then another, she found him wearing nothing but the light that fuzzed the edges of her vision.

One foot rested on the floor, the other on the chaise lounge that was supposed to be in their bedroom. Her stare wandered all over him, his thick shoulders and down his legs.

"Take off your clothes," he said, and intense waves of heat washed over her skin. Without moving, she stood in the middle of the room.

She hadn't been naked in front of him with the lights on since Clinton was still president. And even then she'd always been a lights-off kind of girl.

"I can't," she admitted, wanting him to hold her so bad that it hurt.

"Why?"

Her chin fell, and with it, her ability to look him in the eye. She twisted and turned the rose-colored slip in her hands.

"Nely, why do you keep hiding from me?"

She shook her head. She really didn't know. She loved him, wanted him, was ready for him, and yet it felt wrong. Even though he'd never refused her the few times she'd come to him, she feared the first time he would. And with the way she looked now . . .

She didn't want him to see her yet. Not until she got back to the way she'd been. The fear of his rejection was like chains wrapped around her shoulders, twined around her throat.

"Nely, I can't keep coming to you," he said softly. "You have to come to me. You have to show me you love me."

She pulled up the slip. Stop wondering what he'll really think when he sees you. *The hem brushed the tops of her thighs.*

Stop telling yourself that when he closes his eyes, he'll think of someone prettier than you.

She dropped the slip and it brushed over her knees.

"I don't know if I—" She looked up, and he had this funny smile on his face, one she didn't see too often. He smiled as if he knew what she was trying to admit. "Can't you meet me halfway?"

"I'm right here, baby. I won't go anywhere."

Swallowing hard, she turned to the door. She rose up on the balls of her feet but couldn't take a step that would take her out that door. Sweat shined off her hands. She drew up her slip until it shimmied along the bottom curve of her behind. Her skin erupted in heat as she felt his eyes tracing her every curve.

"Do you want to see more?" she whispered over her shoulder.

He strangled the word, "Yes."

She slipped her thumbs under the waistband of her thong panties.

"You have to look at me," he demanded. "I want you to see the way I look at you."

Her breath hitched up in her throat, the slip balled in the grip of her hands. Put on a good show, she told herself as her feet squeaked on the bare floor.

Simon's eyes were filled with love, with lust, with the honesty that made them partners. She touched her eyes with his and saw that there was no one else in this room or in his mind but her.

Her hands slid up, her thumbs brushing out from under her panties as she traced her waist and belly. He leaned forward, his jaw clenching under the skin. Cupping her breasts, she pushed them up in offering. His eyes narrowed and his hands curled into fists at his sides.

Her own power rising, she asked, "Do you want to know what they taste like?"

"That's—" He cleared his throat. "—not fair."

Nely stepped closer as she nudged down her panties inch by inch over her hips and then stopped. Blood surged under her skin as wet heat collected between her thighs.

With a hiss of breath he forced himself to recline on the pillows.

"Get down on the floor," he told her. "Open your legs for me."

"Touch me."

"On the floor."

Her knees hit the cold floor, her hands balled in the crease of her thighs.

"Please," he added as if he bore a terrible weight.

She kept her knees and ankles locked tight as she eased her legs out from under her behind. His erection twitched but he didn't touch himself to ease the tension.

Drawing out his anticipation, she spread her feet and then her knees. Before he could tell her what to do next, she reached around the back of her thigh and with one finger pulled the crotch of her panties aside. A low hiss passed through his teeth, the muscles in his legs clenching into tight lines.

She savored the decadence, the power of teasing a heated male.

"You like playing with me like that?" he growled, planting his other foot on the floor beside her ankle. His length stood rigidly up from his lap, the veins marbling the pink brown flesh. She wanted to kiss him, lick him, and suck him so deep inside her. With her index and middle fingers, she peeled her lips apart and a deep pulse of desire whooshed the breath out of her lungs.

He struck without warning. He used his body to force her onto her back, while his hands snuck under her bottom to lift her hips. His shoulders wedged between her thighs. She recovered just quick enough to meet that feral gaze directed at her core.

His finger slipped under the soaked panty crotch and she whimpered for him to touch her. But he deliberately brushed her ever so gently with the back of his knuckle, sending sparks of pleasure right before her eyes.

"Simon," she warned and begged at the same time.

He jerked the material against her thigh, and then the tip of his tongue traveled up to the spot that sent those sparks in a swirl.

A cry shocked out of her, and he dipped his finger into her mouth. "I told you I wanted you," he whispered, kissing her thigh.

She swirled her tongue over his finger and he moaned against her. She had nothing to clutch onto as he danced his tongue over her. Her hips leapt up, offering everything that he took.

This was how she had always wanted it but had been too shy to ask. She felt carnal and dirty, straining to hold her legs wide for him. His eyes dared her to keep biting down on the eruption that tensed her spine into a bow. His kisses and gentle bites urged her to come so hard that her screams would break the windows.

"God damn it, Simon," she ground out.

And he shouted, "Yes!"

In a brutally swift motion, he pushed her legs up. He took himself in his hand, aiming right into her throbbing wetness. He pushed himself in, and the shock of it jolted through her.

She could hear his groans through the fantastic noise coiling in her body. She latched her arms around him as he planted his hands on either side of her head. He drove into her relentlessly until she came so hard that she thought her soul had been yanked from her very skin. He fused himself completely with her, his mouth opening in a perfect O as his release poured into her.

Her muscles twitched from the aftershocks, holding him inside and never wanting to let him go.

They murmured I love yous as they nuzzled and dropped kisses wherever their lips could find. His mouth found hers as he slipped out of her.

Her fingers brushed the damp hair over his neck as they languidly kissed each other out of the haze of desire.

"When are you coming home?" he whispered. "I miss you so much."

Twenty-five

When Kevin started the car, Johnny Cash blasted from the radio, singing a song that cut straight to the bone.

"I'm not the one you want, babe. I'm not the one you need."

You're done, Johnny Cash, Kevin thought. He pushed the eject button and the system took forever spitting it out. He flung the CD out the window, and the BMW kicked up dust as he pulled out into the street.

Tires screamed and a horn blasted as a black SUV swerved around him. He hoped that a healthy dose of cussing and derogatory hand gestures would let off this pent-up steam. It didn't.

Even though he'd come home late from the restaurant and spent most of the night in front of the TV watching demonstrations of stain removers, Kevin drove to work early. For a month he'd managed to avoid running into Aggie. But their bedrooms shared the same wall, and he'd taken to sleeping on the couch, unable to sleep knowing just a few inches of wood and plaster separated them.

Watching Pierce drive himself nuts over proposing still bugged the hell out of him. Something about the whole deal rankled, and no amount of stain removing power could stop him from thinking about it.

He pulled off a risky U-turn in front of Pannikan and managed not to die. The car jerked to a sudden stop and the engine groaned as he put it into reverse and backed up to wedge himself between two cars.

The air was redolent with pungent dark roasts and steamed milk. There was no line. He refused to look around for her. Thinking about her only darkened his mood.

At the very least Aggie should've told him that she wouldn't be getting them coffee in the morning. Common courtesy dictated some kind of notice.

"Kevin? Is that you?" Someone with a sultry voice asked in front of him.

He looked up from the floor he'd been staring holes into, and she looked familiar.

"It is," he said, not bothering to remove his sunglasses.

She didn't get the hint that he wanted to be left alone and held out her hand. "Bianca. We met a month ago at your place."

Slowly her face emerged from his memory. But then the corners of his mouth turned down when he remembered he'd met Bianca the night that Aggie brought a date into his restaurant.

"Nice to see you again."

"Here." She offered him her coffee cup. "You look like you need this more than I do."

Speechless, he just took it and then, realizing what he'd done, tried to return it. "Wait. I can't take your coffee."

"No problem." She waved away his concern. "It's a large French roast black. I didn't touch it so it's cootie free."

"Then I need to get one for you."

"Kevin, take the coffee."

He could just thank her, make small talk, then thank her again before leaving. Or he could say, "Then I need to make you dinner."

To his surprise, his sleep-deprived brain made him say that out loud.

Her green eyes snapped wide with delight. But she wasn't faking it. She treated him like a pal rather than a conquest.

Unlike Aggie, he thought, who'd treated him like clothing lint.

"Oh, but wait," Bianca said. "I'm a vegetarian."

Alarm almost made him drop the coffee. "What?"

"Kidding. I'd love dinner. But just so you know, I don't cook."

It was all so damn cute that even he had to crack a smile.

Nely parked the car, said hello to each and every single person she encountered on the sidewalk, her briefcase swinging purposefully. She met the day renewed by great sex with her husband. It had been the-baby-isn't-sleeping-down-the-hall kind of sex . . . even if it had been dream sex.

She shivered, remembering waking up at three-thirty and thinking it had actually happened. She felt his big, hot body spooned against hers and his whisper against her ear, "When are you coming home?"

Her throat tightened with emotion. She didn't trust this kind of giddiness. It always let disaster through the door.

But the air smelled sweet and fresh, the sun caressing the earth with a golden hue.

And then she opened the door to Pannikan and saw Kevin smiling down at a stunning blonde.

He certainly wasted no damn time. If Aggie hadn't been in love with him—after her outburst last night, she wasn't fooling anyone—Nely's fists would not be heating with violent anger.

She let the door slam shut. Today was still going to be a wonderful day, even if it killed her, or she killed Kevin.

It was harder to smile when she arrived at work. Just as she had originally believed, Aggie didn't need Kevin. She could do so much better. The blonde probably deserved him.

No, she didn't. No woman deserved him. She should've told that poor woman to run, run for the hills! And then slipped her a card to Lola's with the promise of a discount.

When the front door opened and La Cacuy trilled, "Nely? Oh Nely?" Aggie seriously considered diving under the table and staying put until the evil one went away. But that old woman would just sit on the couch and wait.

"Hi, La—Simona," she said, pretending the plastic hadn't been removed from the couches and the drapes pulled down.

"What happened to the living room? Nely, look what Audrey has done to the couch!"

Actually, she was the one who spilled the juice, but she'd let Audrey take the blame.

"We'll just squirt some stain remover on it," she replied. "Is there a reason why you're here?"

La Cacuy sputtered. "We have to go to class!"

"We?"

"I'm planning the Halloween party."

"You are?" Aggie toyed with her. She'd miss that when she went back to her old life. "I thought I was doing it."

La Cacuy clasped her talons in front of her. "We want the party to be nice," she pontificated. "Remember Audrey's first birthday?"

Aggie thought the cowgirl theme had been cute. And those frozen taquitos were surprisingly tasty.

She was pushing it, but it was so easy. "But I already went to Costco," she lied. "They had a special on the chicken toes you liked."

When La Cacuy sashayed into the recreation center, Aggie gave Audrey one last pep talk.

"Don't be nice," she told her. "Be real. No one respects a nice girl. But if you're real, they'll fear you, and a little fear is good."

She waved at Pema, who hunched over Naveen while he pushed a plastic grocery basket around the room.

"And finally, choose your friends carefully. Sometimes a bad one can slip in, and when you figure it out, cut her out. For the next seventeen years your primary focus is survival. You'll get a brief reprieve in college, unless you join a sorority. It'll start all over again when you go into the work world."

"Hey, Nely," Pema greeted her, with a genuine smile.

"You look tired, is everything okay?" Aggie asked after she have Pema a hug.

"Oh God," Pema sighed. "Naveen's molars are coming in. I can see them just under the surface—"

"I'm so sorry about that," Aggie cut in, repressing a shudder at the thought of tiny teeth breaking through gums. "I wanted to ask you something."

"Of course."

"I might need someone I can trust to watch Audrey a couple of times a week. Would you be willing to? I'd pay you, of course, and provide Audrey's food—"

"I'd love to," Pema offered.

"It won't be all day, just half days, so—"

"What won't be all day, Nely?" La Cacuy appeared.

Pema pressed her lips tightly together to keep from saying another word, and Aggie appreciated her consideration. "We're planning a play date."

"Oh. Should Audrey be playing with a boy?"

"Think of it as target practice," she replied, and Pema doubled over in a sudden coughing fit.

"I should—" Pema choked on her laughter, then cleared her throat. "—follow—heh heh—Naveen."

"Nely," La Cacuy hissed when Pema stumbled away. "You really should make more of an effort to befriend Leila. She's more our—" She lowered her voice. "More our kind of people."

Aggie's mouth dropped open.

"I'm not being racist," La Cacuy stammered. "I'm just saying—" Suddenly, she frowned. "Where's Audrey?"

Aggie's gaze flew down to her stroller, which was now empty.

She grabbed the first little girl she spotted in a red jumper.

"Hey, put my daughter down!"

She took a second look. *Fuck!*

"Do you see Audrey?" she asked La Cacuy.

La Cacuy froze in the face of fear.

There were about eleven kids toddling around the room, but none of them were Audrey.

Her heart lurched when she saw that the door was propped open. "Audrey!" she screamed.

She'd lost Nely's child! At Miss Cheryl's, in front of all these mothers looking at her as if she'd been caught freebasing in the bathroom. She nearly took out a small child in her single-minded bolt for the door, and then everything she had ever feared happened right before her eyes.

Audrey ran out in the street just as a silver BMW came around the bend, too fast to stop when it happened upon the baby.

All went silent within Aggie as she watched Audrey about to die. But then she distinctly heard her mama's voice shout, "Run, damn it!"

The next thing she remembered, she was holding Audrey in her arms.

"Oh my God!" she whispered over and over again. Somehow she had made it down the sidewalk, through the parked cars and to the lot, in time to save her.

The relief was so swift and unrelenting that it felt like she'd fallen through a frozen lake. She locked Audrey against her, thanking God, Great Spirit, Allah, the Force—whoever was listening—that Audrey was alive.

A breeze kicked up, bringing with it the smell of jasmine at twilight. But jasmine wasn't planted in the park, and it had been her mama's favorite scent.

Aggie smiled as tears seeped out of the corners of her eyes. Her mama had come through when she'd really needed her. Maybe this was her way of letting her know that she'd been around in a tight spot.

"I'm so sorry," Aggie said, righting Audrey on her feet

and dusting off her outfit. "I'm so sorry. Are you scared? Are you okay?"

Audrey sized up the situation. Sensing Aggie's guilt and the opportunities it would afford her, she said, "Due, choco!"

"Have you ever heard of Samantha Runion?" Leila hollered across the park, apparently more annoyed than concerned for Audrey's welfare. "Danielle Van Dam? How could you let her out of your sight?"

Aggie didn't get many moments of grace in her life. Leila's compassion withered the edges of what should have been a moment of transcendence.

"What you did was pure negligence," Leila spat as she clattered across the street in ridiculously out-of-style platform wedges. "No wonder your daughter can't talk."

Aggie looked Audrey in the eyes. "You will never have to come here again."

The roaring in Aggie's head drowned out Leila's blathering. She walked right up to the bitch and the sound of her hand making contact with Leila's face echoed through the park.

Someone gasped, but no one so much as moved.

"It was an accident," Aggie said calmly, as she successfully crossed over from the girls to the women. "And she does talk. Her favorite word is bitch."

As she walked Audrey to the car, she heard Pema say, "It's about time."

Twenty-six

Aggie spent one of the best days she'd ever had with Audrey. They were the first to ride the merry-go-round at Balboa Park. They ate half-and-half ice cream cones from the snack shack by the theater and then walked along the Prado chasing fat pigeons to the sounds of a street saxophonist.

It was the kind of thing Aggie had done with her mama. Just the two of them, alone without family, living in a trailer that gave them a perfect view of the drive-in movie screen.

Now she and Audrey had bonded as rebel girls who skipped out of Death's path and then bitch-slapped a mean girl's mama. It was awesome.

"There you go," the temporary tattoo artist said, patting Audrey's arm.

As they pulled up to the house, Audrey sleeping open-mouthed in her car seat, Aggie saw Simon and his mother outside and didn't have to wonder why he was home so early.

"There she is," Simona charged when Aggie approached, carrying still-sleeping Audrey.

"Mama . . ." Simon warned.

"I've stayed quiet all this time and now that she has endangered my granddaughter, I will speak."

Aggie glared at her sleeping partner in crime. Audrey let her take the rap solo.

"Oh yes," Simona answered the unspoken question. "I was there. And then she ran off. Leaving me there. Humiliating me in front of Miss Cheryl—"

"*Mom!*" Simon shouted. He turned to Aggie. "Carry Audrey inside, will you?"

Eager to escape, Aggie fled the scene.

Simon could not yet bring himself to look into his mother's eyes and say what he needed to say.

"She slapped another mother in front of everyone!" Simona cried. "I don't think Nely should be around the baby. What is she like when we're not around?"

He sucked in a deep breath and then asked, "Mom, why are you doing this?"

"Why? Because I love you and Audrey and Nely is completely out of line and I—"

"No, Mama, you are."

She blinked. Before she could recover, he said, "I'm sorry, Mama, but you have to listen to me. Nely is my wife and the mother of my daughter. I know you have your ways, but when it comes to my house and my family, Nely's way is how we do things."

"But she let your daughter wander out into the parking lot!"

"It was an accident," he said. "It could've easily happened to me. And you were there, too, weren't you?"

His mother lifted her chin, stubborn in her denial that any of the fault was hers.

"I know she is up to something," she hissed. "I've been watching her very closely and she's up to something with that friend of hers."

"Nely doesn't deserve this," Simon added, refusing to admit to his mother that he, too, had his doubts. "Especially from you."

"Then she'll break your heart, *mijo*. But I'll be here for you, just as I have been all these years. How could you do this to me?"

"All I'm asking is that you respect me enough to stop interfering."

"Is that what you think of my concern? Everything I do is to protect you, Simon," she said roughly. "She's proven over and over again that you can't trust her."

His mother never failed to bring up the past.

"That was a long time ago," he growled, "and none of your business."

"When it concerns you and Audrey, yes, it is my business. And once a cheater, always a cheater. Don't fool yourself into thinking she isn't up to something, Simon. Did she tell you about the night that friend of hers was over? She snuck out the back door right before you came home."

Simon filed that away.

"What do you think you'll gain from all this?" he asked. "Do you want to lose me and Audrey? I'll do whatever it takes to keep my family together, even if I have to move away from all this—"

"You can't take Audrey from me," she rushed in. "I'll die if you do."

"Mom, you know I don't want to do that," he said quietly. "But maybe we're too close. Maybe we need our space."

"Oh. Well. I see," she choked, holding her hand to her mouth.

He hated making her cry. But what else could he do? There was no other way to get through to her. He sighed, wishing she had a boyfriend or someone to focus on rather than him.

"Are you going to be okay by yourself?" he asked, holding back from reaching out to hold and comfort her. If he did, she'd see it as weakness and start working on him with the guilt.

This was his fault. He'd let it go too long, too far. If he'd nipped this in the bud way back when his mother had gotten between him and Nely while they were dating, he wouldn't be standing on his front lawn breaking his mother's heart.

His mother straightened her spine as if she would walk to her funeral pyre on her own two feet.

"I will be fine," she said roughly. "I learned a long time ago how to take care of myself."

Aggie snuck up the stairs before Simon came in and caught her listening.

She thought she'd feel triumph when he finally put his mother in her place. Instead, she felt sorry for the woman. In fact, she was a little ashamed of having slapped Leila. Did this mean she was becoming a better person? If so, it really blew.

"Did you hear any of that?" he asked when he did finally come in, and stood in the doorway.

"Some of it," she said.

"Is Audrey all right?"

She nodded, preparing herself for the lecture.

But he asked, "Are you all right?"

"Better. Simon, I'm so sorry. She's never gotten out of her stroller like that before—"

"Hey," he said, moving up the stairs. His knees popped as he got down on the step below hers and took her hands in his. "It could've happened to me." He looked down, thinking about something, then looked up at her. "Remember when you left the house for the first time when Audrey was eight weeks old?"

That would be no. But she kept it to herself.

"I was walking out of the bathroom with her and I misjudged the doorway and she— She hit her head on the doorjamb. I didn't tell you because . . . well, you remember."

She didn't because she was Sham Nely. By standing here, hearing his confession, she realized was taking another moment away from him and her friend. Abruptly, she began crying and couldn't stop.

"You got her in time. She's okay."

"But what if I hadn't?"

"We're not going to think about that."

She let him hold and comfort her, never expecting that he'd kiss her. He brushed his lips against her temple and then her cheek. She jerked back, and he dove in for her lips, capturing the back of her head with his hand.

He worked magic with his lips and his tongue. The only thing that kept her from pushing him off was the thought that this was how Kevin probably kissed, and with her eyes closed, she pretended it was him.

His hand caught her breast, and that's when logic slapped her upside the head.

"Wait. Don't," he whispered against her neck. "Don't push me away."

For the first time since she'd been here, she tried to send telepathic messages to Audrey to start crying, screaming . . . anything! But she also knew that she wanted this. She wanted to comfort him for standing up to his mother, for temporarily losing his wife. To pretend he was Kevin.

Simon's touch was hot and rough, reverent and gentle. She could hold onto those strong shoulders for the ride and cling to his lean hips with her thighs. This wasn't her body, it was Nely's. But she wasn't Nely, she reminded herself. Simon didn't belong to her.

If she pushed him off, it would further widen the divide he thought was there between them—or rather, him and Nely. If she let him stay, she'd live with the knowledge that she had betrayed her best friend. She might be able to bear the secret for the rest of her life, but it would be the end of their friendship. Knowing what she'd done, she couldn't look Nely in the eye, and she'd lost so many people that she couldn't lose her best friend.

"Stop," she whispered against his whisker-rough cheek.

"No," he groaned, sliding his hands up under her shirt.

"Simon," she said, stronger, arching her back away from his hands.

"Nely, please," he begged.

"I said get off!" She shoved him back, then curdled inside when she saw his eyes filled with hurt.

He staggered back, rolling onto his butt. They stared at one another, their lips wet from kissing, their skin buzzing with unfulfilled desire.

His face tightened with fury and distrust, he pushed himself up off the floor.

"Sometimes you make this marriage impossible," he growled before stalking out.

Nely made it to her car alive and headed uptown to Banker's Hill. She had a dinner meeting with the head of the management office at Laurel, across the street from Balboa Park.

He'd already apologized profusely for Jeff's conduct and then had the windows and front door cleaned. He now wanted to make further reparations and reassure her that they had never planned to raise her lease.

Nely left the Charger with the valets.

French jazz tinkled softly in the air as she entered the black and white, Miro-themed restaurant. Swarovski crystal chandeliers hung from the ceiling, and mirrors with an arabesque motif reflected the pre-theater crowd.

She was seated on a chartreuse banquette as waiters whisked past with plates of stylish, sexy food.

But Nely reminded herself she held all the cards and she couldn't afford to fritter away her chance to keep Lola's alive and well. In just a few more days, she would be home.

"Aggie? I'm Hugh. You haven't waited long, have you?"

"I haven't," she answered crisply. "How are you?"

Maybe she would come here with Simon. She imagined him stroking her fingers while frowning at the menu prices and trying not to show it. Every day that she'd spent in Aggie's shoes was a day she'd missed with him and her baby. If she learned anything about being a mother, time sped up and the baby you brought home was calling someone "dude" when you weren't looking.

But she smiled at him in spite of the cold, aching homesickness. *Pull it together,* she told herself, and then got to business.

"This is a list of improvements that we'd like to be done immediately," she said, handing him a crisp printout she'd made that morning.

"Done," he said, flicking the paper with his finger. "You've been a great client and we think you're an asset to the Gaslamp."

Damn right we are, she agreed silently. But outwardly, she merely nodded.

"The space next door is closing," he said expectantly. "I've been talking—"

"Don't believe anything she says," Jeff burst in. "She's a liar."

"What—" Hugh started.

"She's making this up so you won't raise the lease!"

"Ms. Portrero, I'm so sorry—"

At first taken aback by the creep's appearance, Nely quickly recovered, realizing that it could work to her advantage. She stood up, about to walk out, when Jeff stepped in, crowding her onto the banquette.

"Sit down!" he snapped. "You're going to pay for doing this to me!""

"I— What? You are, asshole."

Diners gasped and a waiter almost walked into a chair because he, along with everyone else, had been watching them.

"I know everything about you," Jeff hissed, his stale breath nearly knocking her against the wall.

"Hey—" Hugh stood up and got between them. "Buddy, you need to leave now."

"Only if she comes with me."

The way he said it made Nely's stomach clench. She began shaking, trying not to show it, which only made it worse.

A light shone in Jeff's silvery eyes, one that promised he'd never go away until he fulfilled whatever sick thirst he had for her. He'd had access to her personal information. He probably knew where Aggie lived, maybe even watched her windows until she turned off the lights.

Nely's anger sputtered to life, struggling against the icy fear crystallizing in her gut. She watched as if in a bubble as the manager came over with two WWF-sized men to escort Jeff away. She felt someone touch her arm and flinched.

"He's gone," Hugh assured her. "Do you want to call the police?"

"No," she said unsteadily. "I want to go home."

"Let me walk you to your car."

Outside, the sunless air smacked some of the life back into her. "He trashed the front of my store—" she burst. "We never did anything to him—"

Her teeth chattered as the wind blew against the back of her neck, sneaking under her coat and coating her skin with goose bumps.

The valet brought her car.

"If you'd like, I'm happy to follow you home," Hugh offered.

"No, but I want you to hire security to watch my store."

"Um, okay—" he stammered. "Maybe you should keep your cell phone close. If you want, dial nine-one, and then if anything happens hit one and it'll automatically dial emergency."

"And a security guy, a great big one, to escort me to and from my car."

He nodded in acknowledgment, then gestured to the car for her to get in. After she drove off, she realized, with morbid amusement, that she should've asked for a pony.

Twenty-seven

"Who's the blonde?" Sandra asked. "The one I saw you walking out of Pannikan with, before you ask what I'm talking about."

"Her name is Bianca."

"The one who brings her clients here?"

"That's the one."

She leaned over the counter, propping her chin on the bridge of her threaded fingers. "What do you think of her?"

He paused in chopping chocolate for a mole recipe he was playing with. "She's all right."

"You know what I think?"

Kevin knew he'd find out whether he wanted to know or not.

"I liked how you two looked together."

What about Aggie? he immediately thought. Sandra had

been on him for weeks not to give up. Had she changed her mind? Why?

Ugh. He sounded like a woman. "Thanks," he answered.

"And?" she prodded.

"This is killing you, isn't it?"

"Fine. You've been so miserable over Aggie that it's good to see you not so pissy for a change."

"Did you talk to our fruit vendor?"

"I did. They have a better understanding of what we need."

He nodded and continued working.

What he kept to himself was that he'd been thinking about how he could use Bianca as leverage with Aggie. He wasn't proud of it. But watching what Pierce went through busted some screws loose, making Kevin wonder how far he would go to make Aggie see him as—

"Kevin, I hope this one works out for you. I don't know what happened with Aggie because she's been ignoring me for the past month, too."

"You think it's just the business?"

Sandra straightened. "I walked right by her on the street and she pretended like she didn't see me." She shrugged as if the slight hadn't hurt her feelings. But Kevin knew her better than that.

"She could be embarrassed to talk to you about it," he offered.

Sandra cleared her throat, shifting her weight uneasily. "I don't think that's it. She, uh . . . she knows how loyal we are to each other, and she's probably cutting me out of her life along with you."

He might as well stick the knife in his hand, he thought. It would hurt less than the yawning vacuum in his chest at the thought that Aggie was cutting them off. Maybe in a few months she would be one of those people they'd wonder what she was up to, and talk about in the past tense as if she were just someone they once knew.

A few months? He'd never been a kidder, much less kid himself. No one could fill the void Aggie would leave.

"I'm making some changes to Friday's special menu," he managed, turning to look for a towel to clean the knife and not let her see the pain. "And I'm thinking about taking a tasting trip back East."

He heard her hand squeak across the stainless steel counter and then he felt it rest on his shoulder. "Let me know whatever you decide to do."

Nely wanted to squeeze her head and make all of this drama go away.

She'd driven to her neighborhood and slept in the car, parked across and down the street from her home. No one answered the house phone or her cell phone. But she'd watched the windows. Someone stayed up late in front of the TV, while the other one went to bed upstairs.

Now, still wearing the clothes she'd put on yesterday morning, she turned the corner to cross F Street and nearly tripped over her own feet when she saw Simon standing in the doorway of Lola's.

She wanted to run straight into his arms, leaving Aggie's crazy life behind. Her body erupted in a fine sweat, remembering that powerful dream. When had she forgotten that he was so damn hot? Why had she not been doing him on a regular basis?

"You have a moment?" he asked as she approached.

She remembered to roll her tongue back into her mouth.

But that tough guy cop thing had her smoking. "Uh, yeah."

"I need to know what the hell you and my wife are up to."

"Excuse me, what?"

"Why did she cut you a check for a hundred and twenty-five thousand dollars?"

"She offered it as her investment in the business."

"I didn't even know she had that money. Did you?"

Nely almost answered yes, then remembered she needed to answer as Aggie. "She told me she had it when she offered the money. I'm the one who told her to tell you."

He backed off, shaking his head. "I don't know what the hell is going on. Every time I talk to her, it's like she's not there." He looked back to her. "If you knew something—if you knew she was going to do something—you'd tell her not to, wouldn't you?"

Tell him the truth. Tell him now.

"Simon, there's something you should know."

He seemed to go absolutely still, as if he waited for the executioner's blade to slice through his neck.

"Can we go inside first?" he asked.

Why didn't she just shut up before she made this worse?

"Aggie!" he snapped.

She sucked in as much air as she could before diving in. "When Nely was in labor with Audrey, right before she got her epidural, *Lord of the Rings* was on TV."

"I know that."

"I know you do. That's what I'm trying to say . . ." She shook her head to clear it, to press on. "When I say Nely, I mean me . . . It's me." She pressed both hands to her chest. "This is me, Nely, in here. I couldn't tell you before because I didn't know how—"

"You're out of your fucking mind," he hissed, advancing on her, intimidating her back against the store window. "Stay away from my wife, my daughter, and my house—"

"Simon, listen—"

He slammed the palm of his hand against the door frame, inches from her ear.

She shoved him back. "When we went on our first date, you wore that black corduroy jacket that I later told you I hated." She spoke as fast as she could, intending to spill out all of their most private moments, things she'd never spoken of to another person. Not even Aggie.

And still he didn't see her.

"Simon, I dreamt of you, of us," she said and went on to describe in graphic detail everything they'd done. With her face on fire she said, "I've been here all this time."

"What did I say?" he asked hoarsely. "At the end?"

"You asked me"—her voice broke and hot tears blurred his face—"when I was coming home."

He reached for her, resting his forehead against hers. "Oh God, Nely."

"I know," she said, crying as relief poured through her. "I know."

"I thought I was losing you, that I—" He pulled her into the safety of his chest, wrapping her with arms that wouldn't let go. Life hummed all around them, but they were the only two people on that street. They were two shipwreck survivors who thought they'd lost the other.

She heard his heart pounding in his chest, felt the trembling of his whole being.

"Don't ever do that to me again," he finally whispered

She didn't mean to, but she laughed at that. "I'll never leave you again."

She slid her fingers through his short, bristly hair to bring his lips to hers. But then he jerked back, startled by the face looking back at him. "Nely, I'm sorry," he apologized. "I can't. Not like this."

He shoved her away, hitching his hands onto his hips, unable to look at her as if she were some hideous, one-eyed freak.

"I know," she said, trying not to choke from the rejection. "It took me a while not to have a heart attack every time I looked in the mirror."

She backed away, still shaking from the shock that he believed her, that she didn't have to carry on this masquerade. And yet, she tried to loosen the rock that had lodged in her throat. She told herself that she understood why he couldn't touch her. But it didn't stop the icy cold hurt.

"Let's sit down," she suggested. "I need to tell you how this happened."

"You can go back, right?"

She nodded, still unsteady. "We have one more day till the full moon. Guru Sauro promised to switch us on the full moon."

"I have to ask you something, and I need you to answer me straight."

She met his eyes, and a grin touched his lips.

"There you are," he said softly. "If I look in your eyes, I can see you."

Sobs jerked up from her chest and she had to look away. "I was not having an affair," she said, her voice ragged.

"That wasn't my question," he replied quietly.

He looked like a little kid who dropped a fly in his teacher's soup. "Does Aggie think I look good naked?"

Twenty-eight

When Aggie swept open the curtains, she yelped at the un-expected sight of La Cacuy sitting at the patio table like a cat waiting for someone to let her in.

With a sigh, she opened the sliding glass door.

"Why didn't you knock? I've been home," she said.

La Cacuy gave her a martyr's smile as she straightened her spine, not getting up from her chair. "Ever since my son asked me not to interfere, I thought I would wait."

The full moon is almost here, she reminded herself. Then again, Nely was going to have a hell of a mess on her hands.

"Would you like to come inside and have some coffee?" she invited, hoping to soften some of the edges. "It's kinda cold out here."

Simona was about to answer when her face softened. Audrey muscled her way between Aggie's leg and the door opening. "There's my *mijita*!" La Cacuy called, holding her arms wide.

She reached for Audrey and held her in a tight hug. "Do you know how happy it makes me to know you love me?" she gushed to Audrey. "That you're so happy to see your *abuelita*?"

Dude, this woman played dirty and had no shame about it. Aggie crossed her arms and leaned on the door frame, watching La Cacuy use her own grandkid to guilt her daughter-in-law.

"It's so cold, why isn't she wearing slippers, Nely?" La Cacuy asked, carrying Audrey to the door.

"I have some fresh coffee," Aggie answered with her best impression of La Cacuy's patronizing smile.

"Oh well, I couldn't trespass on your privacy."

"Trespassing is when you walk in without being invited. I'm inviting you in."

As La Cacuy's eyes watered up with tears, Aggie wished she could cry on cue. She'd tried many times, but it was a skill someone had to be born with. La Cacuy pulled it off better than any Mexican novella star.

"No, no. You made it quite clear that I am no longer welcome in your home." She primly unzipped her briefcase and plucked out a file. "This is my checklist for the Halloween party if you decide to go through with it."

"I'm not going to Miss Cheryl's Toddler Time."

"Well," La Cacuy sighed. "I hope you take this much more seriously than you have been. It's Audrey's reputation at stake. These will be her little friends all the way through school, and I don't want her to be an outcast. Since you hadn't stepped up, I assumed—"

"You assumed too much. This is—" She almost said Nely's, but stopped herself. "This is my turn to be a mother."

For a moment La Cacuy looked human. "Then know this: You have no idea how fast time will fly by. One day you're chasing after Audrey, wondering when you'll get a moment of peace and quiet. And then you're chasing your adult child, wishing for just one moment when you could be the most important person in his life, to be the one person he needs all the time."

Aggie wanted to take those words to heart, but she didn't trust the woman. La Cacuy always had a biting comment to whip out at any moment.

"I'll try," she answered carefully.

"And just more thing," La Cacuy said in a quivering voice. "I know you don't want to hear it from me, but you're just going to have to. I see my son trying very hard to please you. You better think hard about what you have to lose."

"Look, unless you go to bed with us every night—"

Simona held up her hand. "Trust me, when Audrey's your age and her husband isn't good enough for her, you'll say something, too."

Aggie opened her mouth. Yes, Nely probably would. She might not always speak up for herself and take a bunch of crap in the process, but Nely would most definitely stand up for her daughter. And when it came time for her to become a mother, she would do the same for her kid.

"Sorry about what happened at Miss Cheryl's," Aggie said, remembering she needed to make nice for Nely's sake. "And thanks for the advice."

"Go inside and get ready for your day," La Cacuy said. Just when Aggie started burning with shame for thinking the woman had another trick up her sleeve, that she'd actually been genuine in sharing her wisdom; La Cacuy struck again. "Did Simon sleep downstairs?"

Aggie went still, like a rabbit sensing the slither of a hungry snake. "No he didn't," she lied.

"Hmm. I thought I saw the TV flickering through the windows," she said, which meant that La Cacuy saw straight through her lie and couldn't wait till Simon left his wife.

Aggie sneered a silent *Bitch*, and slammed the door. Then, as an extra *f-you*, she flipped the lock.

"Come on, Audrey," she said, plucking her up from the floor. "We've got places to go and people to see."

Nely and Simon crossed the street when the light at the corner turned green. She felt lighter on her feet, freer now that he knew. He was still reluctant to touch her, which relieved any insecurity that he had a thing for Aggie's body. But it also hurt at the same time. Still, he knew the truth and she was almost home.

"Your sign said that you would be closed at six."

She turned, and Guru Sauro stood there, behind them. With him was his assistant, Claudine.

"It's only fifteen minutes till eleven," Nely said. "Did you have something in mind you wanted to buy?" she asked, then introduced him to Simon.

Guru Sauro shook his head at Simon's offer of a handshake. "Where's the other one? I need to switch you now."

Nely's heart soared. "Now?"

"No, next week," he spat sarcastically.

"She's at home, I mean at my house."

"Where's that?"

"Half an hour from here."

"Have her come here. It's too far."

She exchanged glances with Simon. "Aggie's apartment is five minutes from here," she told Guru Sauro. "I can have her meet us there."

He jerked his head that her suggestion was minimally acceptable. "I'm hungry. Let's eat there," he decided, and pointed to Sazón.

She sighed. It never could be easy, could it?

"Don't we need to go to the apartment?" she asked. "I could get takeout."

"You said it would take her thirty minutes to get there. I don't want to just sit around and wait."

"But that restaurant isn't open."

Guru Sauro snapped his fingers at Claudine. "Call them and have them open for us."

"You really don't want to eat there," Nely tried one last time.

"I didn't ask your opinion." He proceeded down the street, expecting them to follow.

Simon touched her elbow. "What's up?"

"You know the guy you thought I was having an affair with?"

"No."

"Well, Aggie's in love with him and . . . " She told herself that tomorrow at this time, Kevin would no longer be her problem. "It's so complicated I don't know where to begin."

"Since it involves Aggie, I think I have a good idea."

She jerked her thumb at Guru Sauro. "Can't you just arrest him or shoot him?"

He brushed the strands of hair out of her eyes, tucking them safely behind her ear. "You want to come home, don't you?"

Nely watched Guru Sauro march up the steps to the doors of Sazón while Claudine talked into her cell phone.

"I'll be there with you," Simon said. "You're almost home, Nel."

I'm going home, Aggie told herself as she turned on Via La Cuesta, where Pema lived.

Her heart weighed like a stone in her chest as she thought about leaving Audrey, Pema, and the girls behind. She wished she hadn't made friends with them because once she became Aggie again, she wouldn't mean anything to them.

She glanced in the rearview mirror at Audrey, who looked away from the window and smiled at her.

"Will I still be your dude when I go back?"

Audrey grabbed the armrests of her seat and tried to scoot to and fro as if she could make the van drive faster.

"Your mama will put you to bed tonight and—" A lump formed in her throat when she thought about having to sleep in her place all by herself. "But she won't let you eat as much chocolate as I do. You'll thank her for that one day. So don't be too hard on her."

She made a U-turn at the end of the cul de sac and then stopped at the blue-shingled, single-story house. White impatiens smiled up from the planter underneath the French bay window, and a Halloween wreath of black roses hung on the front door.

Brown needles crunched under Aggie's shoes as she walked up the brick steps to the front door. Naveen's stroller was parked by the door.

"Nely," Pema greeted her.

"Thank you so much for taking Audrey at the last minute—"

"Oh, just come inside. We'll take good care of her, won't we, Naveen?"

They settled in the living room that had been cordoned off with a childproof fence. Naveen and Audrey planted themselves on the floor, keeping a curious but shy distance.

Now that she was here, Aggie didn't know what to say.

"Nely, just because you, uh, slapped Leila the other day doesn't mean we can't be friends," Pema said.

"I know, it's just that—" How could she say good-bye when Pema thought she was Nely, whom she'd probably see at Starbucks next week?

"I'm so relieved," she said, chickening out. "I didn't want to make things awkward for you guys, and—"

"Don't worry. After you left, Miss Cheryl took her into the kitchen. Everyone sided with you. They thought she was way out of line, and she was." Pema leaned forward. "And from the way she looked when she stormed out, I don't know if she'll be around much."

Aggie leaned forward. "Why are you whispering?"

Pema giggled. "It's silly, I know, but she lives across the street."

Aggie craned her neck to peer out the front window.

"Which one?"

Pema gave her an exasperated look. "Which one do you think?"

She picked the 1950s ranch-style house done as a faux Victorian, complete with tacked on gingerbread and tacky, white wrought-iron furniture that a lady would never sit in because of the pattern it would leave on the back of her thighs.

A few minutes later they walked outside.

"There he is," Pema whispered with minimal lip movement. "Don't look yet! Okay, you can look."

Aggie watched an overweight man with plenty of gold around his neck and wrists march across the lawn. His guayabara shirt billowed out at the hem and he wore khaki green pants with woven leather shoes.

She wondered if Leila would have to pour water on his blow hole to keep him alive.

"Leila!" he bellowed. "You comin' with that coffee?"

Leila ran out with a travel coffee cup. He swung around and his briefcase smacked against her hips.

"You spilt on my briefcase," he yelled, cradling it like a newborn infant. "Clean it up!"

"It's only a little drop—"

"Clean it!"

Birds were startled out of the trees.

Nely and Pema tried to hide as Leila's husband berated her, criticizing how she wiped the briefcase, how stupid she was to spill on it, going on and on. Leila kept apologizing, which only seemed to aggravate him.

"You fucking embarrass me, Leila," he said, with one leg in the gold Escalade. "You embarrass me."

His door slammed and the Escalade heaved from side to side as he futzed about the inside of the SUV.

A memory long since forgotten was dislodged from Aggie's memory.

One of the rare times she spent the night at Lauren Bruner's house, she watched Lauren's dad do the same thing to Mrs. Bruner. She didn't have to wonder if Mr. Bruner did the same thing to Lauren, made her mean just like he was.

Something felt all light and fresh inside of her. She wasn't about to run over an give Leila a big ol' hug and forgive her for what she'd said about Audrey.

But she'd be forever grateful to Leila for shooing those old demons out the door. Aggie was ready to go home.

Twenty-nine

Nely stiffened at the shock of Simon's whisper in her ear, "You know, Aggie's really going to owe you when this is over."

"What was that?" Guru Sauro said, negotiating a mouthful of steamed chayote.

Simon answered with a bite of his food while squeezing her thigh under the table. She took some confidence in that Simon was completely unfazed by Guru Sauro.

"Why are you switching us now?" Nely asked.

Guru Sauro's eyes met hers over the rim of his glass. He set it down and went back to his lunch.

Nely turned to Claudine, who sipped her tortilla soup daintily. "Why are you both avoiding my questions?"

Claudine ever so subtly shook her head at Nely to stop asking.

"How do you like the soup, Aggie?" Sandra asked, saying *Aggie* like it was a synonym for bitch.

Nely hadn't ordered soup, but Sandra had served it anyway.

"It's great," she replied. "Thank you."

"You're welcome. It's *asado de bodas*. My brother made it especially for you." Sandra gave Simon a pointed glance, then went back to Nely, questions boiling in her gaze. "We haven't seen much of you lately."

"But you'll see more of me soon," Nely promised.

"How do you know each other?" Sandra challenged.

"I met Guru Sauro—"

"No. I meant *him*." Sandra's razor sharp eyebrows came together in a thunderous frown.

Simon volunteered, "I'm her—"

Nely side-kicked his shin to keep him quiet and gestured toward Guru Sauro with her knife. "He's his police protection."

"More wine," the guru demanded. Sandra grabbed his glass but didn't budge one inch from their table.

"Is he *your* police protection, too, Aggie?" Sandra could see Simon's hand resting on Nely's thigh.

Simon shook from suppressed laughter, and Nely positioned her heel so she could stab the top of his foot with it.

"What's the matter with you?" Guru Sauro demanded. "I'll need a stick to shovel all this food down my throat. Go!"

Nely slumped with relief when Sandra left the table.

"Excellent food but noisy service," Guru Sauro said.

Simon went back to his food.

"I'll ask again," Nely started. "How come you want to switch us now?"

He focused all of his attention on his food.

"You made it sound like nothing was possible without the full moon."

He shrugged and kept eating.

"How long have you been working for your father?" Simon asked Claudine, the assistant.

She jumped at being directly addressed. "Six years."

Guru Sauro banged the side of her bowl with his fork. "Go get me some *jamaicha*."

Claudine left the table.

"No more questions," the guru said. "I have my reasons."

"You're dealing with her life," Simon said, a threat vibrating softly in his voice. "With my daughter's mother and my wife."

Guru Sauro regarded him quietly. "Women make men weak."

"A weak man is weak no matter what," Simon countered.

"Women only give men something to lose. My wife is the one who made me build that resort and all the books and . . . and then she went off and died on me. She left me with all of it."

Simon leaned forward. "Switch her back," he said simply.

Guru Sauro shifted his eyes to Nely and then back to Simon. "Tell Claudine to get the bill."

Out of habit, Aggie walked through the back door of Sazón. She sensed Kevin nearby. Maybe he was in his office or she'd turn the corner and practically walk into him as he made his rounds of the kitchen.

She straightened one side of her chocolate-colored cardigan and then ran her fingers over her eyebrows.

Sandra whizzed by and then backed up. "Can I help you?"

Aggie opened her mouth but nothing came out. "Sorry I—I'm looking for, uh, Aggie."

Sandra's smile collapsed. "Oh. She's in the dining room." She stopped short when she saw Simon at the table.

Nely looked up and then walked over.

"What's going on?" Aggie said, keeping a wary eye on Simon.

Nely lowered her chin, staring at Aggie like she'd just sprouted a third head. "He's right there," she murmured, jerking her head toward Guru Sauro.

"Not him," Aggie snapped. She mouthed, *Kevin*.

"He hasn't come out of the kitchen. They think you're with Simon."

Aggie couldn't keep up. "What's Simon doing here?"

"I told him."

"You what?"

"He believed me. And he . . ." Nely paused. "He's taking care of the bill."

"So does Kevin know you're here?"

Nely shook her head.

"All this time and he hasn't tried to seduce me?" Aggie asked, strangely hurt, yet also relieved that Kevin hadn't hit on Nely.

She tugged her sweater down and smoothed it as she casually glanced at the mirror until the air seemed to heat. A low hum started in her ears, drowning out the sounds of footsteps and chairs groaning against the floor and of murmuring voices. A figure moved into the reflection and then disappeared out of the frame. He was near and her awareness of him paralyzed her.

Heart trampling around in her chest, Aggie stared into the mirror, too afraid to see him in the flesh and yet dying for just one look. Her ears twitched up at the cadence of his decisive footsteps, his long chef's apron flapping against his legs. And then his reflection joined hers. But his eyes were riveted to Nely.

"Who's that?" his deep voice demanded.

Kevin flicked his eyes over Aggie, which would normally have frightened small children.

"That's Guru Sauro," she answered dismissively.

"No. The other—"

"Hi, Kevin," Aggie heard herself say. "How are you?"

Kevin glanced over at her, realizing someone else was actually standing there. "Hi, how are— Do I know you?"

Words scrambled in her head. Aggie's breath tightened into short, hard pants.

"We should go," Nely said, and Aggie felt a tug on her arm.

"I'm dating someone," Kevin told Nely, and Aggie's face went cold. "I thought you'd want to know."

"Oh," Nely breathed, and Aggie couldn't look at the confused pity on her face.

"I'm tired of this, Agg," Kevin said. "If you want to move on, then move on. But don't do it under my nose."

Simon, finished taking care of the bill, came up to Nely and Aggie. "We have to go," he said, then took notice of Kevin.

"Kevin, I'm so sorry, but—" Nely tried to keep up the pretense but couldn't. She'd run out of energy for it. "Aggie," she said, sending her a silent apology.

"Come on," Simon urged, and Nely walked out with him.

Kevin's face hardened into an expressionless mask. He made an abrupt turn.

Aggie caught his arm before he walked off. "Kevin—"

His eyes met hers and for a moment she thought she saw them flicker with recognition. But then he tore his arm away from her grip, looking at her like she was nuts. She'd seen him like this only once before, back when he tried not to cry as he returned the gifts he'd bought for his mother.

"I'll come back to you," she promised. Somehow, she moved her feet from there to the door and then out to the sidewalk. When she snapped the buckle of her seat belt in the minivan, she realized her hand was still warm from touching him.

Kevin still hadn't moved. The one who said she would come back . . .

He wanted to physically reach into his head and pull that moment out so it would stop playing over and over.

His cell phone burred in his pocket.

"Yeah?"

"It's me."

The voice didn't immediately strike a bell.

"Bianca," she teased. "Are you busy? Is this a bad time?"

"No," he said, pressing his fingers against his forehead. "What's going on?"

"I don't know." She giggled. He hated giggles. "I just wanted to call and say hey."

"We're still on tonight for drinks," he said, to get her off the phone.

"We are. Make it a great day, all right?"

"Right." He snapped the phone shut, went back into the kitchen and wondered what he was supposed to do next.

Thirty

"Aggie, please get up," Nely murmured to the lump on the bed.

"I can't."

"Kevin was confused. He thought you were with Simon and—"

"How come Simon knew it was you?"

Nely's hands trembled from the need to shake her friend. She didn't have time for this. Not now. They were so close, so close. "I told you, I told him—"

"And he believed you?"

"Aggie," she said. "Please pull it together. I've missed almost a month of my daughter's life. I'll never get that back and I just want to go home."

"And leave me with this mess?"

Nely proceeded cautiously. "The store is getting back on its feet and I'll help you bring it back. As for the . . . well—"

Aggie shot up. "Did you get my wax like I told you to?"

"Well, not really." Nely fought back a grin. Aggie was coming around.

"You didn't shave it, did you?"

"No! I'm not touching you down there. Have you touched me down there?"

"I should've taken you in out of spite."

Nely cringed.

"Now it'll start growing in," Aggie whined. "I'll have to start all over again."

"Does that mean it will hurt more?"

"Yeah."

"Good."

Aggie swatted her arm. "Hey, we made a promise. I'd take care of Audrey and you'd take care of my bush."

"Maybe Kevin prefers a natural look. If anyone can get him to come around, it'll be you."

Aggie shook her head sadly, but at least she didn't start crying.

"Anyway," Aggie sighed, "I don't want to talk about it anymore."

"You know what's funny?"

"If our men don't work out, we could be like Mrs. Muir and—"

"Don't you start thinking I'm living with you," Nely said, reaching for Aggie's hand. "You're too picky."

"Shut up."

They were quiet for a moment and then Aggie let go of Nely's hand.

Aggie sighed. "My work is cut out for me. He's one ornery bastard."

Nely nodded, deciding not to tell Aggie that she was the

woman he was dating. "Just so you know, the older they get, the worse they get."

Aggie swung her legs off the bed. "Let's go. But I need some chocolate first. I think I have a box of Snickers in the freezer."

Nely quirked her lips guiltily. "I ate those."

"All of them?"

"You made my husband think I was cheating on him."

"Yeah, but—the whole box?" Aggie whined, and looked down at her chest to make sure she wasn't bleeding from the daggers coming out of Nely's stare.

Aggie blew out her breath. They were moments away from getting on with their lives. She had woken up every morning thinking it was one day closer. But then, somewhere along the way, she wanted to hold onto those days rather than hurry through them.

If only she wasn't wishing she was at Nely's house, with Audrey messing around. It had become easier taking Nely's ready-made life than making it happen herself.

He had them sit facing each other with a shallow bowl of water between them. All the shades were drawn and doors closed. Nely couldn't pull in enough air to fill her lungs. The anticipation, the fear that it would hurt—because it had— seemed to strip away all of the oxygen.

She gripped her hands, feeling her finger bones fight the crush. Simon was waiting with Claudine in the bedroom. When she saw him again, she would be herself.

"I'll be right in there," Simon had murmured to her. She'd been afraid to let him go and hadn't needed to say it. "Don't think about anything but switching back, okay? This will all be over with soon."

Nely touched her cheek where Simon had kissed her. Guru Sauro began walking around them with a bundle of smoking herbs.

"This is the smoky mirror," he intoned, "a tool of the *naguals* to—"

"Yeah, we know," Aggie interrupted. "Let's get this over with."

"—to see the reflection of the soul," he continued, emphasizing the words to keep her quiet. "I draw the sacred circle counterclockwise to undo what has been done, to open the doors to these souls so they may return to their rightful places."

Nely looked at Aggie. Her body seemed slimmer than she remembered. Had Aggie been starving her?

"Close your eyes and listen to the drum," he instructed, then swatted the air near Aggie's ear. "Stop scratching your nose. Pay attention."

His leathery hand smacked a small, primitive drum as he walked the circle.

Nely shut her eyes, waiting to be lulled into the same state as on the night they were on the top of the mountain. What if she saw Helen again? What would she say to her?

She readjusted her posture. The rug itched her behind. A motorcycle roared down the street.

She released her hands and set them on her knees. Nothing was happening. She pushed all thoughts out of her head. No more Simon, Audrey, or Kevin, or any of it.

She squeezed her eyes tighter. She bore down. *Focus*, she told herself. She didn't have any ruby red slippers to get back. Guru Sauro was her only way home.

Then why wasn't anything happening? Why wasn't she—

A horrendous noise shook the floor. Her eyes snapped open, expecting to see the gold light outlining her body. She looked in the bowl of water. But she didn't see her reflection; Aggie's face stared back at her.

Aggie scrambled up to her hands and knees and scrambled away. The bedroom door swung open.

"What happened?" Simon asked, Claudine standing behind him.

"Shit. I don't think he's breathing," Aggie said.

Simon ran over to Guru Sauro, who had been the horrendous noise that shook the floor.

"No pulse, call 911," Simon said.

"Papa!" Claudine cried, shaking his hand as if to wake him up.

"*What?*" It was more of a rush of air from Nely's lungs than a word.

Aggie twisted around and grabbed the phone.

"Nely!" Simon called her.

She looked at him, her breath caught in her chest like a bird trying to fly through a closed window. His shoulders slumped when he realized she was still in Aggie's body.

"Go in there with Audrey," he said quietly.

She couldn't bring herself to watch Simon pump his hands against Guru Sauro's chest. Lying next to his hand was his eagle feather. She rose up and then her knees gave out.

"One of mama's boyfriends once had a heart attack on her," Aggie said, just to keep talking while Claudine climbed into the back of the ambulance. "He was fine after a few weeks. But mama dumped him when he couldn't— When he was incapable."

Nely flinched when the ambulance doors slammed. The lights danced over her pale, stoic face, which looked like marble in the gray twilight.

Aggie refused to think about what they would do if—

"He will be better by the next full moon," she insisted. "We can do this. Simon knows, and that will be more helpful—"

"Simon won't touch me," Nely said quietly. "Not like this."

Her first thought was an indignant, *Why not?* But then she imagined Kevin making love to Nely in her body and the only thing she could say was, "I'm so sorry Nely, I—"

Nely spun away and walked off.

Aggie began to shake, the muscles in her face leaping and bucking as she strained against the tears. She held it in because she knew that crying wouldn't do her any good. It wouldn't help her with the store or to get Kevin back. The one way back, the *only* way for them to have returned home, was now gone.

She looked out at the city, the downtown towers twinkling against a sky of dark lilac. Her skin prickled from the sudden breeze, and she wondered what Kevin was doing at that moment. Was he thinking of her, or, no matter what would've happened, was she too late?

Nely had no destination in mind as she turned into the courtyard garden. Vintage homes the color of lacquer jewelry boxes had been reconfigured on a plot of land. In the center garden, lemon and orange trees were planted in a miniature grove. Sunflowers were held up by tall stakes, like old women leaning on canes. The air smelled thick of lavender and mint.

Her feet crunched on the gravel path, and she'd just registered someone behind her when heavy arms wrapped around her, one around her waist and the other her neck.

"There you are, bitch."

Before she could scream her feet rose off the ground and Jeff carried her, the garden retreating from her line of vision.

She twisted and kicked and the pressure on her throat choked off her air.

"You die here or—" He paused to tickle the shell of her ear with his pointed tongue. "Or you see what I have for you."

Nely cringed from his breath and the moisture it left on her skin. She went limp, and he toppled over to keep his grip. She broke free, the gravel biting into the palms of her hands as she crawled away, hoping there was a way out of the courtyard. She made it to the sunflowers and looked back over her shoulder. She didn't see his fist coming until her head swung back and a light exploded in her right eye.

Nely heard someone yell, "Hey!" and then she stumbled, throwing her hands out to catch her fall.

Jeff caught her around the waist, her backside cupped by his hips. Her stomach heaved at the feel of his body draped over hers. She tried to scream, or maybe she did, but the pain in her face seemed to paralyze her whole body.

"Come on," he said over and over again, dragging her to the street.

"Wait," she whispered as he walked her to a car, his grip on her wrist squeezing the blood out of her hand.

Where was Simon? Aggie? Why weren't they helping her?

She heard the *thunk* of the car doors unlocking and dug her feet into the ground. "No," she sobbed, leaning her body away from the black Mercedes.

"Fuck," he cursed, then tugged her so hard her feet skidded. It happened so fast. The back of her head bounced off the headrest, and the car door shook the whole car after he slammed it.

"Wait," she said, slapping her palm on the window. "Wait!"

She tried the door handle but it was locked. She tried to look for the button to unlock the doors but couldn't find them on the door.

He slid into the driver's seat, his shoulder bumping against hers. He stabbed the key in her face, aiming it right at her eye. "Don't," he ordered, and she went still. "Do not."

"Jeff—" She gasped when he thrust the key closer. She blinked and her eyelashes caught on the metal point.

"You will not speak until I say you can." He waited, making sure she heard him. His excited breath warmed her cheek. "Now put on your seat belt."

She reached up over her shoulder and his eyes latched onto her hand, following it as she pulled the seat belt across her body. His eyes lingered on her chest, his nostrils flaring. Saliva filled her mouth as she smelled his breath.

"Much better." His smile was almost eerily normal.

"Nely!" She heard Simon yell through the window.

Jeff swung the giant sedan into the street as she turned to the window, catching a glimpse of Simon's face as he chased the car.

But Jeff barked, "Don't!"

She jumped in her seat, her heart beating up a frenzy that was almost painful.

"Look straight ahead," he told her.

She obeyed as sobs clogged up her throat. She should've fought harder. She should've screamed her head off. She never should've gotten into his car, now her cage. He could take her anywhere. He could do whatever he wanted to her.

Oh God, what if he killed her? What would Simon do? What about Audrey?

They sped down the hill, not slowing as he swung them onto the south 5 freeway.

"It didn't have to be this way," he said calmly. She suppressed a flinch when his hot hand squeezed and released her knee, like a pulsing starfish. "You could have made this much easier."

Her skin suddenly erupted into chills as adrenaline seeped into her bloodstream. Her heart beat at a steadier rate. When they arrived at wherever he was taking her, she would fight. She would claw at his face until her fingernails were ripped out; she would scream till her voice gave out. She would survive whatever he would do to her.

Thirty-one

"Did you get his license plate?" Aggie yelled, running after Simon.

"I'm with 911 . . . Hey, this is Detective Mendoza . . ."

A fear so cold gripped her very bones as she listened to him call in Nely's kidnapping. She watched the brake lights of the Mercedes flash and then the car turn the corner at the bottom of the hill.

Then they were in Simon's minivan and the engine came to life, the wheels squealing as he punched the gas with his foot.

A truck swerved around them as Simon pulled out. She braced her arm on the dash as he zoomed up to the truck, tailgating it, blaring the horn, determined to catch up with

Nely before she disappeared. The truck driver deliberately slowed down, rolled down his window and flipped them off.

"Not now!" Simon shouted, and floored the accelerator to shoot around it.

Where in the hell are the cops when you need them? she thought, remembering the times she'd been pulled over for speeding.

But in the back of her mind she admired the way Simon maneuvered around the truck and sped through the intersection just in time for them to see Psycho Dick's Mercedes head up the freeway ramp. The light turned yellow and Simon sped up, though they were still half a block away.

"You all right?" he asked tightly as the digital bars on the speedometer climbed.

Aggie pressed her back against the seat, praying for one more miracle from her mama. "I can handle it if you can."

Simon gripped the steering wheel as he sent the van into a blur of silver.

Tires screamed as he cranked the wheel to the left, then he caught the wheel before the back fishtailed into a spin.

Seeing Nely in that car, the white look of fear on her face, his uselessness ached so deep and vicious that it almost squeezed the breath out of him.

The van bounced as he hit the dip in the street and then flew up the on ramp. He prayed that psycho fuck didn't know they had his tail. He might try to hurt her.

"Do you know where this guy lives?" he asked Aggie.

She shook her head.

He popped out of the lane to speed around a Volkswagen going the speed limit.

What was he going to do without Nely? How would he raise Audrey, how would he ever tell her that he—

The things he'd done and hadn't done wound their tentacles around his throat.

They flew up the Coronado Bridge, climbing higher and higher over the wavering bay. The suicide prevention signs and the downtown skyscrapers were just a blur in his peripheral vision. There were just two lanes going to the island, to accommodate traffic heading to the mainland.

Simon methodically planned what he would do when they arrived wherever this asshole was taking his wife. His gun was hidden under his clothing.

A sound shot out of Aggie's mouth when the Mercedes up ahead swerved toward the low-lying barrier that kept cars from falling into a watery grave hundreds of feet below. Sparks exploded from the car scraping against the concrete wall.

"Simon!" Aggie shouted. "Do something!"

"Call 911 again," he yelled back.

He sped up alongside the Mercedes. Nely's face was contorted with rage as she clawed and punched at the driver.

"Oh sh—" Simon said, and hit the brake before they headed into the back of a Ford F-150.

The Mercedes swept forward, and he jumped back into the right lane.

A helpless sound erupted from his tightly coiled control. He hadn't wanted to cry for help since he was in the fifth grade and Paul Lopez kicked him in the nuts at recess. Just as he clamped down on his rising panic, the brake lights of the Mercedes flashed as it careened into the back of an SUV.

* * *

The Mercedes jerked back toward the center of the bridge and then shuddered as Charles fought to right it.

Nely had been prepared to bide her time, but then his sweaty hand crept up her thigh and he tried to feel if she was wearing panties under her skirt. He thought he'd scared her enough that he could do whatever he wanted to her.

Rage exploded, and as silent as death, she grabbed a hunk of his hair and yanked as hard as she could until he lay halfway across the car.

She spewed a litany of the foulest words she could think of as she smacked him with her open palm, hitting any part of him that she could get.

"Stop! Stop!" he cried.

She slammed against the door when the car hit the side barrier, momentarily knocking her out of the black fury. The horrible screech of metal scraping concrete hurt her teeth.

Jeff managed to sit up and right the car. Then he turned to her, eyes glazed with lust and hatred.

"You—"

She blocked the elbow he aimed at her face, hardly feeling the pain in the fleshy part of her arm.

"Don't," she repeated as she pounded her fists on his shoulder and the arm he was using to protect himself.

As her fists went numb and her arm muscles ached with fatigue, Nely fought for Audrey and Simon as well as herself. It no longer mattered that she wasn't in her own skin. She might never get to go home again, but the instinct to survive erased all of that from her mind.

"Stop!" he yelled over the screaming rage in her head as she pummeled him. "You're going to kill us."

"I'm going to kill you, you fuck," was the last thing she said before a horrible eruption threw her forward, the edges of the seat belt biting into her skin as white exploded against her face.

"You're quiet tonight," Bianca said. "Is everything all right?"

Kevin stifled a yawn to pop his ears again. He hated high rises, but Bianca had made a reservation at the Top of the Hyatt. They were tucked away at a table for two, right against the glass overlooking the Coronado Bridge stretching across the bay that danced with lights from the shore.

He didn't know why or what, but some unknown thing tickled the back of his neck. He wanted to look over his shoulder to see who watched him. And yet, he knew no one would be there. It was a sense that something was off, like he'd hit his head and lost a part of his life.

"Sorry, something with the restaurant," he lied to Bianca, to ease the worry straining the corners of her smile.

"Ah, yes. Don't tell me you're one of those types who never stop working," she begged jokingly. But there was no joke in her eyes. "I must have a sign on my back that attracts workaholics."

It hit him that she was hoping there would be something between them. But he squirmed with guilt that he'd told Aggie he was dating someone. He never lied, never played games, but he'd done it to see what she would do.

He took a deep breath, determined to be a gentleman with Bianca. He just wasn't feeling it, and she seemed like a nice woman who didn't deserve to be strung along.

"I've been accused of staying focused on work." He softened that with a grin.

"That's one way of putting it. What do you do when you're not at work?"

Bicker with Sandra, golf with his brother-in-law, he ticked off in his head. Cook dinner for Aggie.

"Are you involved with someone?" she asked, and then forced down a swallow of her wine.

"Yes . . . no . . ." He sighed.

The answer was yes. Yes, he was involved whether he liked it or not. He had to find Aggie. He just had to lay it all out on the line and tell her how he felt. No more games or screwing around. "I'm sorry Bianca but—"

"Don't," she snapped, her smile flipped upside down as she grabbed her bag. "I'll let you finish your drink."

He opened his mouth to protest, then realized she didn't want to sit through the awkward silence or be the one left sitting at the table.

He should say something profound, he thought, something that would keep her from thinking it was her fault. But he had nothing.

He stood up when she rose from her seat. "I wasted your time," he apologized. "I'm sorry."

She smiled, just a movement of her mouth, and avoided looking into his eyes. "Don't be. You're just one more man who doesn't fit."

That was one way of looking at it, he supposed, waving at the waiter for the check.

His cell phone rang in his pocket. Damn it. Sandra got to it again and changed his ring tone to the *Sex and the City* theme.

"What?"

"Where are you?" Sandra asked.

"At the Hyatt, why?"

"I'm coming to get you."

"What? Why?"

Her breath shuddered, and in the background he heard his brother-in-law tell her it would be okay. Kevin felt the building sway, or maybe it was his knees.

"It's Aggie," Sandra managed. "Her friend Nely just called and said she was in an accident. We have to get there now. It's that bad, Kevin."

Thirty-two

"What do you mean you won't talk to me?" Simon demanded. "She's my—"

"Simon!" Aggie shouted before he said anything more in
front of the E.R. doctor. She pulled him away, which was
like trying to drag a wall.

"Simon, they think she's me," she said. "Let her talk
to me."

"Why?" He forced his breath through his bared teeth, and
she told herself not to be afraid of him. She'd never seen
him like this.

"I made Nely my emergency contact. They think they
have me in there." She shuddered at the thought of her
body in the other room. But she kept herself together. Barely. "They'll talk to me, so just stand with me, okay?"

He whipped away from her, walked straight toward the
wall and slowly, deliberately, hit it with his fist.

"If he doesn't calm down," Dr. Mahal warned, "I'm calling security."

Aggie hurried over. "He's her hus—fiancé. He loves her and they— Just tell me everything."

With another cautious look at Simon, Dr. Mahal told her that Nely had three broken ribs, a broken femur, and a minor concussion. They suspected internal bleeding, and she'd been taken into surgery.

"We'll keep you updated," Dr. Mahal finished. "Please wait here and I'll find you as soon as I know anything new."

"Thank you," Aggie whispered, and pulled Simon away.

"This is your fault," he said, yanking his arm out of her grip. "Don't touch me again."

He sat on one side and she sat on the other, tight as a knot, with arms hugging her middle, legs crossed at the knee, and ankles locked tight. She'd gnawed at the inside of her mouth until the flesh tasted coppery with blood.

If she lost Nely, she'd lose everything. Kevin was lost to her. He hadn't seen her when she tried to tell him. Simon wouldn't let her anywhere near him or Audrey. Without Nely, she would have no one.

The doors swept open, letting in another gust of cold air and letting out a father whose son now wore an arm cast. Those left waiting were worn-down with boredom or shell shocked with terror.

Each click of the second hand on the clock next to the TV felt like an hour. The doctor promised she'd come out when she had news. How much longer would it take?

"Are you asleep?"

She hadn't realized she'd fallen asleep when her eyes flipped open to Nely bending over her.

"I thought they were— Wait." Aggie realized her eyes

were shut but somehow she was awake. "What's wrong? What are you doing here?"

"I don't know. I just woke up here."

Aggie stared up at Nely, who flared with light; light poured off her face, her shoulders, and dripped down her fingertips. She trembled at the sight, not sad nor afraid to see her friend, because surely her body had given out and released Nely.

"I just wanted to go home, Aggie."

Aggie knew if there was any chance, *any*, it was up to her. She could stay in Nely's body and live. Or she could let Nely go back to her husband and her daughter.

"When we were on the mountain, I could see you like this," Aggie said, knowing that Nely's window was closing with each passing moment. "When you touched me, we switched. Touch me now."

"But you won't make it, Agg."

"I know," Aggie said, her throat swelling with tears. "If I don't make it, maybe I can hang out and see who's in labor. I always said I should've been born to a rich family."

She had always thought that when she faced her end, she would be terrified. But now she realized that she might see her mama again, and Simon would have Nely, and Nely would have Simon and Audrey. When she left, everything would get back to they way it should.

But then Kevin's face appeared in her mind, the way he looked asleep in her bed on that morning she woke up laying next to him. And she thought of what could have been, of her missed opportunity. She felt no fear, only sadness that she would go without being able to tell Kevin that she loved him from the moment she met him.

"Just touch me," Aggie said before she lost the guts to do

what was right. "I'll try to hold on but—" She looked at Nely, and there was so much love in those eyes. "If I don't make it, name your next kid after me."

"What if it's a boy?" Nely asked.

"Get creative."

Nely reached out slowly, wanting to draw out this last moment. When her hand handed on Aggie's, she watched Aggie slowly lose color. "It's not that bad," she heard Aggie say.

The moment was quiet as Nely felt herself falling. Aggie's voice was no more, but Nely read her lips as she told her *I love you* for the last time.

It felt like cool water trickling under her skin as Nely opened her eyes, now sitting on the bench, staring across the room at the healthy food posters mounted behind plexiglass on the wall.

Voices calling for doctors and patients squawked out of the PA. She blinked against the green-tinged light that bore down on her eyes and went still when she saw her hands clasped in her lap.

Oh God. She lifted them up, stretched the fingers as much as she could stand it, and then curled into fists. Her gaze popped across the room, searching for him.

She shot up to her feet, stumbled but caught herself from falling. He sat at the farthest corner, bent over, elbows on knees, clutching his head between his hands.

Tears stung her eyes as she moved toward him as silent as a spirit. No one looked at her like a miracle occurred. A woman crossed in front of her and a man pulled his feet back from the walkway.

"Simon?" she called down to him, reaching to touch the hair

that was shaven in a ruler straight line over his dark neck.

He swatted her hand away. "I'm not interested in talking to you."

"It's me, babe. I'm back."

His head shot up. He stared at her for what felt like forever. He surged up to his feet and wrapped her in his arms.

He shook so bad that he couldn't talk.

"Aggie and I—" She tried to explain but the loss of her friend choked her up. "She came to me and—"

"Oh my God," he said over and over again. "Oh my God."

"I never meant to leave you and Audrey. Please don't think that I didn't love you."

He grabbed her head and kissed her, sealing his mouth over hers as if she would save his very life.

"I thought—" he tried, but then couldn't get the words out.

"Excuse me, Mrs. Mendoza?"

Nely broke from Simon's hold. A doctor stood there with a mask dangling from her neck, surgery cap still affixed over black hair.

Nely wiped her tears off her face, searching for some clue as to what news she was about to hear. But this doctor's young, serious face gave nothing away.

"Would you sit down with me, please?"

"Of course," Nely murmured, holding onto Simon's hand to keep from sinking into the floor.

"Are you Nely?" Kevin appeared out of nowhere with Sandra on his heels.

"I am," Nely choked out.

"What's going on?" he demanded. "Where is she?"

"I'm about to find out."

Kevin realized the doctor was standing right there. A tremor visibly shook him, and then his face turned into a mask. Nely watched him prepare himself for the worst.

The shadows moved and then shrunk as the light broke through. Kevin's voice murmured somewhere in the room, and Aggie followed it through the shapeless mass of dark and light before her eyes. The voice then changed to Nely's, who said, "It's me."

With a snap, Aggie was there, floating above the room.

Her body lay on the gurney, hooked up to machines. Doctors and nurses pumped air into her chest, while barking at one another in a single-minded quest to save her life.

Aggie knew this was it. She looked around the room, hoping to see the light or Mama coming to get her.

Well, now what? She took another look around for Mama or the tunnel. Nothing.

She stared down at her body. Bruises and cuts marred her face.

"Well?" Aggie said out loud to no one in particular. "Am I supposed to wait around?"

Suddenly her eyes snapped open, staring back up at her. One of the machines sent out a long squeal made familiar by many episodes of *ER*. Her body had flat-lined. Game over. Stick a fork in her. She was done.

She tried to think about the bright side. She could talk someone into letting her be Heaven's official cocktail hostess, or she'd finally be born to wealth, as she had always wished.

But really, she would've liked to grow old with all of them.

"Dr. Mahal, do you want to call the time of death?"

At that moment the reality of death didn't seem so enlightening and peaceful. What was so wrong with her that she couldn't make it back? This was the age of modern medicine, when they could separate two-headed kids and stuff like that.

Suddenly the atmosphere changed, the air moved. Aggie felt something—a presence—enter the hospital

"What's going on? Where is she?" Kevin asked.

Kevin was here. He'd come for her and it was too late.

But her vision flashed and then slowly faded. She fought to stay focused, to pull against the chains shackling her legs, if she had them, to the ceiling. They dragged heavier and heavier the harder she tried moving closer to her body.

But she was getting closer, inch by excruciating inch.

She suddenly froze, paralyzed when she hovered within reach of the bed. The dark closed in from all sides as the doctor looked up at the clock on the wall and then back down at her.

Fight, fight, Aggie told herself as she reached out with her arms, stretched her fingers until they shook with the strain to touch her foot.

"Hold on," Dr. Mahal muttered, pulling the back of her hand over her forehead.

Aggie's vision lost all color and everything went gray. Her strength gave out, flowing out of her like someone had unplugged the sink. She began to sink to the floor.

With what little shred of strength that she had left, she rose up on her toes, giving her just enough leverage to brush the tips of her fingers against her foot. The dark swooped in and a horrible pain shattered her into millions of pieces before she could even think to say one last good-bye.

Thirty-three

They found Claudine on her cell phone, sitting in one of the phone booths by the front door.

Nely knocked on the glass, startling her.

"You signed a waiver of liability form," Claudine was saying, "when you—"

"Is Guru Sauro all right?" Nely asked, cutting into her legal defense.

Claudine touched her throat and fought to swallow. She could only nod her head.

"We switched back," Nely told her. "Is there something you could do for me?"

Claudine stiffened as if she had no choice but to take the blow.

"He took my friend's rhinestone star pendant," Nely managed through the emotions clogging her throat. "I want it back. For her."

Keeping the phone wedged between her ear and shoulder, Claudine leaned down and picked up a bag off the floor. A crinkling of plastic and then she held out her fist to Nely.

Nely placed her open palm under it and caught Aggie's pendant.

"He was going to give it back," Claudine said. "My dad was a good man but—" Her lips trembled as tears seeped down her face. "He said that a woman was haunting him at night. She'd pull off his bed sheet and tell him to give it back to her baby. That's why he showed up so unexpectedly. I think she really freaked him out."

Stunned, Nely closed her hand over Aggie's pendant. So Helen had been looking out for her girl.

"Is he going to be okay?" Nely asked.

"They think so. It was a heart attack. I kept trying to get him to come to the doctor, but he wouldn't." She cleared her throat and then asked, "Why are you here?"

Nely swayed on her feet but Simon's steady hand gave her strength. "It's a long story. But everything's going to be all right."

"You're not going to sue us, are you?" Claudine asked.

"No," Nely said, and shook her head. She walked away with Simon at her side. The main doors swept open for a pregnant woman in a pink jogging suit followed by her husband carrying an exercise ball and two overnight bags.

"Hurry up," his wife barked over her shoulder.

As the couple hurried by to deliver their baby, Dr. Mahal's words came back to Nely. *I've never seen anything like it. Your friend is a real fighter.*

Standing beside her, Kevin had made a noise like he'd been

punched. Sandra bent over her knees, her hands covering her face. But Nely had smelled jasmine in the air. Somehow, some way, they had all made it.

The memory kicked her knees out from under her, and Simon stopped walking, pulling her against him so she could cry it out again.

"At this rate," he murmured into her ear, "we're never going home."

"It feels wrong to leave her here alone."

"You think Kevin's leaving her side? That guy'll piss in a coffee can if that's what he has to do."

A laugh came out of her from nowhere.

"Come on," he urged. "Audrey's waiting for us."

The only way Aggie could describe it was that her mind was a like computer that finally snagged a wireless signal and came back online.

"Am I dead?" she must have murmured, because someone jerked beside her and then grabbed her fingers.

"Not yet," came Kevin's voice.

That got her attention. She forced her eyelids open but could only manage the tiniest slit. She remembered then what her face looked like on the gurney. *Crap*.

"Stop worrying about how you look," he snapped impatiently. But there was a tremor in his voice. "I've seen you in your underwear. That'll hold me for a while."

"Is it that bad?"

He cleared his throat. "They said you might be thirsty. You want some water?"

Well, at least she hadn't scared him away. She nearly moaned when the cold water hit her rough throat.

"How bad am I?" she persisted after finishing off the cup.

When Kevin listed her injuries, she bravely told herself it was nothing that Vicodin and champagne couldn't take care of.

"I love you," she said without thinking, without pretense. Hey, she knew how easily, how quickly, it could all end. And when it all went black in the O.R., she figured she was dead.

So just in case, she thought, she might as well get it out of the way.

"The guy is supposed to be the first one to say it," Kevin replied.

She smiled even though it burned the left side of her face. "Then that makes you the girl in the relationship."

His breath hitched on a sob. She wanted to reach out and touch him, to comfort him and let him know that she was whole, she was here, and she was his.

"This is it, Agg," he finally said, the intensity of his gaze burning through her slitted gaze. "There's no one else for either of us. It's all or nothing."

Suddenly everything in her fluttered into tiny golden pieces and then settled into something solid, something she'd take with her no matter what happened to her. For the first time ever in her life, she felt like she was just beginning and all the shit that had happened in the past happened to someone else.

She squeezed his hand with all her might, unable to summon words to match the happiness that seemed too big for her body.

"I'd kiss you but it would probably hurt," he said. "I got

something for you—Actually, Nely got it." He peered into her face. "Can you see me?"

"Yes," she said, with an eye roll he probably couldn't see.

Her rhinestone star caught the light from the window and twinkled as he held it up for her.

"You know what your mom once said to me?"

She couldn't speak.

"Out of the blue she told me that I could marry you if I wanted."

"What did you say?"

"I asked her how much she'd been drinking." That bad little boy smile brightened his face. "And then I thought she jinxed me because I started seeing you differently. But she was right. We were the ones stumbling along like idiots when we were right there beside each other."

Sappy moron, Aggie thought, then sent a thank-you up to her mama.

"I promise, Agg, I'll do whatever it takes to make you happy."

But he was her sappy moron.

She ignored the pain in her fingers when she squeezed his hand.

"You already have."

Thirty-four

One year later . . .

"He won't let me see what they're doing," Aggie complained when Kevin kicked her out of his kitchen. "I just want to make sure everything is perfect."

"You think he won't make it perfect?" Nely asked, oddly pleased that her high-maintenance friend had married a man who was quite possibly even higher maintenance.

But then, there was no one more dedicated than Kevin, who was working his crew to their early demise so that Sazón's catering was impeccable for his bride's major event.

"Do you see the box cutter?" Nely asked.

"Here. Take mine. Before I kill my husband."

Nely accepted the box cutter and went back to work setting up the new and improved Whatever Lolita Wants: a combination of the old boutique with the flare of a hip maternity section. The launch party was an hour away, and a shipment of Tarina Tarantino jewelry had just made it in time.

For the last two weeks, women had been salivating over the mannequins posed before the ceiling-to-floor, red velvet curtains in the window. A local morning news anchor fueled buzz about the boutique by wearing some of the maternity clothing they would be selling. Invitations had been mailed as the word got out, and calls poured in from people asking to be invited.

Nely drew in a deep breath. This was going to work even if Kevin and Simon hadn't warmed to each other like she and Aggie had hoped.

Apparently, Kevin hadn't gotten over seeing Aggie—who had been Nely, at the time—with Simon. And Simon didn't entirely believe Nely that Kevin hadn't done anything with her when she was in Aggie's body.

She shook her head. They'd have to get used to each other, or learn to avoid each other now that she and Aggie were business partners.

"Need a hand with that?" Simon asked.

"No," Kevin groaned as he pushed the metal cart heavy with hors d'oeuvres through the back door of Lola's. "I got it."

"Let me hold open the door for you."

"I said I got it."

"Just go through the door."

Kevin was the first to end the stare-off. *Cops. Harassing anyone they could find.*

Simon went back to screwing in a shelf unit. If Kevin

hadn't been busy breaking in his crew for Sazón's second location, he knew he would've had that unit up in half the time.

The screw grinding into the wall made Kevin clench his teeth.

"This could work to our advantage," Simon said quietly.

Ignoring him, Kevin ripped open the sheet of plastic wrap.

"If they think we're buddies, they'll use it against us," Simon continued.

"How so?"

"They'll set us up to watch football at the house but then leave us with the kids so they can go shopping."

Kevin grunted and then went back to his hors d'oeuvres.

"And on the off chance that they actually *let* us go to a game, they'll want to know what we talked about. Word for word."

"What are you talking about?"

Simon cleared his throat and then took his time drinking from a Big Gulp cup. "You haven't been married very long. But you'll understand in a few more months."

"Hey, buddy, my wife doesn't keep me on a leash."

"Umm-hmm," Simon replied neutrally. "I give you six months, at the least, eighteen at the most." He sniffed the air. "What've you got there?"

The chef in Kevin couldn't help himself. "*Panuchos* with fried egg, chicken in red sauce, and frijoles colados," he explained, pointing to the top shelf of his cart. "Sopitos with shrimp and chicken. You want me to go on?"

"What about dessert?"

"*Crepes de carjeta*, sopapillas—"

"What are you two doing in here?" Aggie demanded.

"Nothing," they answered in unison.

Simon gave the cart of food a look of longing but went back his shelves. Kevin cleared his throat and went back to unwrapping the trays.

"No, really, are you guys okay?" she persisted.

"Yeah. I'm just trying to set up here but he's got wall dust all over the place."

"You want to help?" Simon barked over his shoulder.

"And let you eat all my doughnuts?" Kevin argued, watching Aggie's eyes ping-ponging between the two of them. "We're serving food and we need things clean around here."

"I'll just go back out and help Nely," Aggie said, making a hasty retreat. "You two figure it out on your own."

A moment passed. "She's gone," Kevin hissed.

Simon set the drill on the desk. "Sorry about the mess, man."

"No problem." He handed him a *panucho*. "So what are we going to do?"

Simon took a bite. "They'll figure it out eventually." Then he took a sopita and the napkin Kevin offered him. "But after what they've put us through—"

"You know what, man?" Kevin interrupted.

"What?"

"I want you to know something about me."

Simon waited.

"I hate sports and I never kissed your wife."

"We'll be okay, man." Simon held out his hand and Kevin took it.

A+

AUTHOR
INSIGHTS,
EXTRAS, &
MORE...

FROM

**MARY
CASTILLO**

AND

AVON A

Q&A with Mary Castillo

Okay, what were you smoking when you came up with the idea of two best friends switching bodies and living each other's lives?

Nothing, I swear! In fact I was maybe three weeks pregnant when I experienced this very strong moment when I wondered if I was truly ready to incubate, birth, and then civilize another human being. Don't get me wrong . . . this baby was planned because I really wanted a Virgo (but ended up with a Leo, just one week short of the cut off). Anyway, I started to think about my life and how I had met my husband at twenty-one and never had the single life that you read about in a lot of chick lit books. From there, the story and the characters evolved. I sat on the idea for months because I thought my agent and editor would laugh at me. But they loved it.

Why do best friends drift apart during major transitions in each other's lives?

The best explanation I've been able to come up with is that some people simply serve their purpose until you graduated or got married, pregnant, divorced, etc. They're not bad people; they just had a specific role in your life at a certain time. However, my closest friends are my soul mates. We were meant to be.

Is Simona based on your mother-in-law?

How did I know you would ask that question? No. The first thing my mother-in-law told me when Ryan and I were engaged was that he couldn't come back home. No matter what, he was mine to keep! She respects me as a wife and mother of my own little family, and I respect her as my husband's mother and my son's grandmother.

On the other hand, Simona stomps all over Nely's boundaries because Nely has the family that Simona never got to have. I really had a tough time writing Simona because there are aspects of her character that come from me, believe it or not. Now that I have a son, God help the woman who breaks his heart!

Anyway, I needed the ultimate antagonist for Nely, and, well, Simona had a dirty job to do. But if you hated her while reading this book, then I think Simona did her job and did it well!

Which one is based on you: Nely or Aggie?

This isn't a copout, but they both are.

Aggie is a reflection of me when I was in my twenties and writing was the first priority. And yet, before I met my husband, I had these moments of panic when I'd search around wondering if I'd ever meet the one special guy who would be closer to me than anyone else in the world.

Nely is me at this stage in my life where my son and husband are my first priorities. But at the same time, it can be a struggle to make room for the writing and have a place in the world outside the home.

How could *you* tell them apart when they were in each other's bodies?

The challenge of writing a story with two strong heroines is making them fully complete and unique human beings. Some days Nely was really strong and I'd only write her scenes; other days Aggie would take over. Some days neither one wanted to come out and play. Jina Bacarr, author of *Blonde Geisha*, advised me to wear a piece of jewelry or a blouse unique to each character. That simple solution made rewriting much smoother!

Why does it seem like when you get a group of women together (i.e., the baby play group) there is so much cattiness?

Insecurity, plain and simple. When I was nine years old, there was a girl on my soccer team who made me the target of her wrath all because I was "well developed" (whereas you could wash laundry on her chest). My mom told me till she was blue in the face that some girls are mean because they can't have what others have. If I had listened to her way back then, it would've saved me a lot of heartache.

Now that I'm a thirty-three-year-old mother, I see that we're all plagued by insecurity and act on it one way or the other. As a writer, I revel in the presence of real neurosis because that is the flavor and spice that makes great characters.

Is Sazón a real restaurant in San Diego?

I based Sazón on a restaurant called Taléo Mexican Grill in Irvine, California. Nic Villarreal, the founder and president, allowed me to spend some time with him and in the kitchen, which was invaluable to the writing of this story. Kevin had been an illusive character until I did my research. Suddenly, he made a lot more sense when I was able to see, smell, hear, and taste the inner workings of a professional kitchen, as well as talk to Nic and his chef, José Acevedo. Now when I go out to eat, I have a deeper appreciation for the food that arrives at the table. By the way, if you're ever in town, go try the *carnitas* at Taléo. That and the margaritas!

Without spoiling the surprise for your readers, why do you have two characters from previous books appear in the story? Should we expect a sequel in the future?

Every now and then, especially when I'm super deep into the writing, I dream of a town where all my characters live together. Tamara is my sentimental favorite because she was the first character who was born from real emotional honesty. So when I got to that part of the *Switchcraft*, she and Isa just walked into the scene. That scene has only been edited once because it worked into the rhythm of the story and yet gave us a glimpse into their lives.

As for a sequel, I'm not sure. But when I am, I'll let you know.

What's next?

As I'm writing this (January 2007), I don't know! But if you check in at my website and blog, www.MaryCastillo.com, you'll find my previous releases and news of my upcoming books.

The *Switchcraft* Soundtrack

When I write, I always have music in the background. As I was writing *Switchcraft*, this soundtrack evolved and I was surprised to see the strong country flavor with bits of pop and jazz. Just like I never know where a story will take me, I never know what kind of music it will bring into my life.

"Bad Moon Rising," *Creedence Clearwater Revival. When I first imagined Aggie and Nely taking off for their girls' only weekend, this song immediately popped in my head.*

"It Ain't Me Babe," *Johnny Cash and June Carter Cash. This is the song that plays in the café when Kevin is licking his wounds from Aggie's rejection. When I saw* Walk the Line *and heard Joaquin Phoenix and Reese Witherspoon perform this song, I almost stood up from my seat because it perfectly described the complicated dynamic of Aggie and Kevin.*

"(You're the) Devil in Disguise," *Elvis Presley. You can never go wrong with Elvis. I struggled to find a song to help me capture Simon's confusion and frustration that somehow, somewhere, along the line he had been emotionally disconnected from his wife. When I played this CD for my son and heard, "You fool me with your kisses," I immediately put it on my playlist.*

"Baby of Mine" *from* **Dumbo.** *I made the mistake of renting this movie for my son because when we got to the scene where Dumbo visits his mother in elephant jail, I balled like a baby. My son, by the way, just wanted to fast forward to the parts with the clowns and the crows. So when I needed to get into Nely's heart,* *especially the scene where she has to leave her baby with Aggie, I'd play this and try to type and wipe my eyes at the same time.*

"Truth No. 2," *Dixie Chicks,* Fly. *The greatest challenge of this book was the relationship between Aggie and Kevin. I wanted them to be together, but with her living Nely's life, that was almost impossible. Kevin is a very straightforward guy. His personal life is clearly defined and he doesn't tolerate much gray between his black and white. So with Nely pretending to be Aggie, and Aggie unable to come out and tell him that she's in someone else's body . . . well, I wondered if I could pull it off. But this line from the chorus, "Sing me something brave from your mouth," gave me the courage to give Aggie and Kevin a happily-ever-after.*

"These Arms of Mine," *Otis Redding. This was the song I played when writing the one and only love scene in the book. Well, maybe one and a half. Anyway, I need to be in the mood when writing these scenes. I can't write them in public. I have to put the baby to sleep, close the door to my office, light some candles, and quiet all that performance anxiety in my head (what will my mother think, is it sexy enough or is it too out there, blah blah blah).Getting into these scenes take time and effort . . . but they're well worth the effort!*

"Gone," *Madonna,* Music *"Selling out is not my thing, walk away. . . ." These words could've been written for Aggie at this time in her life. I won't say anything else because I can't spoil the ending for you. Just listen to this song when you get to page 268.*

"I'm Glad There Is You," *Sarah Vaughan. My bestest friend danced with her husband to a different version of this song at her wedding. When I listen to this song, I think of the relationships in this book—Nely and Aggie, Nely and Simon, and Aggie and Kevin. They all begin with a bond, a friendship, and grow from there.*

How to Survive Your Best Friend's Baby

Just when you think, *Thank God, no more wedding invitations,* your friends announce that they're having a baby. When you're still single, or nowhere near babyville, how do you cope with your best friend's pregnancy and baby? I've been on both sides of the coin: the clueless but well-meaning friend, and now the clueless but well-meaning mom.

So based on my experience, here are my five tips for keeping your friendships strong and everlasting.

1. And you thought she had bad PMS . . . be prepared for hormonal fireworks before and after the baby! One moment she's chatting away, and then one wrong word later she's talking like Linda Blair from the *Exorcist.* I was the grumpiest pregnant lady ever and tried to hide it. But after I had my baby, everyone told me that I wasn't fooling anyone. (God love them, they even forgave me, too!) So don't take it personally.

2. Don't be offended if she never takes you up on your babysitting offer. A new mom might be very particular who takes care of her baby—I only trusted Daddy and Grandmas with my Little Dude. Now that he's approaching the terrible twos, it's open season.

3. Do baby things scare you? Baby showers put you in a panic? Throw a mommy shower where everyone brings a gift for the mama like that gorgeous maternity top that she'd never buy herself. (Or this book! Sorry. It just came out.) When it's your turn, she might even lend it to you.

4. Look with your eyes, not your hands. I know bellies are irresistible to some people, but please, on behalf of pregnant women everywhere, ask if you can feel her up. I was once in the grocery store and a woman reached from behind me to pat my belly. I "accidentally" stepped on her foot. Heh heh heh.

5. Don't show up in the delivery room (unless you've been invited). It's very hectic and a little scary, not to mention *really* personal. Trust me, unless you want to take a chance that you'll walk in while the nurse is checking to see how far she's dilated, stay in the waiting room, or better yet, call her mom to see how she's doing.

6. I know I said five tips, but this one is important, too. Around her eighth month, ask your friend who you should call when the baby is born. I had just nodded off after being awake for eighteen hours—twelve of which were spent in labor—when my friend called my room. I love her for wanting to know if I was okay. But in that moment, if I could have, I would've reached through the phone and smacked her.

If you want more tips and tricks, visit my blog, "How to Survive Your Best Friend's Baby" at bestfriendsbaby.blogspot.com.

MARY CASTILLO's first two books, *Hot Tamara* and *In Between Men*, were both named Top Romance Book of the Year by *Catalina* magazine for two consecutive years. She lives with her family in Orange County, California. Please visit her website at www.marycastillo.com.

Mary Castillo